Intrusion

Intrusion

a novel

MARY McCLUSKEY

Little
a

This is a work of fiction. Names, characters, organizations, places, events, and incidents are either products of the author's imagination or are used fictitiously.

Published by Little A, New York
www.apub.com

ISBN-13: 9781503953062 (hardcover)
ISBN-10: 1503953068 (hardcover)
ISBN-13: 9781503953048 (paperback)
ISBN-10: 1503953041 (paperback)

Cover design by Kimberly Glyder

Printed in the United States of America

PRAISE FOR *INTRUSION*

"This novel raises comparisons to *Gone Girl* and some of the other recent stories about characters who aren't who they seem, but McCluskey's beautiful prose elevates it above most of them . . . Haunting and lyrical, understated and true." —*Kirkus Reviews*, starred review

"Mary McCluskey paints a delicate, deeply convincing portrait of a marriage riven by the loss of a child. *Intrusion* is both a classy thriller and a psychologically acute tale about the vulnerabilities grief can open up in us." —Pamela Erens, author of *The Virgins*

"In this stunning psychological drama, the choppy waters of grief and pain rock the stillness of a fragile marriage and a nearly-forgotten friendship. I was gripped by McCluskey's authentic characters, daring prose, taut story, and deft plot twists. *Intrusion* is an utterly compelling debut!" —Ellen Meister, author of *Dorothy Parker Drank Here*

"Gripping and emotionally complex, this heartfelt novel talks of loss and of how we deal with it, of the long shadow of grief, and of the havoc that can be caused by a need for retribution. It's a dark tale, beautifully told. It will linger in the mind and heart long after you have closed the book." —Charles Lambert, author of *The Children's Home*

For Nick, with love

ONE

The narrow hotel bar, with its dull, disguising light, ran alongside the crystal ballroom. Kat Hamilton, seated on a barstool at the far end of the room, sipped her fourth gin and tonic and wished that she could fade like a ghost into the wall. The formal attire pinched. She had worn only casual clothes since the funeral; on bad days she wore her nightshirt all day. On this evening, the classic black dress chafed against her skin, like a winter sweater on sunburn.

Her husband, Scott, had visited her twice, stealing sips from her drink, taking deep breaths as he surveyed the room. He hadn't tried to persuade her to join him in the glittering ballroom: he knew she would say no. Scott was to receive a Los Angeles Lawyers Pro Bono Award for negotiating a lease for a halfway house run by a local priest and reformed gang members. Kat had not wanted to come.

"Just for an hour, sweetheart."

"Why? The partners won't notice if I'm there or not."

"Not for the partners. For the kids."

"The kids?"

"Yep. They've worked hard."

"Okay. One hour."

She could see Scott at the far side of the ballroom, Glenda Lilley, his smart female associate, at his elbow, Father O'Connor jubilant beside him. Scott shook hands, smiled, appeared in control. He had never lost control. Not even when their world imploded at 10:31 a.m. on a Saturday morning twelve weeks and three days ago when Kat lifted the phone to hear a police officer's voice say, *I am very sorry to have to tell you, ma'am, that your son, Christopher . . .* And after an enormous whoosh, when the air was sucked out of the universe, she had screamed and screamed until Scott ran in from the garden, took hold of her shoulders, and held her tight to his chest. The officer's words resonated in her head every day. She wondered if Scott still heard screaming.

"You plan to hide out in the bar all evening?"

James Dempsey draped his long body onto the stool next to her. An attractive young black man they had befriended when he was a summer clerk, he was now a hotshot associate, trying hard to make partner.

"Hi, James. Not *all* evening. I suppose I have to be at the table when they make the award. Then, I hope we can just slip away."

He took her hand.

"Not getting any easier for you, Kat?"

"No. It's not."

"Scott doing better?" he asked.

"Scott has admirable self-control. And a stiff upper lip."

They both looked over at Scott, still holding court in the center of a group. *A typical urban lawyer,* Kat thought, *even to the serious eyeglasses.* Still a handsome man, though, at least to her.

"I thought you Brits had the prerogative on that," James said. "But I guess it's the manly way."

"Manly?"

"Yep."

"What's the womanly way?" she asked. "Tears?"

"Tears are fine, Kat. You're in pain."

"Yes," she said. "Pain. You know, Chris's death hurts more physically than his birth did. *Physically.*"

Kat knew she was talking too much, four drinks were hurtling around her bloodstream, but she could not stop.

"It's like someone took a knife and just scooped out everything—heart, guts. We're the hollow ones, now, Scott and I. All scooped out."

She looked helplessly at James. He reached out and placed an arm around her shoulders.

"It's grief, Kat. It's normal."

"But if I'm normal, what's Scott? I can't move, and he can't stand still. He's working twelve hours a day."

"That's maybe his way. He's doing great work for this project."

"I know that."

A young black man with a shaved bullet head, an earring, and a solid buffed body stopped beside them and stared at James.

"Hey, what's up, brother?" he asked. James grinned.

"Well hello, Chiller. You here to support your buddies?"

"Man, I'm here to receive my award. I'm a fucking *recipient.*"

Kat was sure that James knew this, but he pretended surprise.

"I'm looking forward to seeing that. I'll be cheering."

"Damn right. You better be cheering, bro."

Chiller swaggered off. James, still smiling, turned back to Kat.

"We better get in there. You're at the main table. Behind the podium."

The awards ceremony began immediately, while people were still eating, which meant, Kat noted gratefully, that the evening would soon be over. She was having difficulty swallowing. When Scott's name was called, he accepted the small plaque with a simple thank-you, bowing graciously, and Kat applauded with the others. But there was some whispering between Scott and the MC, and Scott returned to the podium again. He smiled as he took the microphone.

"Well, I also get to *present* an award this evening. And it's a big honor for me. It's to a young man from Compton. While we were negotiating contracts, doing the easy stuff like the leases and the paperwork, a group of kids were out there working fifteen hours a day, painting, rebuilding, fixing. Making it safe. Making it home. Representing that group today—Chiller."

Chiller headed toward the podium and Scott began to read from the card he was handed.

"I am proud to present this award to Christopher . . ."

Scott faltered, stared at the card in his hand, his face ashen. Kat's heart leaped. How could this be? Christopher was a blue-eyed, smiling teenager. A boy with fair hair and freckles, just like her own. The hushed audience waited. Chiller turned, frowning. Scott began again. He said the words carefully now, with rigid deliberation.

"To Christopher Richard Washington, aka Chiller."

The applause was loud and exuberant. Chiller, grinning as a press camera flashed, took the silver trophy and waved it at the audience, holding both arms above his head like a prizefighter. Scott looked over at her and Kat saw that the ice had splintered, the armor shattered and fallen away. His eyes were bleak as they met hers, then he looked away, staring into an impossible future.

In the car, Scott was silent.

"There's magic in a name," Kat said quietly. "The Indians knew that."

"I know," he said.

He glanced at her, swallowed. She thought again that she could feel her heart breaking.

Once they were home, Scott said he was going to bed. Kat understood this. Understood well the need to burrow and hide. She pulled on her nightgown and then made tea, taking a cup to him as if he were an invalid. He sipped it, and then looked at her strangely, as if he were embarrassed.

"Do something for me?"

Kat nodded.

"Of course."

"Lie on me."

She hesitated.

"Just lie on me," Scott said. "Flat. So I'm weighted down. Nothing else."

She climbed onto the bed and lay down on him; her head reached his shoulder. His body was cold at first. She could hear his jagged breathing.

"That okay?"

"Yes," he said. "That's fine."

So Kat lay quite still, weighting him, anchoring her husband to the warm earth, as his tears dampened her hair.

TWO

The next morning, Kat, propped up on pillows, watched Scott as he dressed for the office. His movements seemed easier, calmer. Last night's emotion had been a kind of catharsis for him. In the dresser mirror, his eyes met hers.

"Did you sleep?" he asked.

"A bit. Did you?" she asked as he turned from the mirror.

"Yes. Some."

She picked up the newspaper, glanced at the headlines, put it back on the bed. He had brought it in to her, along with a cup of coffee. He came to sit on the edge of the bed and took hold of her hand.

"You see the therapist today?"

"Yes. This afternoon."

He was really asking, she knew, whether she planned to go out at all. He worried about the inertia that held her in the house. She had not been back to work since their son's death, had no idea when she would return.

"I'll be home as early as I can," he said. "But there's a lot going on."

Kat nodded. She listened as he left the house, tracking his footsteps on the stairs, before she moved from the bed to the window to watch him walk to his car. A slam of the car door, the sudden loud life of the engine, and then he was driving away. She waited until the sound faded as he turned the corner and was gone. Ten hours until he returned, maybe twelve.

Distracted by the whine of a garage door, Kat looked across the street to see Brooke leaving for work in her red Miata convertible. Her neighbor's blonde hair was tied back with a glowing gold head scarf, and she wore large wraparound shades, though the early-morning light was still dim. Brooke glanced toward the house—must have spotted the shadow of Kat behind the blinds because she waved—then touched her fingers to her lips to blow a kiss before gunning the car engine, heading off into her busy day. Kat, aware that Brooke could not see her clearly, waved to her friend anyway.

In the kitchen, Kat stood at the window looking at the garden, neglected these past weeks, thinking about what Scott had said two nights ago. It's incredible, he said, how a small thing can so change a life that nothing will ever be the same again.

"Like a truck blowing a tire on the Coast Highway?"

"Christ, yes. That, of course. But things that seem insignificant at the time. You know—an ad for a job, an introduction to someone. Little things."

"A strange English girl looking at you?" she had asked, wondering if he was regretting everything in his life. If he had not met her, he would not be grieving like this. They had been lying in bed and he had turned to look at her.

"A drive around the city—and a whole chain of events follows. Who would have guessed? Little thing like that."

"Oh, I would have guessed."

But Scott was right. A drive with an attractive UCLA student so many years ago had changed every aspect of her life: her job, her friends, even her country.

She had been happy enough with her London life until the Los Angeles assignment. Her editor gave her six weeks to write about a new band of young filmmakers in Los Angeles: a plum job, causing some resentment in her office. She had loved LA at once—the sun, the mountains, the palm trees, the energy, and the glitter. She was amused by the enthusiasm and arrogance of the creative young people she met, who believed with their very souls that this was where it was happening. This was the place.

She met Scott, two weeks into the assignment, at a party held by a group of USC film students. She noticed him at once: a tall young man, hair rather long, dark blue eyes, a wide, warm smile. He studied Kat.

"So, Miz Brit," he said. "What have you seen so far?"

"I've seen Sunset Strip, Beverly Hills, Santa Monica, Malibu," she told him. "Just about everything."

He laughed out loud.

"Everything? No kidding? Hey, come see a different LA."

She thought he was an actor; he was as good-looking as the other young men around and was dressed the same way: blue jeans, T-shirt, hair falling into his eyes. What amazed her was that he noticed her among all those sparkling starlets, with their gazelle legs and pouting mouths.

The next evening, he drove her to Old Pasadena, then on to the San Fernando Valley, through the town of San Fernando, with its Spanish buildings and charming town center, and to Pacoima, with its early flickers of menace and youth gangs.

Back on the freeway, he took her through the streets of downtown Los Angeles, right by The Midnight Mission, and the alleys that housed humanity's lost and rejected. Then, to a hillside just north of Malibu, where they sat silently, watching the ocean.

"Damn, I'm sorry, but I got to get back," he said after a while. "Finals coming up."

"You're still at university?"

"Second year UCLA law school."

"You're going to be a lawyer?"

"Yep."

"You don't look like a lawyer."

"Thank you. I guess."

He leaned over, kissed her softly on the mouth.

"Pick you up tomorrow at seven," he said.

She should have demurred, said she had other plans, for she did, in fact, have a number of people to see. But she nodded. It was already too late: too late to change the shape of her Los Angeles assignment, too late to change the direction of her life.

"I'll be ready," Kat promised.

Two nights after their first date, he took her back to his cramped room near the UCLA campus, and she knew, as she stepped through the door, what she wanted to happen next. Kat had stripped off her T-shirt and bra and was fumbling with the zipper of her jeans when Scott came back from the kitchen, tugging at the cork on a bottle of wine.

"Jesus, you are so beautiful," he said, placing the wine bottle on an old bookcase and coming forward to take her in his arms. "I love fast women."

"I've never behaved like this in my life," whispered Kat.

"You were waiting for the right moment," he said.

They made love with a hunger Kat could never have imagined and a tenderness that left her terrified. She could not conceive of living without him now. They were married the following year. Chris was born three months after their first anniversary.

"A son," Scott had said immediately after the birth, holding the loudly protesting baby in his arms. "A son with stunning good looks and a big voice."

She remembered their pride and amazement at having produced such a remarkable infant; she remembered Scott's wide smile.

Now, sighing, Kat turned away from the window and began to make more coffee. It seemed impossible that they had been so young, so full of hope and self-confidence. That attractive young man and woman, those proud young parents, appeared to her now like people she had known a long time ago, in another life.

She had poured cereal into a bowl and was adding milk when the phone rang. She lifted the receiver uneasily, praying it would not be a colleague from the PR agency of Waters & Chappell, wondering when she would be back to work. But it was not a colleague; it was Maggie, her sister, calling from the UK.

"Thank God," Kat said when she recognized her sister's voice.

"Thank God for what, sweetie?"

"That it's you."

"Me indeed. And I've got a surprise."

"What surprise?"

"Look, I know you *think* you don't want to do it. But you will, darling, because I've paid for it already. And booked my flight."

Kat froze.

"What have you paid for?" she asked.

"Five days at a spa. In Palm Springs. It will do you so much good."

"I'm not sure I want to be done good," Kat said.

"It will do me good, too," said Maggie. "Do it for me."

"But what about Scott?"

"I checked with Scott," said Maggie. Kat felt immediately betrayed. "He thinks it's a super idea."

There was no way out. She knew it and listened to her sister's chatter about body wraps and massages with a slowly mounting dread.

THREE

Martha Kim, a tiny, immaculate Korean woman with clear skin and narrow bright eyes, had been appointed as Kat's grief therapist through Scott's insurance policy. Kat had never visited a therapist before and Martha was not at all what she expected. During their first session, she had simply indicated the box of tissues and allowed Kat to cry for twenty minutes before beginning a gentle questioning. She showed no emotion at all, no sympathy, no empathy; she was a practical woman. Now, she said, "Your sabbatical must be up. They gave you three months?"

"Yes."

"And have you thought about returning to work?"

"Thought about it, yes."

"They are still paying you?"

Kat balled up the tissue in her hand and looked at Martha. Was this really any of her business?

"No. That ran out."

Martha nodded.

"So when do you plan to return?"

"I'm giving notice today," Kat said.

As the words fell from her mouth, surprising them both, she realized that she was never going to return to Waters & Chappell. She did not want to continue with work that had been fulfilling once but seemed totally meaningless now.

"And what will you do?" Martha asked.

"I don't know. I have to think about it."

"How does Scott feel about this?"

"I haven't told him yet," Kat said.

Martha's expression did not change in the slightest, but Kat was certain she saw disapproval in the small brown eyes.

"Are you getting out of the house at all?"

"To the library. Once, to the grave."

"Oh? And how was that?"

Martha settled back in her chair. Kat began to speak, felt her throat tighten. She reached for the box of tissues automatically. *How was that?* How could she describe what it was like to see her son's name on a piece of hard granite? *Christopher James Hamilton, Good Night, Sweet Prince.* It was impossible. She did not believe the clichés about his soul being in a better place; she knew only that his body, his long, clumsy, beautiful seventeen-year-old body, was there in the ground. She imagined his hands, the long fingers that played the piano so beautifully, there in the ground. But *he* was not there.

"I didn't feel him there," she said to Martha.

"No?"

"I suppose if I were religious. If I believed in a God, maybe."

"You have no spiritual beliefs at all?"

"No. None."

"Did you ever?"

"I was brought up Catholic. Attended a convent school. I grew out of it, I think." She stopped. "Not entirely. I suppose you never really grow out of it."

For how could she explain to Martha her prayer each night, as she looked at the picture of her son: *God, if there is a God, take care of my Chris. Please.* An irrational prayer to a God she no longer believed in.

"You don't feel his presence at the grave. Where do you feel closest to Christopher?" Martha asked unexpectedly. It was odd to hear his name on her lips. Usually she said *your son.*

"In his room. Or by his piano. Or when I play his music."

"Music he loved?"

"Yes. Or music he composed himself."

Martha raised an eyebrow. She was impressed by this.

"He composed music?"

"Yes."

The tears streamed down Kat's face, but she realized that she was learning to talk through them, to ignore them.

"And your physical health. You are sleeping better? And eating?"

"Sleeping a bit. Eating too much."

Martha did not show the disapproval Kat had expected. Instead she said, "You feel hollow inside? And you think it's hunger?"

"Yes. Exactly. That gnawing, empty feeling. But food, well, of course it doesn't help. But still, I eat anyway."

"And thoughts of suicide?"

Martha regarded Kat steadily. Kat had been waiting for this question, knew that a certain box must be ticked in the forms submitted to Scott's insurance company.

"Occasionally," Kat said.

She looked at the therapist, frowning. She was not going to share with Martha the fact that she had hidden, at the back of her underwear drawer, one unopened bottle of prescription sleeping pills. A full bottle. Just in case.

"It's not that I want to die, Martha. I just don't know whether I want to live." Kat paused, thought about it. "No. It's that I don't know *how* to live. I've forgotten how."

Martha tapped her file.

"I think we need a plan for you. Exercise certainly. Perhaps a better diet. Some physical changes might help you move forward."

Kat sensed impatience in the woman—enough of this, let's have a plan—so she told the therapist of her sister's idea for the Palm Springs visit. Martha was so approving of it that Kat, for one paranoiac moment, wondered if Maggie, Scott, and Martha had all actually conferred.

As she left the parking lot outside Martha Kim's office, Kat did not turn right, toward home in Porter Ranch at the northwestern tip of the San Fernando Valley, but instead began the drive to Forest Lawn without consciously deciding to do so. The conversation about the grave site had unsettled her. Surely, she should feel *something*? Kat wondered why she felt nothing but emptiness.

The stone that marked Chris's grave, still so shiny and new, gleamed in the sunlight. It was a shock to see his name written on it. It gave Kat a physical jolt. She wondered if years from now she would be used to it. A tall glass vase, containing purple and white tulips, had been placed at the edge of the grave. Kat stared at the flowers, seeing them precision-etched against the green of the grass: the dark ones, a rich ecclesiastical purple, a little decadent, a little corrupt. The white ones, more delicate, bowing their neat, supplicating heads. A shaft of sunlight cast their shadows on the stone. A card was attached to one of the stems.

Kat hesitated a moment before, deeply curious, she crouched down to read the card. Shrugging away the feeling that it was wrong and intrusive—for surely a handwritten note, even in this public place, was a private communication meant only for her son?—Kat turned the card over.

We miss you—Chloe, Vanessa, Ben, Matt, and Teddy

Ben, Matt, and Teddy were Chris's oldest friends; all three had been with him on the night of the accident, and Ben had sustained minor injuries. Vanessa was a good friend from high school. But Chloe? She couldn't recall a Chloe. She thought back to the service, the girls in a huddle at the back. Was she one of those? Perhaps.

"I miss you, too, Chris," Kat murmured before she walked back to her car.

At dinner that night, Kat confronted Scott.

"You didn't tell me you talked to Maggie about this Palm Springs spa thing," she said.

"Only once. For a minute. She's worried about you."

"Why didn't you ask me if I wanted to go before you agreed to it and made it seem like a great idea?"

"Well, I thought it might be good because"—he paused, seemingly intent on slicing a cherry tomato into minute pieces—"there's a Palm Springs client thing coming up. The opening of the new country club. So I thought it might work."

He looked over at her. Kat stared, horrified.

"And we have to go?"

"I do. The Rancho Mirage group—remember Ted Lafitte? He's an old client."

"And you asked Maggie to arrange some spa thing?"

"Hell no," he said. "Of course not. Maggie asked if it would be a good idea to take you on a small vacation. And I remembered this Palm Springs opening. We're not all in cahoots behind your back, you know, planning evil things to do to you. It's not a stay in a salt mine. It's a few days in a spa with your sister. And drinks at a country club with me. How bad can that be?"

He sipped his wine. His eyes, meeting hers, were worried. Kat smiled, finally.

"Bad," she said. "Very bad."

FOUR

"This is so nice, Kat. Well!"

Maggie looked around with clear approval at the double room in the Palm Springs Desert Spa Hotel. Furnished in the inevitable creams, pinks, and soft greens of the desert style, it had two queen-size beds.

"And look, a mountain view. How super! And a microwave, and a fridge. And golly, our own bar. What will you have, darling? How about a gin and tonic?"

Kat rested the suitcase against the wall and sat on the bed. She felt out of breath.

"Already? It's only four in the afternoon."

"Not in England, it's not. It's midnight there. Come on."

Kat felt as if some dynamic force were dragging her in its wake. Maggie, two years younger, had once been her shy little sister—marrying young, giving birth to a son, Adam, when she was barely twenty. But as her husband's company became successful and their social circle widened, Maggie became bolder. She wore her red hair long these days, and fashionable clothes with confidence.

"Don't you just love this?" she said to Kat. "A whole bucket of ice. They're so civilized, these Americans."

Kat watched as Maggie poured two large drinks. She took one from her sister and sipped it. Then, Maggie flipped open her suitcase to pull out a silky black swimsuit.

"We can go sit in the spa. The natural one. You did remember your suit?"

Kat took another mouthful of her drink.

"Yes," she said.

But when she tried on the swimsuit, it felt old and worn and tight. It pulled at the crotch, created deep ridges of flesh in her shoulders.

"How long have you had that suit, Kat?" asked Maggie. "Since you were ten?"

"Years and years. It does feel tight."

"Here. Try this one."

Maggie pulled another garment from her case and handed it to Kat. It was kingfisher-blue and made of a shimmering nylon, but it, too, was snug.

"You've put on a little bit of weight, love," Maggie said.

Kat sat on the bed and found that the tears she had held back all morning were now sliding down her face.

"So what?" she said. "So what if I have. What do you expect?"

The words caught in her throat. Her sister was by her side at once, pulling her close with slim arms. Kat could smell her perfume, the shampoo in her hair.

"Shush," Maggie said. "Shush. It's all right. It will be all right. Hang on, love."

"How's it going to be all right?" Kat whispered. "How? Can you bring Chris back? Can you? Because that's all I want. I just want him back."

Maggie rocked her gently. She wiped her own tears away with a trembling hand and waited out the crying bout, holding Kat until the shuddering ceased, then fumbling for a box of tissues. They took a bunch of tissues each, blowing noses, dabbing faces, taking long, deep breaths.

"We'll go to the spa later," said Maggie. "Finish up your drink."

Kat was unable to reach Scott until late that night, and his voice on the phone, so tired and tentative, made her want to be home. Though the spa water was soothing after all—and the expensive dinner in a popular Palm Springs restaurant the first meal she had actually tasted in weeks—she wanted to be in her own house, in her own bed.

"You sound tired," she said to Scott. "Did you work late?"

"Yep. Did some catching up. Couple of contracts had been hanging. They're done now."

"You have dinner out?"

"Got a meatball sub on the way home."

She smiled at this. "I miss you," she said.

"I miss you, too. The house is so quiet."

And, like a blast of cold air, came an understanding of how it must be there at home, with no son, no wife, no one.

"Come sooner," she said. "Come on Thursday. When is the opening?"

"Friday night."

"Come on Thursday," she said again. She sounded urgent.

"I might. I might."

That night in bed, she missed him, the warm body next to hers, his awareness. The fact that she had only to move slightly, make a sound, and he would reach to take her hand. They would talk, on those long nights, in whispers.

"You want to ask *Why me?* But really—why *not* me?" Scott said.

"The real question is *Why him?* Because he was special in some way? Chosen?"

"He was special all right," Scott said. "Everyone thought so."

"Do you feel that, well, we could die now," she had asked him on one of those nights. "That we've had our life?"

"Yep. It's odd how death isn't such a big deal anymore."

"It's still a big deal to me," Kat said, thinking of the hidden pills, her own dark secret. She knew the strongest reason she hadn't taken the pills yet was the further pain her suicide would cause Scott.

"Of course it is," Scott said quickly. "No. I mean my own death. Doesn't scare me so much. If there's anything to be learned from this, that's the only thing. Chris led the way. If there are any mysteries out there, he knows them now."

Kat and Scott had not made love since the night before Chris's accident. That night, after their son left to stay at the beach with friends, they had gone to bed early, relishing an empty house with no need to stifle their cries or be concerned about the vigorous creaking of their old bed. And they had made the kind of knowing love that long-married people make: lovemaking as warming as a summer sun, as nourishing and ordinary as rain. The last time. Kat couldn't imagine it now. Could not imagine ever wanting again any kind of sexual joining. There would seem no point to it.

In the Palm Springs hotel room, her sister snored softly. Kat stared at the window, watching the lights flicker on the shades from the traffic passing by. She was thirsty. She edged carefully out of bed and moved toward the bathroom, then *Ouch*—a hard stub; her toe had caught the suitcase or a chair.

"Kat? Are you all right, love?" Maggie sat up in bed. "What's the matter? You can't sleep?"

"I'm just thirsty. And I haven't been sleeping much."

"Shall I make a cup of tea?"

"Go back to sleep, Mags. I'll get some water."

Kat poured a large glass of water, gulped it thirstily, and then returned to bed. Soon, Maggie's soft snoring began again. Kat closed her eyes, imagined her son, tried to visualize him. His face would not come into focus. She remembered a line from a book Martha had given her: Think of him doing something, think of him active in some way, then you will see him. There! There he was at the piano. He turned to look over his shoulder at her. And he smiled.

"Mom, listen! Listen to this."

She let the tears dry on her face. She did not want to move and wake her sister.

Scott arrived early on Friday morning, hugging Kat hard as she stood, still wearing her dressing gown, in the doorway of the hotel room.

"You look better," he said. "Rested."

"She looks great," said Maggie. "And look, she's even got a little bit of a tan."

Kat smiled at her sister.

"A little bit is right," she said.

But she did feel better, right up until the early evening when she pulled on the black dress for the country club cocktails. Scott was already dressed, sitting on the balcony sipping a scotch. Maggie, in the bathroom, added finishing touches to her makeup. Kat stared at herself in the full-length mirror. The dress felt uncomfortable. Her hair was dry and out of condition, and she had shadows under her eyes. She looked tired and she looked old. She was reminded of a quote from *Paula*, Isabel Allende's memoir about the death of her daughter. Isabel wrote that she had studied a photograph of herself taken just a month earlier: *A month ago, at this very hour, I was a different woman . . . a century younger than I am today. I don't know that woman; in four weeks, sorrow has transformed me.*

"I can't go," Kat said.

Scott turned his chair around from the view of the mountains. "What?"

"I can't go. I just can't. This dress looks awful. *I* look awful."

Maggie emerged from the bathroom immediately.

"You look lovely, Kat," Maggie said. "Let me play with your hair a little bit. Your dress is classic. It's perfect. And here—" She tugged at the sapphire-and-diamond earrings in her own ears. "Wear these. Just what you need."

Kat bit at her lip. Maggie had stayed an extra day to accompany them to this function, and her sister was now dressed in midnight-blue silk and looked stunning. Maggie's face, as she regarded her sister, showed clear concern.

"Oh, damn," said Kat. "I'm sorry. I'm so sorry."

She held the earrings in her palm.

"I can't wear these, Maggie. You should wear them."

"Of course you can, Kat. Please."

Kat thought that she should never have agreed to any of this; not to the spa, not to Palm Springs, not to the country club. She should never have asked Maggie to come with them to this opening. Scott and Maggie watched her warily, waiting.

"How long do we have to stay?" she asked, aware that she was acting like a sullen and difficult child.

Scott considered this.

"Just long enough to say hello to Miyamoto and his wife and a couple of the partners. And to say hello to Ted Lafitte. He wants to introduce us to the head of a European consortium. Could be a big client. Miyamoto's really excited about it. So maybe you could stay for that? Then, you and Maggie can come on back. Say an hour and a half?"

"Okay. But that's all."

"Let's just put our best foot forward and see how it goes," said Maggie.

"Oh, Mags. Please," Kat said.

FIVE

The private ballroom of the spa hotel, designed with Italian marble and crystal lights, had French doors running along one side that were open to a pool, softly lit and surrounded by rocks, palms, and cacti. Kat, nervous, paused at the entrance.

"Come on," Maggie said. "It's an open bar."

A couple of dozen people milled around, sipping cocktails, and the noise level was at an animated conversational pitch. Mike Miyamoto, the managing partner of Scott's law firm, stood just beyond the open doors with his wife, Phannie. He greeted Kat warmly, welcomed Maggie.

"Thank you so much for inviting me," Maggie said. "It's an impressive place."

"It is indeed," said Miyamoto, before turning back to Scott. "Lafitte's here already. We should make introductions."

Scott glanced at Kat. She read his concerned expression and nodded.

"Go ahead. We'll get a drink."

"An excellent idea," said Maggie.

Kat found that with Maggie close by, and a regular supply of drinks, she was able to survive the first hour with surprisingly little discomfort. She endured the bear hug from one of the older partners, and a tight, sad hug from his wife, their sympathy for her making them virtually inarticulate. Most of the younger partners and their wives said hello, chatted a little, and then moved on. Glenda, Scott's bright, Harvard-educated associate, came over, kissed Kat on the cheek, murmured a welcome, and then drifted off toward easier company. A few minutes later, one of the young male associates did the same.

James Dempsey found them eventually and stopped to talk. Introduced to Maggie, he studied her, shaking his head.

"It's amazing. You two are not a bit alike. Not in looks, anyway. One blonde, one redhead. My brother and I are just peas in a pod. Of course," James added, grinning, "you're both gorgeous."

Kat and Maggie exchanged looks and smiled just as Scott joined them.

"Going well, boss," James said. "Ted Lafitte's pleased. Where's the head honcho of that European group? I thought we were getting an introduction."

"It's a woman," Scott said. "Miyamoto said she's on her way. Wait, is that her?"

James turned and looked in the direction of the door.

"Oh, Christ. Oh, bloody hell," said Maggie sharply.

Kat turned to look. There was an obvious stirring at the edge of the room from the arrival of a late guest. A slender brunette stood alone in the entrance. She posed with her chin tilted, as if expecting photographers. Her hair was swept to one side, held back with an emerald clasp, and she wore an elegant cream silk gown. A beautiful woman, quite used to attention. She smiled serenely as Miyamoto, his wife close behind, hurried forward to greet her. Kat, rigid with shock, simply stared. The same smile, the same air of absolute confidence. A natural grace that Kat had once envied and tried hard to copy. Sarah Cherrington, twenty years later.

"Sarah," she whispered. "I don't believe it."

"What the bloody hell is she doing here?" asked Maggie.

Scott looked from one to the other. "You know her?"

"Knew her years ago," Kat said. "We were at school together."

"Hey, that could be good."

"Do not be so sure," Maggie said.

"Think she'll remember you?" Scott asked.

"Oh, yes," Kat said. "We were at the convent school together. Then, at university we were flatmates. We were best friends once. Good grief, what a surprise."

"Shock, more like," said Maggie.

Scott placed an arm around his wife's shoulders. "You moved in gilded circles, sweetheart. She's a possible new client."

"I thought it was a conglomerate or something," Kat said.

"It is. She heads it. She's Sam Harrison's widow. She inherited the entire estate."

"Well, that makes sense," Maggie said. "Sarah was destined to marry some old geezer and inherit everything."

Scott looked at his sister-in-law, frowning.

"He was not exactly an old geezer, Maggie. He was in his fifties, I think, when he died last year. Had cancer. And she's quite the businesswoman herself, according to Miyamoto."

Maggie, unrepentant, shrugged, and Scott caught the look she flashed to her sister.

"You don't like her?"

"No. I don't," said Maggie. "But don't mind me. A client's a client. Rich widow or not."

"Mags," said Kat in an undertone, "she's probably changed."

They both looked over at Sarah, smiling warmly at the group surrounding her. The clear green eyes, slanting slightly, the golden skin, had seemed exotic, Kat remembered, to the other schoolgirls with their freckles and English rosebud looks. Rumors about her had swept the convent school regularly. It was said she was from one of England's oldest aristocratic families, that she had been expelled from four previous schools, including Elmwood Hall, the exclusive girls' school in Sussex. She was an orphan; there was talk of her mother's death as a suicide and speculation as to her real father. She had been thirteen years old when her mother died, just one year before Kat met her. At fourteen, she had riveted an entire convent school. At twenty, as a university student, she attracted both gossip and envy, and had almost as many enemies as friends. But she had always commanded attention, just as she did now at the Palm Island Country Club. Sarah looked older but essentially unchanged.

"You want to go over and say hi?" Scott asked.

As he spoke, Sarah turned her head. She seemed to stiffen, looking hard at Kat, then she gave a smile of recognition and a small shake of her head. She patted the arm of Mrs. Miyamoto, excusing herself, and moved across the room, the green eyes never leaving Kat's face.

"Caitlin! Dear gods, how is this possible?" she asked, hugging Kat.

The voice was the same: low and melodic. A voice so soft it indicated gentleness and was dangerously deceptive. Sarah was unusual at St. Theresa's Convent School because she had no discernible accent: not the cultured caw of the upper-class girls, nor the rough Midland of the few day girls. Private tutors and a mother educated in European finishing schools had modulated her voice.

"Sarah, you look exactly the same," Kat said. "I don't believe it."

"Nonsense. I look older. And so do you."

Sarah held Kat's shoulders and stood back to study her.

"Though you're still lovely."

Maggie's voice, clear, loud, interrupted her.

"Hello, Sarah," she said.

Sarah turned, frowning.

"Maggie? Maggie, too? Oh, my goodness. This is just unbelievable."

Maggie's smile remained in place, and she extended her arms so that the two women hugged stiffly, barely touching.

"Quite a surprise," Maggie said.

Sarah looked at her steadily. "Well, well, dear Maggie, you haven't changed a bit."

"Honestly?" Maggie asked. "I thought I'd grown."

"You don't appear to be blushing, however," Sarah noted. "I seem to remember you did that all the time."

"I only blush with pleasure these days," Maggie said.

"Of course you do," Sarah said, and turned back to Kat. "It's been, heavens, how many years since we—?"

Her question was directed at Kat, but Maggie answered.

"Twenty-one. Twenty-one years come the twenty-first of June."

Sarah turned to look at her.

"The last time we saw you," stated Maggie, "was on my wedding day. And our anniversary is June twenty-first."

"Oh, you're right," said Sarah slowly. "Your wedding. I do remember. You were so young, Maggie."

"Old enough," said Maggie. Though her sister was still smiling, and her voice controlled and pleasant, Kat recognized her look. Maggie was alert, wary, clear dislike in her eyes. "Doesn't seem like twenty years, does it, since you turned up on our doorstep that night?"

Kat, aware of Scott at her side, interrupted quickly.

"Sarah, do meet my husband. This is Scott."

"Scott Hamilton," he said, reaching to shake Sarah's hand. "One of the partners involved in the project."

"Really?" Sarah said, appraising him. "Delighted to meet you."

"And this is James Dempsey, my associate."

James shot forward, holding out his hand.

"Pleasure, ma'am."

"Oh, don't call me ma'am. It's Sarah. Please."

Sarah shook his hand, but her attention moved immediately back to Kat, and very lightly she tugged at Kat's arm to move her away from the group.

"If you will excuse us? We haven't seen each other in such an age," Sarah said.

"Of course," said Scott.

Kat allowed herself to be led away, risking a quick glance at Maggie. Her sister watched Sarah as one would a snake or a rabid dog.

"We must talk," said Sarah, squeezing Kat's arm. "It's been too long."

Sarah led Kat into the corridor. They were outside a conference room, in an open hallway lit with crystal wall lights and furnished with long linen sofas. She sat down on one of them, pulling Kat down beside her.

"So? Tell me everything," she said. "How are you?"

Kat returned her look, noting now in the cooler, brighter light, the small age lines, a weariness in the eyes not apparent before.

"Oh, fine. It's just—" Kat paused, not wanting to go on.

"It's just? It's just what? I knew there was something wrong. Knew the moment I saw you. That lost look. Tell me. What's happened to you, Kat?"

"It's—our son died," Kat said. "In an accident."

"Oh no. I'm so sorry."

"I really can't talk about this now, Sarah."

Sarah moved to touch her hand.

"Of course not. Not here. You must tell me later. When we have time. When we're alone."

"Yes. You've had a difficult time also? Scott said you lost your husband," Kat said.

"I did. But I was prepared. He was ill for some time."

"But that's hard, too. A long illness."

"Yes. Those last few months—" Sarah shivered. "He was at home, you see. I had help, of course. And a delightful doctor who came every day. But my nursing skills? Well, you can imagine. But please. Go on. Tell me other things. You're still a journalist?"

"Not anymore," Kat said. "I work in a PR agency now. Press releases, brochures. Not the kind of writing I used to do."

"Then why do it? You were so talented. And such big dreams."

"The hours are regular. Nine to five. Better than newspapers. When Chris came along, I wanted something less demanding," Kat said. "And you? What about you?"

"My dreams were rather different from yours, remember? White weddings. Children. No. Not for me. I was tired of being poor. I wanted to change that. And I have."

Sarah gave a small smile and looked down, twisting the cabochon emerald ring off her finger, then holding it for a few seconds, as if checking its weight, before replacing it.

Kat remembered clearly then, the day before her sixteenth birthday on the cliff edge near Brighton. A gusty, gray day; the Channel had been choppy, a few boats making their rolling way to the Brighton Marina. They had been staying with Sarah's aunt Helen, at Lansdowne, her huge mansion near the Sussex coast, and the young Sarah wore her weekend outfit: old blue jeans; a thick, black knee-length sweater with holes in the sleeves. She had been pulling at the grass, and whispered in a small, harsh voice.

"I wanted to buy you that pearl ring we saw in the Lanes for your birthday. But I didn't have enough allowance left. I hate this. Not having enough money. Hate it."

Only Kat, of all Sarah's teenage friends, knew that Sarah's ragged appearance was not, as some of the girls believed, a pose; a bohemian, artistic image that she affected. It was due to lack of funds. Hers was a genteel, aristocratic British poverty, but poverty nevertheless. Kat, even with her working-class, council-house background, had more pocket money to spend.

"Don't be silly. I don't need a ring," Kat had said. And she didn't. She had no interest in jewelry, would rather have had a book or a CD. But Sarah loved Victorian jewelry and prowled the Brighton Lanes and the many antique shops like a hungry cat. Sarah produced the pearl ring a few days later and gave it to Kat with sullen defiance. Kat was quite certain that Sarah had stolen it. The thought both thrilled and horrified her. She was never able to comfortably wear the ring, was nervous about giving it away lest it had been reported as stolen, and so she had it still, somewhere at the bottom of a drawer.

"You're very successful in business," Kat said now. "So says Mr. Miyamoto."

"Mr. Miyamoto who would like me for a client?" asked Sarah, laughing. She had the same rich, full laugh that Kat remembered from years ago. "Well, he's quite right. I am."

She was still smiling when Scott turned the corner. Maggie followed a few steps behind.

"There you are, Mrs. Harrison. Some of my partners are searching for you."

"Oh, call me Sarah, please," she said. "And do take me to them."

Sarah took Scott's arm, leading him back to the ballroom. She was smiling up at him, her chin raised, shoulders perfectly straight. It was a regal posturing that caused Maggie, following behind with Kat, to whisper.

"Will you look at her? Who does she think she is?"

"Maggie—cut it out."

But Sarah had swept Scott into the throng, the guests parting to let them through until they reached Miyamoto and his entourage. Then, the group surrounded them again, like a sea tide ebbing back.

"She's so over the top," said Maggie. "Way over the top."

"That's just how she is. She's always been like that," said Kat. "She's not hurting anyone."

"No? Wait. Just wait and see."

Later, Kat saw Scott standing with the Miyamotos and the previous owners of the hotel chain. Sarah was standing right beside Scott. Kat was swamped by a clear memory that was twenty years old. Then, Kat had opened the door of the small Birmingham apartment she shared with Sarah to find that Sven, the Danish boy she was involved with, had his arms around a girl. When Kat gasped, they both turned. In the dim afternoon light, Kat saw that the girl was Sarah, wearing only a white slip, one strap pulled down over her shoulder so that her full breast was bare.

Kat swallowed, glanced at Maggie, who was talking with James Dempsey.

"You all right, Kat?" her sister asked.

"Yes. Yes, fine."

"Looks like the black widow is saying good-bye," Maggie said.

"Good. That means we can leave," Kat said.

James Dempsey looked at Maggie with amusement.

"Black widow?" he inquired.

"You will forget that I said that, James," Maggie murmured.

"Please," Kat added.

"Consider it forgotten," said James, but he was grinning. "She's something else, isn't she? Cute, though. Very cute."

"Oh yes, indeed," said Maggie with a sigh. "She's cute all right."

Sarah was looking around the ballroom, and after a moment she leaned toward Scott and whispered something to him. His eyes scanned the room until he found his wife and he indicated her whereabouts with a smile. Kat stood, uncomfortable and shy, as Sarah crossed the room. James also jumped to his feet, but Sarah did not look at him or at Maggie. Instead, she reached for Kat and planted a light kiss on her cheek.

"I can't tell you how happy I am to see you again."

"Yes. A surprise," said Kat.

"I'd love to keep in touch. If that's all right?"

The green eyes looked serious. Kat nodded automatically.

"Yes. Yes. Of course."

Sarah touched Kat's arm, a soft pressure, then turned and returned to the group at the door.

"Exit, pursued by a bear," murmured Maggie. "With any luck."

James raised an eyebrow, looked quizzically at Kat.

"Shakespeare," Kat explained. *"Winter's Tale."*

James laughed as he sat down again. Kat found that her hands were trembling; there was a thrumming in her chest.

"Now, we can leave," she said. "Surely?"

In the hotel room, Scott stood and stretched.

"We should think about bed, sweetheart," he said, smoothing Kat's hair. "Miyamoto wants a breakfast meeting before we all head back to LA."

They had booked an extra room for Scott and Kat, with a king-size bed, but Kat still lounged on her bed in Maggie's room as she sipped a nightcap.

"Unless you want to stay here and chat for a while?" he added.

"No. We can chat in the morning," said Kat, swinging her legs over the edge of the bed and fumbling for her shoes. She looked over at her sister, now leaning back against the headboard and yawning widely.

"Besides, Ms. Life and Soul of the Party here is fading fast."

"I am. I admit it," said Maggie. "I think the sight of Cherrington wore me out. *Maggie, you haven't changed a bit.* Bloody bitch."

"You're talking about Sarah Harrison?" Scott asked.

"The very same. She was Sarah Cherrington when we knew her."

"She come from some kind of old-money family?" Scott asked. "James said he thought so."

"Because she acts like the queen?" Maggie asked.

"Maggie, stop. She's from an old English family," Kat said. "But there's no money left, I don't think. She would never talk about her parents. They're both dead."

Kat had asked Sarah about her mother once, tentatively, and Sarah had turned sharply, eyes flashing like knives: *Never ask me about her. Never.* Kat never asked again.

"The partners thought she was charming," Scott said. "Miyamoto liked her a lot."

"Naturally," said Maggie. "And what did Mrs. Miyamoto have to say?"

"She doesn't say much. Oh, okay, I get it. Anyway, time for bed."

Kat, getting to her feet, turned to Maggie.

"What time's your flight, Mags?"

"Not until the evening. We have plenty of time."

"We can have our own breakfast meeting then," said Kat. "I'll come get you around nine."

Maggie stood, still yawning, and walked with them to the door. As Scott strolled toward the elevator, Kat kissed her sister's cheek and turned to follow him.

"Sleep well, Maggie."

"I'll probably have nightmares," Maggie said. "Who would have thought we'd meet that damn woman again?"

Shaking her head, Maggie closed the door.

Kat opened the drapes a little so they could see the sky from the bed.

"Is it too bright?" she asked Scott. "The moon will be shining right on us."

"Leave it. It's nice. Come to bed."

She cuddled in beside him, and he pulled her against his shoulder, holding his arms loosely around her.

"Missed you," he said.

"I missed you, too. It must have been horrible. An empty house," she said. "I didn't think about that."

"It was quiet."

He hugged her closer and Kat became aware of his erection, pressing against her thigh. The first time since Chris's death that she had been aware of any sexual stirring in Scott at all. She stayed very still, tears building in her throat. He was kissing her shoulder, softly, persuasively, and she squeezed her eyes tightly shut, thinking—*I can't. I just can't.* But she did not want to hurt him. He was hurt enough. She lay very still, waited for a minute or two. His penis was rigid now, digging hard and painfully into her. His breathing had changed.

"Scott. I'm sorry. I'm so sorry."

He took a deep breath, held her still and tight.

"It's all right. Of course it's all right."

"I know you want to—"

"Hey," he said, leaning up on an elbow and looking at her. "It's not me. The beast has a will of its own."

She tried to smile, pulled him down to hug him so that he could not see her face. Her body felt frozen into solid ice, impenetrable; icy fear surrounded her.

"Scott, I love you. You know that."

"I know," he said. "When you're ready, tell me."

"Yes. Yes, of course I will."

He moved onto his back. His arm was still around her but she felt a distance between them, and after a time she heard his breathing become even as he fell asleep. Kat watched a narrow ray of moonlight as slowly through the hours it moved across the room. When it lit on Scott's face she feared it might wake him, so very slowly, quietly, she crept to the window, closed the drapes, then returned to the bed. Scott stirred beside her.

"Go to sleep, Kat," he whispered. As dawn began to break, she did.

SIX

Kat woke to see Scott and Maggie at the small table in the corner of the room, sipping coffee and reading newspapers.

"Oh, damn," she said. "Maggie, I'm so sorry. Did I miss our breakfast?"

"Missed the breakfast and the light lunch, too," Maggie said. "Not to worry, darling. I'm barely out of bed myself."

Kat struggled to see the bedside clock.

"You're done with the meeting, Scott?" she asked.

"Yep. It was short and sweet. Ted Lafitte thanked us. Sarah Harrison thanked us. Said it will be a pleasure working with us—she's quite certain we'll do an excellent job for her consortium et cetera, et cetera. And that was that. The associates all grabbed doughnuts and left. So did I."

"So they decided to take you on?" Kat asked.

"I guess she's decided. I think she has to present it to her board, but I kind of got the impression that if she said yes, it's pretty much a done deal. Miyamoto seemed to think so anyway. He was mighty pleased. Grinning like a fool."

Maggie made a slight huffing sound.

"Were they all bowing to her and kissing her ring and everything?"

Scott stared at his sister-in-law with amused bewilderment.

"Maggie, what on earth did this woman do to you to make you dislike her so much?"

"How long have you got?"

"Maggie. Please. Leave it alone," Kat said, wanting to halt what she knew would be a long and detailed diatribe. "Sarah is Scott's new client. It was a long time ago. Forgotten."

Maggie gave Kat a long look, appeared to register the pleading tone in her sister's voice.

"O-*kay*," she said slowly. "One thing, Scott—the very first time I met her, she booted me out of my own room in my own house."

Scott grinned.

"You're not serious?"

"Yep. You remember *that*, don't you, Kat?"

"Yes. Of course."

Sarah's first visit to the Watt home occurred on a day toward the end of the semester at the convent school. Kat's mother studied this girl, with her long braided hair and her upper-class voice, knowing a stranger, and set out a proper tea with the best tablecloth used only for special visitors.

"Why don't we go to your room?" Sarah had whispered afterward. Kat stared at her, astounded: in her working-class world, kids did not use their bedrooms for anything other than sleeping and homework. When Kat and Sarah opened the door to the shared bedroom, Maggie was sitting at the small desk, her books open in front of her.

"Oh," said Sarah. "I didn't realize you— Do you mind if we have some privacy?" she asked.

Maggie's cheeks were crimson and she trembled slightly.

"I've got all my homework out," she said.

"I'm not going to touch your homework, silly," Sarah said. "Golly, look how red you are. Do you always blush like that?"

Maggie stood at once and hurried from the room, leaving her books still open.

"So that's why you dislike her so much?" asked Scott, bemused.

"Oh no. There's a lot more."

"Leave it, Mags," Kat said.

But Maggie took a sip of her coffee, then spoke directly to Scott, ignoring her sister.

"Sarah Cherrington broke the heart of someone I loved and just about ruined my wedding day. Reason enough for a little dislike, don't you think? Reason enough."

"Maggie!" said Kat fiercely. She looked at her sister with annoyance. Maggie returned her look, then added stubbornly:

"Plus, she stole my boyfriend."

"Not Paul?" Scott asked.

"Of course not Paul. Jason. The boy before Paul."

Maggie was clearly not going to be deflected. Kat, sitting up on the edge of the bed, tried to lighten her voice.

"Well, think of it this way—if she hadn't lifted Jason, you might never have married Paul."

"*Lifted* Jason?" Scott asked.

"Yep. That's how she operates," Maggie said. "Light-fingered. She'd take every male in sight if she could, especially if he seemed happy with someone else."

"Come on, Maggie, that's not fair," Kat said. "A lot of guys made a play for her. No surprise, considering her looks. She *was* stunning. It wasn't all her fault."

"Oh, get out. She got away with a whole bunch of crap because she was beautiful, and I bet she gets away with a whole bunch of crap now because she's rich. And Sven? You can't say that wasn't deliberate. And she even came on to Paul, you know, at a party once, out of sheer vindictiveness to get at me. Just after we got engaged. I thought he hadn't noticed, because he just ignored her. You know how vague he is about such things. But years later, we were talking about predatory women and I mentioned her and said, 'Of course you didn't notice that she was coming on to you.' And he laughed and said, 'Maggie, naturally I noticed. How could I not? I was enormously flattered.'"

All three smiled at this. Maggie took another sip of her coffee, then looked at Scott.

"She's a nasty person. Don't trust her."

"Noted," Scott said.

Maggie said nothing more, and Scott, after glancing at his wife's face, began folding up the newspaper and packing files into his briefcase.

"Okay. Here's the plan," he said. "Why don't we get going and have a real breakfast on the road? That way you'll have time to rest and pack before your flight, Maggie."

"Fine with me," said Maggie, looking at Kat in a conciliatory way. "I wish I had more time. Just a few more days."

"We can't keep you here forever," Kat said. "Paul must be missing you."

"I expect he is. And I've got business stuff to do. And Paul wants to take a long weekend in Paris to see Adam. Otherwise . . ."

A sharp pain, an arrow through the heart, shot through Kat. It was such an innocent sentence, she didn't know if Scott, sipping his coffee, even noticed it. *Paris to see Adam.* She and Scott would never say *Paris to see Chris.* Or even *Berkeley to see Chris.* It should have been possible. They raised him, educated him, loved him; above all, they had loved him. He was ready. He had been accepted. He had an academic scholarship, a dorm room, classes chosen. *To Berkeley to see Chris.*

Kat held the coffee cup so tightly with both hands that it began to tremble. She placed it down carefully, telling herself: *Breathe slowly, control it.* She must learn not to break down every time the knife twists. Maggie said something else. Kat did not hear it clearly, but she felt herself calming. Scott and Maggie did not seem to have noticed.

Maggie left for LAX an hour after their return home. As she watched the taxi pull away, Kat heard a voice calling her name and saw Brooke, in a loose wrap and black bikini, across the street at her mailbox.

"Been away, sweetie?" Brooke called.

"Palm Springs."

"Love that place," Brooke said. "I guess you're tired. I won't keep you. I made some of that date loaf Scott likes. Hang on, I'll get it." She disappeared into her house.

Brooke had been baking date loaves as small gifts for them since both Chris and Scott, at a barbecue at her house years before, told her the dessert bread was awesome. She confided to Kat that it was the only thing she could bake.

"I'm hopeless at pastry," she said. "Mine is so heavy it would sink a battleship."

A striking blonde divorcée, with a love of fashionable clothes and impossible heels, Brooke liked to sunbathe in her side yard wearing the tiniest of bikinis. Occasionally, she would remove the bikini top and lie on her stomach, spread-eagled on a beach towel. Chris had been fourteen years old when Brooke first moved in across the street, and he and his friends all stared longingly at this new neighbor as she lay, her skin oiled and gleaming gold, soaking up the sun. The posse of boys raced up and down the street, slowing at Brooke's yard as the teenagers stretched up high on the pedals of their bikes to get a better view, bobbing their heads like meerkats.

"She's going to cause a bike pileup if she doesn't put some clothes on," Scott had said once, laughing as he watched the boys from the window.

The day that the news of Chris's accident swept through the neighborhood, Brooke appeared at the Hamiltons' door with a chicken casserole, a date loaf, and two bottles of wine. Since then, she had been a gentle support for Kat. She visited occasionally, sitting with Kat and talking quietly of nothing very much, always bringing small gifts—a special bath oil for Kat, a single- malt whisky for Scott.

Now, she emerged from her house carrying the date loaf on a baking tray and handed it to Kat.

"It's a bit burnt on the corners," Brooke said. "I got distracted by *America's Most Wanted*." She paused to study Kat's face. "So how are you, sweet pea? How was the desert?"

"Fine. The scenery's so pretty. The hotel was nice."

"But?" Brooke asked, not convinced.

"I struggled a bit with Scott's client thing. All those people. And the big client turned out to be an old school friend, so that was a bit weird."

"Really? Scott's old school friend? Or yours?"

"Mine. She's a widow now. Married some high-powered international investor type. She's very rich."

"Well, that's good, isn't it? To reconnect with an old friend?"

"Not sure. Maybe not this old friend," Kat said. "Anyway, love, thank you for this."

"You're welcome. Tell Scott sorry about the corners."

"He won't mind. He'll wolf it down."

Brooke smiled a good-bye, then headed for her side yard, stripping off her wrap and exposing the bikini even as she crossed the street.

Kat placed the loaf in the kitchen before walking slowly around the house as if reestablishing herself inside it. The air of the house felt oppressive; the very walls and roof seemed heavier. Was it possible for a house to absorb grief, hold it in the walls?

"The house feels heavy," she said to Scott. "Dark."

"We've just come from the desert," he said. "The light is different."

"But don't you feel it? The heaviness? It feels as if the ceiling is pressing down."

He was heading to his den, a file under his arm, but he paused to look at her.

"I'll adjust the air a bit," he said. "It's probably musty."

Kat wandered into Chris's room, sat on his bed, looked at his hard rock posters, his books, his CDs, ran a hand along the papers on his desk. He had left an essay unfinished; the pen still lay on top of it. She opened his closet, touching the shirts and sweaters, holding each one to her face.

She reached for his leather jacket and stroked the soft nap. He hadn't worn it much; he had been saving it for some special occasion. Some date, perhaps, with a girl. It was hard to look back on the day they bought this jacket. He was so excited, eyes bright, kidding her along, knowing that she would eventually give in. It was too much money, Kat said. But Chris knew it wasn't really too much money; they wouldn't be there in the department store trying it on if it were.

He had wanted that jacket so badly, and she had hesitated for a while, really wanting to wait until after Christmas, to see if it would go on sale. *Thank God,* Kat thought now, *thank God I said yes.* He was so happy that day, coming home with the coat on a hanger. He had carried it thrown over his shoulder and walked with a jaunty step to the car. Then, he hung it carefully in the closet, waiting for that special occasion. How many times had he worn it? Twice? Three times? She could not imagine ever giving it away, or throwing it away, but what could she do with it, except stroke it, hold it to her face as if she could breathe him in, breathe him back to life.

She turned from the closet to look at the framed photographs squashed on top of the dresser among open video games, empty DVD cases, books, and dried-out pens. There was Chris with his friends, Vanessa and Ben and another boy, his name gone from her memory. They were maybe ten years old, grinning at the camera. Kat spotted herself in the background, her hair tied back in a ponytail. She was laughing. *Rewind,* Kat thought. *Rewind to that point, right there. Start over.*

Kat, suddenly weak, heart pounding, sat down abruptly on Chris's bed, still holding the photograph. What she really wanted to do was get under the covers, lie where Chris used to lie, snuggle down where he used to sleep. But though she longed to do it, she was also frightened. Her heart might implode with the pain of it. Scott could come into the bedroom and find this just too strange, too crazy. He might fear that she had reached some final breaking point.

A shadow crossed the doorway, and she looked up to find Scott watching her.

"You okay?" he asked.

"Yep. Just looking at these old pics," she said, standing, placing the photograph back on the dresser.

He came to stand beside her, lifted another picture. It showed them camping years ago, in Yosemite. She must have taken the photo herself, for there was Scott, grinning, and Chris and two of his young friends.

"That was a fun trip," Scott said.

"Oh yes," Kat said, remembering the fire that wouldn't start, the tent that wouldn't stay up, the new hiking shoes she had foolishly bought only a week before and not worn in, so that she had blisters on her feet the size of silver dollars. But she remembered, too, late at night under the stars, the boys laughing in their own tent, Scott beside her as they whispered about the happenings of the day.

"It was wonderful," she said now. They stood for a while longer looking at the pictures on the dresser.

"I was hoping you were making coffee," Scott said. "And maybe a sandwich. And a slice of Brooke's date loaf."

"Oh, you are so subtle! Well, keep hoping, buddy." She turned then, to look at him. "I'll make something in a minute. Okay?"

He placed a gentle, closed fist against her cheek for a moment.

"Thanks."

Later, as she carried a mug of coffee and a sandwich into Scott's den, she saw that he was bent over his desk, studying plans and blueprints.

"You almost done?" she asked.

"I'm getting there."

Kat looked over his shoulder; the plans made no sense to her.

"I'm going to have a bath, then read in bed."

Scott glanced at his watch.

"Already? It's barely eight."

"So?" she said.

Scott did not respond. He had returned to the blueprints, had begun to make notes on a yellow legal pad, engrossed in his work.

SEVEN

While Scott showered and prepared for work on Monday morning, Kat carried her laptop through to the dining area, next to the kitchen in their contemporary open-plan home. She placed it on the table, along with a legal pad and pen, and then she made a pot of strong coffee. When Scott came downstairs, dressed for the office, he studied her, puzzled.

"What's this?"

"Job search."

He came to kiss the top of her head.

"That's good, sweetheart. That's really good."

Over the next week, Kat studied prospective jobs, listed agencies, made notes of phone numbers. The few phone calls she made were difficult. She tried to sidestep questions about why she was moving from a job she had done well for five years, that was well paid, to positions that were sometimes described as "entry level."

A recruiter was astonished when Kat, calling about a job for an admin assistant in a school, mentioned her previous salary. Kat decided to downplay the salary, downplay her responsibilities. She did not want a job that involved public relations, or customer service, or any kind of position that meant she had to smile at strangers.

"They want someone perky," the recruiter said. "With good communication skills."

"I am not *perky*," Kat murmured. "I was never that."

Eventually, she stopped making the calls, and instead sat at the dining table reading the online ads, imagining the calls, the interviews, the responses. Occasionally, moments from the past few months would flash into her mind: the funeral, choosing the flowers, the awkward visits of Chris's friends. These memories dropped softly, completely intact, into her mind. Sometimes, they were in strong, primary colors, occasionally in a kind of sepia, like old movies.

One morning, she was transported right back to the room where they chose the coffin. The funeral director took them down in an elevator, an elevator with brass rails and frosted dark glass. It seemed to sink far down, underground, under the earth. When the doors opened, Kat and Scott stepped out into an enormous room. It was ballroom size and it was full of coffins: polished wood coffins of oak and mahogany, metal ones of silver and gold and brass, and tiny ones of white wood, some with satin or silk or ribbon, or elaborate decoration. The light was strange, silvery, ethereal. Scott took her hand and they walked fast through the aisles that separated the different types, the expensive ones first, the cheaper ones at the end of the ballroom. They whispered to each other, saying what about this one, this will be fine, or this, looking at the prices so quickly, barely able to look inside these caskets, one of which would cradle their son for eternity. They chose a light oak one, then walked, with knees that trembled, back to the elevator, and Kat pressed the elevator button so fast that the director had to squeeze in as the doors were closing. Scott recited the number of the casket they had chosen, and the price. He quoted it to the funeral director without moving his eyes from the elevator doors. It was surreal. They were actors in a movie. They were not real. Nothing was real.

Immobilized at the dining table, the laptop open in front of her, Kat waited until these strange dreamlike sequences ended, then began again to scan the job listings.

When Maggie called from England, Kat heard herself telling smooth lies and was surprised at how easily her sister believed her: Yes, she had interviews; there was some work out there. She wanted to be sure, though, wanted to find something that was just right. Maggie agreed.

"Take your time, darling. Might take a little while. How's Scott holding up?"

"Oh, he's doing better. He's busy. Very busy."

In fact, Scott was so busy that he was often distracted and vague or irritable with the brittle edge of exhaustion.

"New client, new challenges," he explained to Kat, apologizing for a sudden snap of temper. "And Jesus, Sarah Harrison has a whole bunch of subsidiaries. Wish I'd known that going in. I've had to farm out some of the routine stuff on my old clients to other partners."

A series of client meetings meant that a couple of suits had to be taken to the cleaners and a new suit purchased. When Kat told him how smart he looked, he told her he felt like a salesman. That when he'd finally been able to revisit the Compton project, young Chiller had told him he should be pimping on the Westside. He was late getting home so frequently that Kat often ate her own dinner alone and left his meal to be reheated in the microwave.

He asked about the job search, and as she did with Maggie, she tried to make it sound active and interesting. She created entire phone conversations with headhunters, pretended that she was setting up interviews. She did not describe the mornings when, once Scott had left for the office, she checked again that hidden bottle of sleeping pills, saved for the day it became too hard to navigate the simple pathways of a normal life. She did not describe the hours at the dining table and the strange dreamlike state that sometimes enveloped her: flashbacks, memories, long minutes lost.

It was on one of these days, when Kat had the laptop open on the table in front of her, that the doorbell rang. She frowned, saw through the etched glass of the front door the shape of a woman. She opened the door reluctantly, ready with her excuses, expecting to see a concerned ex-colleague from Waters & Chappell.

"Hello, Kat," said Sarah.

The sun shone onto Sarah's face, and her dark hair hung loose and gleaming on her shoulders. She held peach roses, a bottle of wine, and a bag of what appeared to be food from a delicatessen. Kat could smell lemon chicken. A green Jaguar was parked at the curb.

"Lunch," said Sarah.

It was a shock to see her there. She looked so polished, a creature from a smoother, shinier world.

"Sarah! So sorry. I'm just on my way out," Kat lied. "I have a job interview."

"Oh, what a bore. You can surely reschedule it," Sarah said, stepping into the house. Her voice sounded warm and light. A young voice. She followed Kat into the kitchen, holding her packages.

"Pretty home," Sarah said, looking beyond the dining area to the living room, with its long leather sofas and view of the garden.

"Thank you," Kat said, aware at once of the stained blue smock she was wearing and the untidy state of her hair.

She found a vase for the roses and turned to find Sarah watching her.

"I was just going to change," Kat said, pulling at the smock. "For the interview."

"You have time for a quick bite, surely?" Sarah asked.

"I don't think so."

Sarah, unpacking the food regardless, continued to look over at her and smiled.

"Come on, Kat. Greek salad and stuffed mushrooms? And can't you smell this absolutely fabulous chicken? Lemon, lime, and herbs. Reschedule your appointment. Tell them you'll come tomorrow."

"I'll tell them later this afternoon," Kat said, snapping the laptop shut. "Excuse me a minute."

In the bathroom, Kat rinsed her face, changed into a cotton shirt, and ran a comb through her hair. When she returned, Sarah had laid out the food on the dining table, found napkins, silverware, and wineglasses. It looked almost festive. She had pushed the legal pad aside. Kat wondered if she had looked at those scrawled notes: *admin assistant, secretary, receptionist.*

Sarah, studying the Rothko print on the wall, turned to her.

"You didn't grow out of him, then?"

At Kat's puzzled frown she added, "You had a different Rothko in Birmingham. The one with fuzzy green and violet and that orangey-red. In the flat."

"Oh, you're right. I did. Why should I grow out of him?"

"He's so popular now. His prints are everywhere."

"And why should that diminish his work?" Kat asked.

Sarah laughed, as if pleased with this response, and waved toward the table.

"Please. Try this wonderful food. And I found this bread on the counter—it looks delicious. You're making your own?"

"No. Brooke bakes it for Scott. We shouldn't eat it. He loves it."

"Brooke?"

"My neighbor. Friend."

"Nice to have a homely baking type for a neighbor."

"She's not exactly homely. Blonde divorcée. Outrageous flirt. Big heart."

"And she makes this specially for Scott?" Sarah asked in a teasing tone.

"Yes," Kat said. "She does."

When they were seated, Sarah did not begin to eat immediately but indicated the notepad she had pushed to one side and said, "You need a job you'll like, Kat. In something you're good at."

"I know. Something will turn up."

"Will you let me help? I know people everywhere. Newspapers, radio, television."

"That's not necessary," said Kat. "But thank you anyway."

Sarah reached for the wine and poured it into their glasses.

"You prefer to stay in public relations? Or would you rather go back to journalism?"

"Not sure right now."

"Remember when you were fourteen and you wanted to be a war correspondent?" Sarah asked.

"At that age—well."

"You wanted to be a war correspondent and you wanted a house that was not a council house and lots of children."

Kat looked at her, surprised. How clearly she remembered.

"Yes," she said. "I did."

Kat could still visualize that fantasy home. It looked like one drawn with precise concentration by a child: a square frontage, symmetrical windows, and a central, brightly painted door. Behind the house she imagined a wild garden and three, sometimes four, laughing children, a leaping dog, an apple tree.

The career dream changed slightly over the years: war correspondent, feature writer, columnist. The house and family dream never did.

"That was then," she said. "I don't know what I want to do right now. I'm still in a bit of a fog."

"Well, of course you are," Sarah said. "Now, try this. It actually melts in the mouth."

Kat spooned some of the chicken onto her plate and helped herself to salad and a rice dish that contained chopped celery and raisins and was flavored with a soft, scented herb. Sarah heaped food onto her plate, making little murmuring sounds of pleasure. Kat was reminded of how Sarah loved to eat, how jealous the other schoolgirls had been that she stayed so slim. She was slender still. Kat tasted the chicken.

"This is good," she said.

"I hoped you would like it."

Sarah paused, studied Kat's face.

"Maggie's still angry, then," she said.

"Why should Maggie be angry?"

"About Sven."

"A long time ago. I don't expect she ever thinks about it," Kat said.

"And you? Do you think about it?"

"Twenty years ago, Sarah. Water under the bridge."

"Did you get back together eventually?"

The question shocked Kat. She looked hard at Sarah, frowning.

"What?"

"I thought you might get back together."

"You . . . you know about the accident?"

"I heard he'd tumbled down some stairs. I left the city, remember. I went straight to Sussex and then on to Antibes."

Kat knew that Sarah had left the apartment they shared and moved to France to stay with an aunt. She believed that Sarah never contacted Sven again. She had simply taken him and then discarded him. She had not returned to Birmingham. It was rumored, some months later, that she was studying in Montpellier. But Kat had always assumed that someone told Sarah how badly Sven was injured that day.

"He fractured his skull," Kat said. "He'd been drinking."

Sarah placed her knife and fork down slowly and stared at Kat. Her face had paled.

"I thought it was just a minor thing. It was serious?" she asked.

"Yes. Very. A fractured skull and damage to the spinal cord. He was unconscious when I saw him. His parents came from Denmark and eventually moved him back there."

"Didn't Paul keep in touch with him?" Sarah asked. "And find out how he was?"

"He tried," Kat said. "But no. No, he couldn't."

Sarah seemed at a loss.

"I didn't know the details," she whispered eventually. "Nobody would talk to me. No wonder you both hate me."

Kat gave her a sharp look.

"I don't hate anyone. Nor does Maggie," Kat said.

Some of the old pain for Sven bubbled back to the surface. And some of the old anger, too. Had it not been for Sarah . . . well, who knew? A tragedy could occur without anyone being at fault. Kat knew that better than anyone. But Sven's accident had caused speculation. He did not usually drink, but he had been very drunk that day. His alcohol level, when tested at the hospital, was phenomenally high. The doctors were surprised that he had managed to get himself home, though nobody knew how.

"What can I say?" Sarah began. "I had no idea he would—"

Kat shook her head.

"Stop it," said Kat. "Please. I don't want to talk about this, Sarah. Not now."

Sarah, nodding, looked relieved.

"You ever go back to St. Theresa's?" she asked.

"No. Never."

"I set up a scholarship fund, you know," Sarah said. "For girls who want to go to university to study business, or economics. A different option. Balance out all those ridiculous funds for teachers and nuns."

"That must have been a first for them," Kat said. "A scholarship for business majors."

"Yes, it was. I tried to set up a fund for working-class girls to attend the school, but Sister Judy claims that things are rather different now. There's still the academic scholarship test, of course. The one you passed."

Kat remembered the three-hour test, the interview in front of a committee of middle-class governors. She could still visualize the chairwoman: a terrifying woman with shaded equine teeth.

"And do you get many applicants for your college fund?"

"Oh yes. I get to choose the winning ones each year. It's fun. Like playing God. They give me a short list and I pick the winners. I choose the ones with a bit of a spark in their school histories. None of those Legion of Mary virgins. Though Sister Judy may have sussed me. Wouldn't surprise me if she didn't throw in a bit of smoking behind the gym just to get me to choose her favorite."

"It's good that you're doing this, Sarah. Really."

"Fun to see the old names come up. The daughters of our old friends and enemies. Oh, remember Bunty Kelly? Face like a glazed ham?"

Kat did. Head girl for one term, and a bully.

"Yes. You had a fight with her over something."

"Monstrous girl accused me of stealing her St. Bernadette medal. Remember that?"

"I remember the day in the showers when she accused you of taking it," Kat said.

"Well, I fixed her," Sarah said with grim pleasure. "Recently."

"Fixed her? Just because of a false accusation?"

Sarah looked up. Her eyes were dancing.

"False? Who said anything about false?"

"So you did steal the medal?"

"Of course I did. She left it there in her locker, right on top of a prayer book, and the locker door wide-open. So prissy. Fake faith. So, yes. I took it. Just to annoy her. But the fact is, she never saw me take it. No one did. There was no one in the gym at the time. So she made that accusation in public, with all my friends listening, when she had *no evidence at all*!"

"So—what did you do to her?"

"Her daughter applied for a scholarship. Perfect candidate. Bunty had been grooming her for years, apparently. I turned her down."

"You turned her down?" Kat asked. "Because of Bunty? But why should the daughter suffer?"

"It's the parents who suffer," Sarah said. "When they don't get the funds. Let Big Bully Bunty pay for the girl. Anyway, it entertains me a bit. I'm involved in a Catholic adoption charity, too. That's rather fun."

Sarah, noting Kat's startled expression, laughed.

"Now, that did surprise you, didn't it? As an alternative to a termination. Well, you know why. You were there. Remember?"

Kat, after a small tremble of shock, gulped at her wine. She recalled the tall Georgian building on a Brighton terrace, the ground-floor clinic, and Aunt Helen's annoyance. Sarah did not want to go through with the termination but had given in finally, demanding that Kat come, too, for support. Nobody else knew about it. Sarah and Kat were both fifteen years old. Kat had waited in a wide corridor, watched as a tall male doctor came for Sarah, placed a hand on the small of her back, and guided her forward as if leading her onto the dance floor. He took her along the corridor and through double doors into the clinic. Helen followed behind, her hands clenched into fists. An interminable time later, Sarah emerged through the double doors with Helen's arm tight around her shoulders. Both looked pale and shaken; neither of them spoke. That night, at Lansdowne, Sarah had been shivering badly, unable to get warm, and Helen gave her a whisky toddy, made with hot water and honey. Kat offered her the duvet from her own bed, piling it on top of the extra blankets that Mrs. Evans, the housekeeper, had produced earlier.

In the middle of the night, Kat woke to hear Sarah whimpering. The sheet and duvet were dark with blood; she had bled right through the bulky sanitary pad.

"I need more pads," she whispered to Kat, her face ghostly white in the dim bedroom light. "I daren't move."

"I'll get Helen," Kat had said, terror causing her voice to shake.

Throughout their school years, and even during college, Sarah rarely spoke of that day, or the surgery that was necessary afterward, and never to anyone but Kat. She referred to the experience always as *that clinic visit*. Kat had never heard her use the word *termination* before.

Now, Sarah waited.

"You do remember?"

"Of course I remember," Kat said.

"Well, the reason I got involved with the adoption charity is not only because of that clinic visit. No, it's so that those nice Catholic girls who make one silly mistake don't ruin their lives by being saddled with a baby. And go on to have a dozen more, just like their mothers. And so many couples want babies desperately and can't have their own. So—perfect. A solution! You're amazed, aren't you, that I should become a charity matron?"

"Surprised. Yes."

"I have a number of them. Sam had his own favorites. Alcohol abuse, drugs, those kinds of things."

She studied Kat's face and smiled.

"There are good solid tax reasons for this, Kat. Ask your husband. I see his firm is involved in pro bono work. Some gangland project. A lad called *Chiller*! Well, that could be fun for everyone."

Sarah reached for the wine bottle to pour more wine. Kat held her hand over her glass, suddenly tired. Since Chris's death, she had avoided social lunches and casual conversation. Sarah's energy and intensity, once invigorating, now felt exhausting.

"Sorry," Kat said. "But I have to get ready for the interview. I rescheduled my appointment for four o'clock."

"You can't cancel?" Sarah said.

"No. I really can't."

Sarah shook her head, then stood and lifted her bag.

"Would you like to meet for lunch in Beverly Hills sometime? Make a nice change for you."

"Maybe in a week or so?" Kat said evasively.

"I hope we can be friends again, Kat. We're going to be meeting from time to time. At least, I hope we are."

Kat was not sure whether Sarah meant to remind her that she was Scott's client, or whether she was hinting at some future social meetings.

"Of course," she said.

Sarah moved to the hallway. Kat held the door as Sarah stepped outside, adjusting the bag over her shoulder, slipping on her sunglasses. As she did so, Brooke's red Miata turned the corner and with a screech of brakes slammed into the driveway across the street. As Brooke climbed out of the car, she looked over to Kat, waved, and then took in Sarah. Kat imagined her doing a swift assessment of Sarah's clothes and shoes.

"And is that big-hearted Brooke?" Sarah said. "You're right. She doesn't look like the home- baking type. Well, so lovely to see you."

"Thank you for the lunch," Kat said.

"My pleasure. Absolutely. I'll be in touch," said Sarah, before walking briskly down the path to her Jaguar.

Kat closed the front door and sat back down at the dining table. Holding her wineglass with both hands, she took a few sips to calm herself. Sven. To hear Sarah say his name had shaken her. Once, to talk of him would have caused tears.

She had heard about the Danish exchange student long before she met him. Paul spent summers with his friend in Denmark and had shown Kat pictures, and so, already interested, she dressed carefully on the day that the blond male was due to join her university comparative literature class. When he walked into the classroom, every girl in the room turned to stare at him. Sven, tall, flushed with radiant good health, seemed to glow. The English boys in the class, pale after a long winter, looked gray and drab in comparison. Kat was surprised when he asked her out, so many prettier girls were flirting with him, and wondered if Paul had suggested it, but Sven seemed genuinely interested and they dated all that semester. They spent a lot of time in bed. In the mornings, she would watch him exercise, a ritual he never missed.

"You're the poster boy for healthy living," she told him once as he measured out ingredients for a breakfast shake. "What are you adding to that now? Eye of newt? Toe of dog? It's a very weird color."

He looked up, puzzled.

"Those are healthy things? This is fruit only. The blueberries change the color. I will make enough for you."

"I'll be the healthiest woman on the planet. All this exercise and fruit shakes, too."

He smiled a white, wide smile.

Meticulous in courtship as he was in everything else, he asked if she was certain before inviting her to bed, was careful about contraception, sexually considerate. When she introduced him to her roommate, he seemed shy and intimidated. Sarah liked to tease him a little, call him the handsome Nordic god, make him blush.

In private, Sarah chided Kat.

"He's sweet. And yes, he's attractive. But, Caitlin, he's so bland, so wooden. You can't be serious about going to Denmark? What on earth will you talk about? Or do you plan to stay in bed for a year?"

It was his strong back Kat saw first, on that dark, rainy afternoon. Then, the muscular shoulders, the blond hair curling at the nape of his neck. He was murmuring to Sarah, the urgent intonation quite different from the voice he used with Kat. He seemed to be pleading.

She stood frozen in the doorway, her umbrella dripping, her hair in her eyes. Sarah and Sven. Kat had raced from the room, gone straight home to Rugby. Maggie's wedding was the next day. Kat never saw Sven conscious again. The next time she saw him, he was just a blank body in a hospital bed.

She recalled the slow-motion minutes during Maggie and Paul's wedding reception when Paul was called to the phone and returned to the ballroom, his face ashen. He whispered something to his new bride and both turned to stare at Kat as she stood chatting with a cousin. She remembered her sister crossing the room to tell her the bad news, her arms already outstretched.

All three had rushed to the hospital, Maggie in a borrowed raincoat over her wedding dress, to wait for hours in an echoing corridor. Paul, usually so calm, was agitated, his eyes bright with anxiety, hassling the nurses and the young doctors. "Why won't they tell us anything? Why can't we see him?" he asked repeatedly. But they were not family; they were not allowed into the ICU. Eventually, a nurse took pity on them and allowed them to sit with Sven, one by one, in the sterile, beeping hospital room.

"This is our wedding day," Maggie whispered to Kat as Paul took his turn. "We should have left for our honeymoon an hour ago."

Then, late that night, Sven's parents arrived from Denmark, so stiff, so formal, and his friends were not allowed to see him again. Sven was moved to a special unit in the hospital. He had a fractured skull, they were told. There was some damage to the spinal cord. Eventually, his parents arranged for him to be taken back to Denmark. Kat never discovered how they managed to do that. He was still unconscious, as far as she knew. His parents would not reply to Paul's calls or to his letters, causing him, and therefore Maggie, considerable distress.

"They blame me," Paul said. "He didn't drink at all before he came here."

But Paul was not to blame—they knew that. Was Sarah? Though Maggie thought so, Kat was never sure. Sven had been very drunk, as the hospital lab report confirmed. Some friends claimed to have seen him in the pub at lunchtime on the day of the wedding, morose and drinking alone. Another rumor was that Sarah had been with him, had actually gone home with him that afternoon, might have been there when the accident occurred. Kat did not believe that. Maggie did. But nobody knew for sure. Sven's fall remained a mystery. The young Dane simply disappeared from all their lives.

Kat sat at the dining table for a while, thinking back to that time. When her phone rang, late in the afternoon, she switched it to voice mail. It was Mark Tinsley, the features editor from a local weekly: an interesting paper, full of well-written articles on the arts, books, happenings in Los Angeles. He would like her to come in for an interview, the editor said. He had a position coming up. Mrs. Harrison had highly recommended her. He was free on Tuesday at ten in the morning if that was convenient.

"My God, Sarah," Kat said to the air. "You don't waste much time."

"So Sarah Harrison brought you lunch," Scott said that evening, spooning the remains of the lemon chicken onto a small plate, creating a starter for himself. "This is really good."

"Yes. You saw her this afternoon?"

"Yep. She was in the office for a late meeting. Man, she's got a good head on her shoulders. She sure knows what she wants. Even Woodruff was silenced for once in his asinine life. I talked to her afterward. She said something about a job? At a newspaper?"

Kat hesitated. "I've got an interview," she said. "On Tuesday."

Scott looked so pleased, his pleasure quite out of proportion to the fact that Kat felt anxiety rising in her gut. Now, she would have to attend the interview. There was no getting out of it.

"Excellent news, sweetheart," Scott said. "Anyway, she wants us all to go look at the model of the country-club estate. Her husband had it set up in their house in Ojai. They don't want to move it."

"She's got a house in Ojai? I thought she lived in Malibu?"

"Malibu is her beach house. I'm hearing that the Ojai place is huge. Anyway, she asked if you would come, too."

"No, I don't think so," Kat said.

"You're not curious about her house? How she lives? James has been out there, says it's quite something."

"No. I'm not curious."

Scott sighed.

"Look, she asked if you would come when Miyamoto was right there in the conference room," he said slowly. "Miyamoto asked if his wife was also invited. And Sarah said yes. I think if you don't go, well, Mrs. Miyamoto might feel uncomfortable. The only wife there."

Kat stood and took a breath before looking into her husband's eyes.

"I don't care if Mrs. Miyamoto feels uncomfortable," she said. "Mrs. Miyamoto has a daughter at Yale. A daughter, alive and healthy and beautiful, who has been home for the summer. Okay? Do you see the difference here, Scott, between Mrs. Miyamoto and me?"

Scott got to his feet at once, moved toward her, and held her by the shoulders.

"Of course I do. But it's just an overnight trip. A small group. You know them. You like them. They like you. It's my job, Kat. It's work."

Kat pulled back. She had become, she realized, so self-centered, so self-absorbed, she could not see anything beyond her own pain.

"Okay. I'll think about it. I'd prefer you went alone though."

"I don't want to go alone. I want you with me."

EIGHT

Scott turned off the 101 and took a narrow road up into the hills. The GPS on the dash showed that they were on the right street, but no signs or numbers were visible and the homes they passed were set way back from the road, surrounded by walls and electronic gates. Sarah's house was right at the top of the hill; James had said it had a distant view of the ocean.

Kat stretched in the car, flexing her shoulders. She wore tailored pants and felt corseted and tethered.

"What exactly did she do to Maggie?" Scott asked unexpectedly. "Sarah Harrison?"

Kat thought for a moment.

"To Maggie," she said. "And to me."

"You?"

He glanced at her quickly.

"A boy I was involved with. Sven. They had an affair."

"Involved? How involved were you?" Scott asked.

"We dated for one semester," said Kat. "I thought I was in love with him. I thought he felt the same about me. I was thinking about doing an exchange-student year in Denmark."

"It was serious, then?"

"It was serious at the time," Kat said, trying to be honest. "I think I might have got bored with him eventually. He was very attractive. But a bit—solemn. Sven was Paul's best friend. They'd been pen pals for years and used to spend summers together, and it was Paul who persuaded him to do the course in the UK. He was going to be the best man at Maggie and Paul's wedding. The day before the wedding, I went back to the flat. I'd forgotten my satin shoes. My bridesmaid shoes. And Sven was there, with Sarah."

"He was with her? You mean screwing her?" Scott asked.

"Pretty much. Sven didn't turn up for the rehearsal dinner that night. Paul couldn't track him down and he was so worried and upset. They had to ask another friend to be best man at the last minute."

She did not want to discuss with Scott the scene in the early hours of the morning of Maggie's wedding day, when Sarah came to their house, sobbing out apologies. Maggie had confronted her, their raised voices echoing between the houses, while Kat stayed crying in the bedroom.

"In the middle of the wedding reception, Paul got a call from the hospital that Sven had been badly hurt," she said. "Maggie and Paul canceled their honeymoon because of it."

Scott gave her a swift look.

"He recover?"

"I don't know. He was taken back to Denmark. We all lost touch after that."

"And Maggie blames Sarah?"

"Yes. She thought Sven was just a pawn in one of Sarah's little games. She's never forgiven her."

"You never talked about this," Scott said quietly.

Kat bit her lip, rested back in the seat.

"No. It was a long time ago."

How to explain to Scott the odd mix of guilt and pain she had felt? The sympathy heaped on her by friends made her uncomfortable, as did their anger at Sarah. They behaved as if her loss was huge, as if her soul mate had been snatched from her. It had not felt like that, she admitted to herself. Not at all. If she had loved Sven, it had been a pale, diluted love compared to what she would feel later, when she met Scott.

"What was he like, this Sven guy?" Scott asked casually, after a minute or two.

"Good-looking. But not as good-looking as you. Not as sexy as you. Not as intelligent, as charming, or as altogether masculine—"

"Fine, fine," he said, smiling. "I only asked."

They drove another half mile along a wooded lane that came to a dead end at a walled estate hidden behind wrought-iron gates. Scott studied the GPS.

"This is it."

He moved forward to the gates, looking for an entry phone or keypad.

"It's like a movie set," he said to Kat.

She stared at the high gates, looking for a bell or button to push.

"Fortress," she whispered. Immediately, the iron gates opened.

"You whisper 'Open Sesame'?" Scott asked.

"Must have an electronic eye."

"With our picture programmed in?"

Kat was not listening. She gazed at the gardens, clouded with a late-afternoon mist, and saw manicured lawns and, beyond them, the glimmer of a lake. The driveway was edged with a series of silver birch and beech trees with leaves that shimmered in the breeze. Far in the distance, a grayish-blue line, the ocean, was just visible.

"Lord, will you look at this," she said.

Scott glanced sideways.

"Pretty yard," he said.

It was all Sarah dreamed of and more, Kat was quite certain. The intense young girl with her patched-up sweaters who wanted so badly to be rich. This was about as rich as any reasonable person needed to be. As they turned a corner, she saw the house: a mansion in the Georgian style, silvery-white in the misty light, with graceful long lines and elegant frontage.

"Wow, it's beautiful," Kat said. "It's just like Lansdowne, the house in Sussex her aunt had. Except newer. And maybe bigger. And in much better shape."

"It's certainly big," said Scott.

A sweeping gravel driveway curved in front of the house, and a uniformed attendant waited for them.

"And valet parking, too," said Scott. "Miyamoto will be a happy camper. He loves this stuff."

As they climbed out of the car, Scott studied the house.

"Make a good country hotel," he said.

Kat smiled, just as Sarah appeared at the top of the front steps.

"At last! Come in."

She hurried forward to hug Kat and shake hands with Scott, then ushered them into her house. Both Scott and Kat paused in the hallway. The house was furnished with French and English antiques, and yet it was a light and airy home with high ceilings and French doors that stretched the entire length of the living areas, showing off the acres of wide green lawn and rose gardens. To the south, a paved path of pastel slate led to tennis courts and a pool.

"Come on, come see your room," Sarah said, leading them upstairs. "It's one of the nicest, I think."

Scott stood at the bedroom door as Sarah held Kat by the arm and led her into the room.

Kat gazed at the four-poster with drifting cream lace and chiffon, the window seat with tapestry cushions, a French writing desk. Casement windows opened to the gardens below.

"It's beautiful, Sarah. It reminds me of Lansdowne."

Kat moved to the writing desk, stroked the smooth wood. A silver bowl containing white roses and gardenias had been placed on it. She could smell their sweet scent.

"Remember the desk in Aunt Helen's bedroom?" Sarah asked. "Took me ages to find one just like it. That beauty had to be shipped from France."

"It's lovely."

"I knew you'd like it. I remember how you just flipped when you saw Lansdowne. And remember . . . remember Aunt Helen's bathroom? The big, grotty old tub with the claw feet? I've tried to reproduce it. See?"

Sarah opened the door to the bathroom and Kat felt disoriented for a moment. It looked just like the old bathroom in the Sussex mansion. But there the paint had been peeling, the tub old and stained. Here, the textured walls were carefully decorated with an expensive color wash.

"It's exactly right," said Kat. She turned to Sarah. "You loved that house."

"Yes. I did. I suppose I cared for Helen, prickly old gal though she was."

"She was a character," Kat said, recalling the patrician Englishwoman, in her pearls and shabby tweeds, pouring tea into porcelain cups. "You couldn't keep the house after she died?"

"No. I really, really wanted to buy it, but Sam said absolutely not. It was triple-mortgaged and had been so badly maintained. It needed everything replaced or repaired. So someone else bought the land, demolished Lansdowne, and built a hideous modern structure. I kept the gatehouse, though, at the edge of the estate. Remember that? Overlooking the water?"

"The little cottage with the view?" asked Kat. "Yes. Of course I remember it. How lovely. Do you visit it?"

"I do. Once in a while I go back and hike the cliffs. It refreshes me."

Sarah laughed, amused at herself, and then turned to Scott.

"You'd prefer something more modern, Scott?"

He nodded.

"Yep. Maybe."

"There's a shower room through this door, just for you."

Sarah opened the door of what looked like a closet and revealed a modern tiled steam shower, pristine, with clear glass doors.

"Perfect," he said.

"See you in about an hour," Sarah said. "For cocktails."

When the door closed behind her, Scott turned to Kat.

"It's not going to be so bad, sweetheart. At least we'll be comfortable."

"Comfortable indeed," said Kat. She had pulled her dress out of the suitcase and was shaking it to remove the wrinkles when someone tapped on the door. Scott moved to open it.

"Steam and press available for evening clothes," said a young woman in a starched apron. "Please give me."

Kat stood, puzzled. Scott took the dress out of her hands, pulled his own suit from the case, and handed them to the maid.

"Thank you."

He turned to Kat as the young woman left.

"Hey, and laundry service, too," he said. Kat, noting his smile, felt a surge of irritation.

"So?" she said.

Scott turned to her again.

"What?"

"Oh, nothing. You're just so happy because you have a maid and a fancy shower."

His eyes had lost their warmth as he regarded her.

"I am not so happy, Kat. And you know that."

She shrugged, turned away.

"I know, I know. Sorry."

It was said ungraciously, and Scott did not acknowledge it. Instead, he put his clothes away, then minutes later stepped through the door that led to the shower. Kat heard the rush of water as the shower gushed. She stood, balling her nightgown tightly in her fists, aware that she was being unreasonable. She remembered the first few days after Chris's death when Scott would answer the phone and say simple things such as *Oh, hello. How are you?* Things one says by rote, automatically, not thinking. And it would incense her because he sounded quite willing to chat. She had never told him about those surges of unwarranted rage. She was glad now that she hadn't. The only time she reacted was when she overheard his conversation with the coroner's office about moving Chris's body to the funeral home. Scott had said, *And you will transfer—the deceased,* and she ran crying into the room.

"Don't say that! Don't say *the deceased*. He's Chris. *Chris!*"

And Scott had looked at her, lost, his eyes so sad, and said, "I don't know what to say. I don't know the language for this."

God, she had been out of control then. She was losing control again. She took a few long, deep breaths, telling herself that she had only to get through one evening, one night and a morning. That was all. It seemed like an eternity.

"Sarah, you have excellent taste," Mrs. Miyamoto said in her tiny, tinkling voice. "I think the English know how to do things."

"Not all of them," said Sarah. "We've been in homes, haven't we, Kat, that one would not describe as tasteful?"

Kat was not sure whether Sarah was making some reference to her family's home or just pulling her into the conversation. They sat around the elegant lounge after a dinner of poached salmon and duck. They had studied the model of the country club that was set up in the wood-paneled den, and they had inspected the grounds. Kat knew that she had said little throughout the evening.

"Taste is so individual, though, isn't it?" she said with an effort. "Scott and I don't agree on a thing when it comes to furnishings."

"Oh, that's not true," said Scott indulgently.

"We should defer to the women in these matters," said Miyamoto. "Right, Phannie?"

His wife gave a shy nod.

"Your aunt's house was like this?" she asked Sarah.

"Yes. Aunt Helen had a home in Sussex. Lansdowne. Beautiful old house."

"And you lived with her?"

"From age twelve on. She was the only one who would take me in. The other aunts couldn't handle me."

"Why couldn't they handle you?" asked James, leaning forward. He and Glenda were both fascinated by this woman, Kat thought. Their eyes were fixed on her. "You were such a bad kid?"

"Very bad. Helen was strong stuff, though. Old school."

"Ah, the British are an interesting people," said Miyamoto. "Right, Scott?"

"Yes, indeed. Once you get over feeling like a Loud Uncouth American everywhere you go."

"My goodness, you felt like that with Kat's family, too?" asked Sarah, winking at Kat.

"Oh no. They were good to me," Scott said. "We got on just fine."

"They were impressed because he got served so fast in our local pub," Kat said, remembering her father's delight. "They didn't realize that the bar staff made a beeline for him because he gave them huge tips."

"Well, I didn't know it wasn't the custom," Scott said. "I had a good time there. A few of those fancy country places, though, I felt like the Marlboro Man. Frontier man. A cowboy. Aware of my loud voice."

"Scott, you *are* a cowboy," said James, grinning, and the group laughed.

Kat realized that Scott had been drinking a lot; he was talking more than he had talked for weeks. As the group relaxed, mellowing in the soft light of the room, Sarah's butler appeared to switch on lamps and bring fresh drinks. Miyamoto sat in an armchair, his wife on the sofa beside James Dempsey. Glenda, her short cap of chestnut hair shining in the lamplight, looked pretty this evening; her angular face was relaxed, and she wore eye makeup for a change, so that her blue eyes sparkled. She perched on the arm of the sofa, her arm draped along the back where James sat, her fingers occasionally brushing his shoulders, just the slightest proprietary touch. Kat wondered briefly about their relationship. They were at least close friends, she guessed. At the very least. And likely more than that.

Kat sipped her white wine, noticing that somehow, without her being aware of it, her glass had been refilled. Deep in the armchair, she thought how easy it would be to get used to this level of comfort, the ease of absolute wealth. To have someone light lights, refresh drinks. At some unseen request from Sarah, a maid came in with cheese, crackers, fruits, and various kinds of pâté and set them down. The drapes were drawn. Sarah need not concern herself with chores to be done or dishes waiting. It was hard to imagine living like this, every day.

Eventually, Miyamoto rose from his chair, yawning.

"If you will excuse us, I think it is bedtime for us. We have an early start."

Mrs. Miyamoto stood delicately, hovered as her husband said his good nights, and then Sarah walked the couple to the staircase. Glenda also stood, stretched, and gave James Dempsey a tap on the head.

"Have to hit the road. Busy day tomorrow. You want a ride back?"

James regarded her with amusement. He, too, had drunk a little too much and he had a sleepy smile.

"We could get an early start in the morning."

"You drove up together?" Scott asked.

"Yep. My car," Glenda said. She turned back to James. "Last chance."

Sarah, coming back into the room, intervened.

"Oh, no. Stay, please. I have rooms ready all over the house."

James raised an eyebrow and looked at Glenda.

"Well?" he asked.

"You stay," said Glenda. "But I gotta go."

"You're not going to drive back with Glenda?" Scott asked James. "It's a heck of a long drive for her alone, this late."

"Really, people, come on! James should stay and Glenda, too," said Sarah.

Glenda remained firm, shaking her head.

"Can't do it," she said, picking up her purse. "I've got a hearing first thing. And an opposition I promised to help with."

"A hearing?" Scott asked. "Not for our department. What's the opposition?"

"Litigation department. Opposition to a motion for summary judgment. For Mitt Lindsay."

"When's it due?"

"Day after tomorrow."

Scott and James both groaned.

"Why do you volunteer for this stuff?" asked Scott, an edge to his voice. "You've got enough to do in our department."

"Because she's just a girl who can't say no," said James. Glenda slapped him playfully.

"Someone can give you a ride in the morning?"

"We'll drop him off," said Scott. "Is the Lindsay case the whistle-blower one?"

He followed her to the door, listening as she explained the problems with the complex litigation.

Kat had noted Scott's stern look from James to Glenda, the irritated tightening of his mouth, and she wondered whether Scott was annoyed because James was staying or because Glenda was going. She knew the signs well, and he was clearly annoyed about something. Sarah refilled James's glass and then waved the decanter at Kat, who shook her head.

"Will Scott have another drink?"

"Probably."

Sarah glanced toward the door, where Scott was still talking to Glenda.

"He's so wonderful with his associates, isn't he?" said Sarah softly. "No wonder they all adore him."

James pulled himself to his feet and strolled to the door.

"Let me escort the lady to her car," he said. Glenda gave him an amused look, but allowed him to lead her out. Scott, back in his chair, sipped the brandy. Kat glanced at him.

"What's up?"

"Nothing."

A few minutes later, James came back through the front door, singing to himself. He opened his arms wide.

"You gotta come look at this," he said. "Come on. Up!"

He opened the French windows so that the lake was visible. Moonlight shone right onto it; shafts of silver illuminated the willow trees at the bank and the rippling water.

"How sweet the moonlight sleeps upon this bank!" James quoted grandly. Sarah moved to stand beside him. Scott and Kat followed.

"This is absolutely one of my favorite views at night," Sarah said. "Do you want to walk around the water's edge? There's a beautiful little path."

James turned in anticipation, but Scott shook his head.

"No, Sarah, not tonight," said Scott. "I think we're all beat. Kat, you ready for bed?"

"I am," she said, turning from the window, promising herself that she would look at the view from the bedroom.

James took Sarah's arm.

"Lead me to the lake, my lady," he said.

Scott's voice was quiet but firm.

"It's late, James. We're setting off early tomorrow. You've got a ride with us, remember."

Sarah smiled at James.

"Maybe another time," she said.

James gave Scott a long, measured look, but Scott stared back unperturbed. Kat realized then that this was a side of Scott she rarely saw: the senior partner, the man who made the decisions.

"Okay, boss," said James.

Scott seemed about to speak, took a breath, patted James on the shoulder.

"See you in the morning," he said.

"You were pretty bossy with James," said Kat when they were in the bedroom. "He didn't like that at all."

"So? I *am* his boss."

She opened the windows so that the soft air scented the room. Kat could smell the ocean. It was a beautiful night.

"What were you so worried about?" she asked eventually, turning to him. "That he was going to make a play for Sarah?"

Scott, folding his pants onto a hanger, looked over at her.

"He should have driven back with Glenda. That's a long trip alone. And you don't start coming on to the client. Okay? I'm sorry, but you just don't."

"He wasn't coming on to her. He was just being himself. Friendly."

"Maybe."

"Let me tell you something, Scott," said Kat, getting into bed. "If Sarah has decided she is going to screw James, she will screw James. And nothing you can do will change that."

"Jesus," said Scott.

Kat woke early, as the sun was rising and the light changing from gray to gold in the luxury bedroom. She had a metallic taste at the roof of her mouth and a slight pain behind her eyes: last night's wine extracting penance. She slid from bed and gazed out the window. The gardens, with their fine morning mist, looked enchanted. She stood still for a while, breathing it all in, until she noticed that the patio doors were open and, as she watched, Sarah, in a cream-silk shirt and loose pants, came out, followed immediately by a maid who laid out coffee and newspapers. Sarah had a telephone in her hand, and after she had dialed a number, she pulled a newspaper closer and began scanning columns, her pen moving down the page. Kat watched, curious. Sarah spoke into the phone, her voice low and serious. She wore small glasses and seemed entirely focused. Sarah Harrison, the businesswoman, at work.

Kat noted the long, salon-pampered fingernails as Sarah tracked something in the paper. In the morning light, they looked a deep burgundy shade, glossy and perfect. As a schoolgirl, and even during their university years, Sarah had bitten her nails savagely, right down to the quick. Kat remembered those stubby fingers, strangely raw at the ends. According to Sarah, one of the meaner nannies of her childhood had tried to cure her of nail biting by painting the ends of her fingers with a caustic, bitter substance. Sarah, in an attempt to remove it, had used boiling water and burned the ends of her fingers, leaving mottled pigment and tiny scars. Kat wondered if the scars were still there, under the perfect nails.

From the bed, Scott gave a low groan and Kat turned quickly.

"Morning," she said.

"Morning to you. You want to try out the pool?" he asked, stretching.

"Not sure. You going in?"

"Yeah. Think so. Clear the head a bit."

"I think I'd rather borrow your power shower," she said.

When Kat, dressed, strolled down to the patio, Sarah was still talking on the phone, her laptop open, newspapers surrounding her. Seeing Kat, she clicked off the phone and waved.

"Morning, Caitlin," she called. "You're not swimming?"

"Not me. I can't bear to see myself in a bathing suit at the moment. The Miyamotos up yet?"

"They left early," Sarah said. "An hour ago. He's an early riser, Mr. Miyamoto. Phannie came down for a tray for him and insisted on carrying it up herself. Such a devoted little geisha." Sarah laughed, shaking her head. "Come on. Breakfast will be a few minutes. Pour yourself some coffee and we can look at the ocean."

Kat poured coffee, followed Sarah to a small curved bench at the far end of the patio. From there, the ocean was visible, a series of changing strands of gray and silver, sparkling in the morning sun.

"Oh. This is beautiful," Kat said, sitting next to Sarah on the bench and looking out.

"Does it remind you of anywhere? The way the coast curves? The rocky areas?"

Kat looked again.

"Of course. The Sussex coast. The view from the house."

"Exactly. Heartbreaking to see that house demolished. I saw them go in with bulldozers. I was staying at the cottage at the time and watched with Mrs. Evans. Remember her? Helen's housekeeper? Sam persuaded the new owner to keep her on, part of the sale package, but she stood with me as they tore the house apart, tears rolling down her face."

"Mrs. Evans was crying?" Kat said, finding it hard to imagine the dour housekeeper showing any kind of emotion. "Really?"

"Oh, I know you were scared of her. She's not so bad. She keeps an eye on the cottage for me. Cooks for me when I visit."

They sat in silence for a few minutes until Kat, uncomfortable, found that Sarah was studying her.

"What is it?" she asked, turning.

"You haven't lost that stillness. It's astonishing."

Sarah had remarked on this, years ago. The first words Sarah had said to her had baffled Kat. The newcomer, exotic and unknown with her clear voice and perfect posture, had been told to sit next to Kat in the advanced English class at St. Theresa's. Although Kat, after two years in the school, had a small number of friends, none of them qualified for this English class, and she was still uncomfortable among some of the middle-class girls. Sarah, for different reasons, seemed equally out of place: they were two outsiders, from extreme ends of the social scale. Kat—intimidated by the glowing confidence of the pampered girls, with their talk of riding lessons, of skiing, of travels abroad—was grateful that at least someone was sitting next to her, that the attention of the bored girls would be deflected.

The young Sarah had turned to her at the end of the class.

"You're so quiet," she said. "And very still. I'm glad."

"You said that years ago," Kat said now to Sarah. "At St. Theresa's. I didn't know whether you meant I was dull."

"Dull? No. God, no. You have this stillness. A serene still point. You were different. Quite different from all those bouncing, braying girls."

"I was different because I was Scholarship. And poor. And worried all the time that I didn't fit in."

"I know. I soon discovered that. But it wasn't obvious. Not at first."

Sarah leaned back against the bench, stretched a little.

"We were both misfits," she said. "My default state, actually. But it was so nice to find another one. Quite amazing in fact. I think we surprised them all when we became friends."

And surprised me most of all, Kat thought, but did not say. Sarah's friendship had caused her life at the school to change in a number of ways. Her status as Sarah's confidante protected her from the more snobbish, terrifying girls at the school who were in awe of Sarah's background. But some of the quieter, kinder girls, who had been her friends before Sarah's arrival, were wary of Sarah's sharp tongue and gradually drifted away. Both outsiders, they had that in common, but Kat and Sarah were such a mismatched duo that even the nuns occasionally remarked on their friendship.

The two women sat in silence for a few minutes longer.

"I know what grief feels like," Sarah said eventually, in a quiet voice. "If I can help you through this terrible time, please just ask, Kat."

"I'm fine," Kat said. "But thank you."

Sarah reached into her pocket, pulled out a card, and handed it to Kat. It had a cell phone number in gold lettering but no name, no address, nothing else.

"My private cell," she said. "Please don't share it with anyone else, not even your charming husband. It's for personal matters. Not for work."

"I understand."

Soon, a young woman called from the patio that breakfast was ready, and Sarah stood.

"Right. I need to call order. Work to be done."

Sarah moved to the edge of the lawn.

"Come along, boys," she called in the direction of the pool. "Let's carpe this pretty diem. Seize it by the throat."

Kat shook her head. *Boys?* But Scott and James both turned, grinning, and began to swim toward the edge of the pool. As they climbed out, Sarah turned to Kat and gave a quick, mischievous smile.

"Such a lovely sight, wet men. See that pleasing symmetry?"

Kat turned, looked at her husband and his associate, both attractive in the morning light. Scott, still slender, solid, with his curling chest hair; James, smooth as stone, a gleaming ebony.

"Yes," she said. Sarah watched them openly, her eyes moving from one to the other, an approving appraisal, before she strolled toward the breakfast table.

Kat turned back for one last look at the view. She experienced a longing then, so intense that she wanted to cry out. A yearning to be by a rough sea, a deserted beach, a wind so wild that it was possible to taste the salt in it. She longed for a sight of the craggy Sussex coast, the high cliffs and rocky promontories, dark sky, constant cloud, rain. A light that was dull or shadowed. Here, the bright light was blinding her.

Later, when they were ready to leave and Scott and James were putting bags into the car, Sarah tugged Kat aside.

"Would you like to have lunch? Perhaps next week? Next Thursday?"

Thursday would have been Chris's eighteenth birthday. Kat planned to do nothing, talk to no one except Scott, but she did not want to share this fact with Sarah. On Tuesday, she had the interview with Sarah's editor friend, Mark Tinsley.

"Not sure about next week," she began.

"Oh?"

"The editor you contacted. Tinsley?" Kat explained. "He's interviewing me on Tuesday."

"Wonderful," Sarah said. "He's a cocky lad but an easy boss, I should think. Well, call me when you're ready. I can easily reschedule my plans."

"Of course," Kat said.

Sarah waved them off as they began the journey back. James, in the backseat of the car, waited until they began the descent down the hill before leaning forward.

"Compton's a go," he said.

"What? You're kidding," Scott said. "When did you finalize that?"

"Early this morning. Sarah said she'll fund the sports center. If we can pick up that piece of land next door."

"Joseph's?"

"Yeah. He's asking too much for it right now."

"We can get him down. She didn't seem sure when Miyamoto and I talked with her last night. You certain? She wasn't just—"

"Nope. She's sure now. Wants to name it for her late husband. The Sam Harrison Sports Center."

"She can name it for Homer Simpson as far as I'm concerned," Scott said. "Damn. That's good."

Scott punched the steering wheel, pleased.

"Father O'Connor will be a very happy man. Young Chiller, too."

Scott turned to James.

"So what did you say, or do, to persuade her?" he asked.

James shrugged, but couldn't hide his smile.

"Nothing illegal," he said.

He pulled a file from his briefcase, was hard at work for the rest of the journey.

NINE

As she waited in the tenth-floor reception area of the renovated offices on Santa Monica Boulevard, Kat realized how seriously she had miscalculated. She wore a smart fitted suit, silk shirt, polished shoes: the outfit she had worn at Waters & Chappell for important clients. She had thought the clothes suitable for a job interview. She did not want Mark Tinsley to report to Sarah that the woman she had recommended looked like a bag lady, missing only a shopping cart.

The outfit was a mistake. Here, she was surrounded by teenagers in blue jeans and T-shirts. They looked no older than Chris. She watched as the kids moved back and forth, calling out to one another in her son's language: *hey, man, wassup?* She could not imagine herself here, with all these bright young things. She felt like an anxious mother visiting a summer camp. She took off the jacket and undid the top button of her shirt. It didn't help.

When Tinsley came out into the foyer and the receptionist waved a hand in her direction, Kat saw him pause, momentarily uncertain. Tinsley appeared to be barely thirty. He shook her hand, though, in a friendly way and led her to a corner office. A confident, cheerful young man, he chatted to her about the newspaper as if he were selling it to her. He gave her résumé a perfunctory glance, saying that Sarah had told him her job history, and then apologized for the low salary.

"I'd get you more if I could, but the fucking board here puts caps on salaries. Pathetic. That's as high as they'll go for features."

He looked at her curiously, waiting. She nodded.

"That's fine," she said.

A number of toys littered his desk, and stacks of video games were piled by his computer. He played with them for a while, as if trying to think of other questions to ask. Kat couldn't imagine him as her boss, as anyone's boss.

"You got any questions?" he asked.

"I think you've answered them all," Kat said.

He leaned back in his chair, placed his fingers together as though imitating a grown-up executive he had seen in a movie, and said, "You're from England, too, huh?"

"Yes. But I've been here quite a while."

"That it? You sound different. Different from Sarah Harrison, I mean."

"Well, we don't really have the same background. Sarah is—"

He nodded impatiently, as if he knew what she was going to say.

"She's an aristocrat, right?"

Kat did not want to disillusion this young man, who was after all doing her a favor by seeing her, and who might one day be her boss, so she smiled.

"Yes. I suppose that's it."

He nodded again.

"Thought so. You got kids?"

The question felt like a hard punch to the gut. Kat sat forward, gripping the edge of the seat with tight hands. She knew that he was simply making conversation; it was not a question that should be asked in a job interview in California. She could not answer it. Her heart thumped in her chest. He stared at her, frowning slightly.

"Yes," she said at last. "A son."

"Oh. Right."

The frown cleared. He waited for her to say more.

"How old is he?" he asked, finally.

"Eighteen. Almost. He's been accepted at Berkeley."

"Berkeley? Pretty smart, then."

"Yes. He is."

Was, was, was—that one word like a stormy echo in her head. Kat felt as if her limbs had liquefied, and she reached to the floor for her bag.

"Just the one?"

She stared, not comprehending.

"Kid," he said. "Just the one kid?"

"Oh," she said. "Yes. Just the one."

He stood up then.

"Okay," he said. "When can you start?"

Kat's mouth was so dry that she ran her tongue over her upper lip before answering and tried to swallow.

"A month? About a month."

"A month? You can't start sooner?"

"No, I'm afraid I can't. I have some commitments," Kat said. Her voice sounded whispery. She coughed, tried to take a deep breath.

He looked bewildered.

"I thought . . . well, Sarah gave me the impression you could come on board right away." He shrugged. "Well, I guess a month. You got a definite date?"

"I'll call with the date," Kat said, moving toward the door. "I'll call you tomorrow."

He walked her to the elevator. When he leaned forward to shake her hand, Kat tried to smile and knew that her mouth trembled. She imagined that her eyes were sparked with fear. He seemed not to notice, waved to her as she stepped into the elevator. She rested against the elevator wall as the doors closed slowly. The claustrophobic sense of suffocation began immediately. The doors took too long to open, and then closed so very slowly, as young people stepped in and out, their bright white shirts blinding her. Kat could not breathe. She felt the panic starting, growing like a prickly ball in her chest.

By the time the elevator reached the ground floor, Kat's silk blouse was sticking to her and a cold sweat soaked her back and shoulders. Her hair felt damp on the back of her neck.

In the lobby she began to tremble and gasp for breath. Only seconds later, her heart started to pound so hard and so loudly that she was certain she was about to have a heart attack. At the edge of this conviction, circling her fear, was an absurd embarrassment: these young people would see her and think she was a crazy person.

Kat stumbled to the front of the building and rested against the wall, concentrating on slowing her heartbeat, trying to take deep breaths. But the more she tried to breathe, the harder it got. She was hyperventilating. She remembered something about breathing into a paper bag, or if that was not possible, talking out loud. She pulled her cell phone from her bag, gasping.

I can't do this, she thought. *I can't do this. I can't live like this. I just cannot go on this way.* She dialed Scott's number out of habit, out of need. He was not available on his cell phone. She dialed his office fast, her fingers fumbling and trembling over the numbers, and at last his secretary answered.

"Nettie?" she whispered. Too quiet. She must try again.

Nettie's voice, so familiar, repeated, *Mr. Hamilton's office.*

"Nettie. It's Kat." Her voice was audible. Nettie heard her.

"Kat? Is that you?"

"Is he there?"

"No, Kat. He's not. Have you been running? You sound out of breath. No, Mrs. Harrison called another meeting and he and Glenda headed out to Malibu—"

Kat whispered a thank-you, clicked off the phone, and closed her eyes. Then, she called Martha Kim.

"A panic attack," said Martha an hour later. "It's not uncommon for these to occur during grief or depressive episodes. Did it begin to abate after you talked to me?"

"Yes," said Kat, remembering the gradual slowing of her heartbeat, the ability after a long interval to take a real breath.

"But it was so terrifying. I thought I was going to die."

Martha nodded.

"Yes, that's common, too. But you won't. No one dies of a panic attack."

Her dismissive tone disconcerted Kat, and Martha, noting Kat's expression, raised an eyebrow.

"I'm not minimizing the discomfort you were in," she said. "Those attacks can be very scary."

"Why is this happening now, though?" Kat asked. "Wouldn't this happen right afterwards?"

"You were in shock then. Numb," said Martha. "It's possible that you are now emerging from shock into a different stage of grief."

They sat in silence for a minute. Kat felt exhausted, as if she had run a marathon. Martha gave a small cough.

"When do you begin your new job?" Martha asked. "That will be a new beginning for you."

"A month," Kat said.

Martha nodded her approval. She shuffled her papers as if already preparing to see her next patient. She had given Kat just thirty minutes, an emergency session. Kat stole a glance at the clock. Martha was right; she was out of time.

"What should I do if that happens again?" she asked Martha. "That panic?"

Martha actually stood.

"The most important thing to remember is that it's simply a panic attack. You are not having a heart attack. You are not going to die. Do your very best to stay calm and wait for it to pass. You will come out of it quite unharmed."

She walked to the door. Kat followed her.

"Call me if necessary," Martha said.

Kat stood in the doorway, hesitated.

"He asked if I had children," she said. "I said yes. A son."

Tears, like the early tears, springing up from nowhere, were on her cheeks.

Martha pulled Kat's elbow gently, slowly tugged her back into the room, and then closed the door. She remained standing, did not indicate that Kat should sit. Instead, she reached for the box of tissues and handed one to Kat.

"You wanted to save him embarrassment, perhaps?"

"I don't know. I don't know!" Kat's voice rose. "What do I say? What can I say? I had a son. He's dead. I was a mother once. Does that mean I'm not a mother now? Does it? Am I?"

Martha took a breath.

"You were a mother. That will never change."

Tinsley's tactless questioning still echoed in Kat's head. *Just the one?*

"I didn't know what to say to him," she said.

"Let's make an appointment for next week," Martha said. She consulted the little red book she kept on her desk and then looked up at Kat. "On Friday? That's convenient?"

Kat nodded dumbly, not caring.

"Eleven a.m. If you feel it's necessary, then please call me before then." Her voice was softer than usual; there was something in it Kat had never heard before. It could even be sympathy.

At home, Kat made tea and took it to the old chair by the window to wait for Scott. The fear she had felt earlier had abated except for a small curling uncertainty, a sense of being vulnerable and in danger. She longed for Scott to come home, longed for his solid presence.

Two hours later, realizing that he was very late, she began to pace, going from window to window, constantly watching the road. When his car finally pulled into the drive, Kat hurried to the front door, watched her husband walk up the path, briefcase swinging. He was so preoccupied that he kissed the top of her head, barely glancing at her, before striding inside. The tension of the day erupted in Kat. She was so angry that she could barely close the door before she said in a harsh whisper, "You're late. Why are you so late? Why?"

He shook his head, bewildered, glanced at his watch.

"Am I? Didn't realize."

"Where have you been?"

"Out at Malibu? Why? What on earth—?"

"Why didn't you call me?"

"Kat, for Christ's sake—"

"I called you. Your cell phone was off. And I called your office. Didn't Nettie say? I needed to talk to you and—"

"I didn't go back to the office." He came toward her, held her shoulders. "Why? What happened?"

"I had a panic—I had that interview."

"Right." He nodded, relieved. "Okay. How did it go?"

Kat pulled herself from his grasp.

"Oh, you don't have to pretend. Forget it. Forget it."

"Kat, please."

"It was an interview. That's all. And then I had a panic attack. While you were out at the beach."

"I wasn't *out at the beach*. I was working. Did you get the job?"

"I had this panic thing. I had to see Martha Kim."

Scott's face finally registered his concern.

"And you're okay now?"

"Yes. Yes. It doesn't matter. I'll get dinner."

Kat poured a glass of wine, gulping it as she grilled the chicken and prepared the salad. She called to Scott when it was ready, took the bottle of wine to the table. Scott, clearly hungry, took a few mouthfuls of food, then looked over at her.

"Better, sweetheart?"

"I'm fine."

"You'll get the job," he said. "Don't worry."

She looked into his anxious face and felt the anger and the fear abating.

"I did get it. He already offered it to me. But he asked me these questions, if I had children. If I had more than one. I didn't know what to say to him."

Scott nodded slowly.

"It's awkward," he said. Kat wondered how Scott answered casual questions about children, whether he simply avoided the subject.

She leaned back in her chair, sighing, then said, "Remember, years ago when we wanted another baby, a sibling for Chris, and I didn't get pregnant again and the doctor couldn't find anything wrong and we were going to have further tests done? Both of us. Why didn't we? Ever? It seems like we just let it go."

"Stop it, Kat," Scott said softly, leaning across the table to take her hand. "Please. It's too late, now. It doesn't help to think like that. Stop it, please."

She nodded, sipped her wine.

"Sorry," she said.

TEN

On the morning of the day that would have been Chris's eighteenth birthday, Kat woke before dawn. Scott rolled over onto his back, murmured something, then drifted back to sleep. *Chris's birthday.* Her mind raced back through years of candles and cakes to the moment when they placed the baby in her arms for the first time: a little angry, red-faced boy. She had gazed down in wonderment, swamped by an avalanche of feelings that included both tenderness and terror. Scott was immediately entranced by the infant.

"He's amazing," Scott said. "He's got way more character than the other babies. They look so bland. They all look the same."

They agreed that their baby had perfect features, but he was also, they decided, clearly smart and *interesting.* They were charmed by his many facial expressions: his frowns; his damp, smirky smiles; the little sucky movement he made with his mouth when he slept; and his wide, unrestrained yawns. He studied his parents with an intense, thoughtful look, as if considering them as possibilities.

"He was hoping for movie stars," Kat said to Scott.

"Or Nobel Prize winners."

Scott leaned down to whisper to the infant.

"Hey there, son. You'll be okay. We'll be fine."

And they had been fine, Kat thought now. They really had. Seventeen birthdays came after that day: with toy trucks and trains and parties with small, noisy friends, video games, Disneyland. Happy birthdays. And then this one.

Scott stirred. She snuggled against him.

"Don't go to work, Scott," she whispered.

He turned his head and studied her. Crease marks from the pillow lined one side of his face.

"I freed up the morning," he said. "But I have to be there late afternoon for a client meeting. No way out of that."

"That's fine. Just the morning's fine. I want to take flowers to Forest Lawn."

It was already a hot day, the marine layer burning off slowly and the air oppressive.

"Like walking into a dog's mouth," Scott said as they left the house.

The morning commuter traffic was heavy on the drive to Forest Lawn; Scott cursed intermittently and turned the news radio on and then off again. It felt like a long drive to Kat, and despite the warmth of the day, she shivered as they arrived at the cemetery.

Scott turned to her. "You okay?"

She nodded, taking his arm as they walked up the steep slope of the long lawns. Kat placed her flowers on the gravestone, next to a florist's bouquet and a tall sunflower in a glass bottle.

She studied the bouquet: an elegant selection of perfect white blooms—gardenias, freesias, orchids—professionally arranged in a curving crystal vase. Kat leaned down to look for a card. The sweet perfume of gardenias scented the air.

"These are classy," she said. "Wonder who left these?"

"A teacher?"

Kat looked at them doubtfully.

"Bit expensive for a teacher."

"Ben's parents maybe. They look like the kind of flowers his mom might choose."

"No clue. There's no card."

The message attached to the sunflower, however, was easily visible.

Love you, miss you—Chloe

"Who *is* this Chloe?" Kat asked Scott. "Don't remember a Chloe."

He shook his head.

"I don't know. A girl from school? Vanessa's friend?"

"She must care about him."

"He used to chat to a bunch of girls after football games," Scott said. "Vanessa and some of her friends. I know there was one girl he liked. I remember when I was giving his buddies a ride home, they were all kidding around in the back of the car, talking about it."

"A girlfriend? Not Vanessa?"

"No, not Vanessa. She was always with that huge guy. The running back."

"Teddy?"

"Yeah. Teddy. That's him."

"So this was a different girl? You should have told me!"

"You would have interrogated him," Scott said.

"I would not!" Kat said, thought for a moment, and then added, "No, you're right. I would."

"I didn't want them to know I was listening," Scott said. "Used to make me laugh. You wouldn't believe the things they'd say. Even years ago, when they were just, well, really little kids, they'd call each other these names: douche bag, dildo."

"Dildo?" Kat said with a mix of shock and amusement. "I hope you said something."

"Nah. Just between themselves? They were just kidding around. Playing the big man. I don't think they had a clue what the words meant."

"Even so."

"I broke my invisible man cover and cautioned them once," Scott said. "But that was—well, over something else."

"What?"

"On a need-to-know basis," Scott said, smiling. "You don't need to know. It was the little skinny guy. Jake? He never said it again."

He stopped, stared for a while at the gravestone.

"Damn," he said.

Another stubby bunch of carnations lay on the ground. It had no note. Kat imagined these flowers were from Chris's old friends; they were tied awkwardly with thick black ribbon and wrapped in smoky-black cellophane paper: the kind of packaging a group of boys might put together.

They must come occasionally, Kat thought. Those friends who were with him the night of the accident. She noticed the cigarette butts around the stone. She could imagine the boys: slouching, uncomfortable, talking of their activities and parties and girls, smoking furiously, embarrassed.

Scott placed his arm around her shoulders, looked at the stone for a moment or two longer, letting out a long, sighing breath before he turned away.

"Do you want to look in the chapel?" he asked.

"If we can."

But a service was in progress, a funeral mass, and the doors were closed. Kat could hear the choir singing *Agnus Dei,* and was transported back to the convent school. The incense and lavender scent of furniture polish that mingled with the gravy smells coming from the school cafeteria; the side chapel with the small altar of Mary, where the more devout girls—to Sarah Cherrington's loud amusement—would say the rosary during their lunch break. Kat recalled Sarah, with much exaggeration, pretending to lift an imaginary hand grenade, remove the pin with her teeth, and then hurl it into the crowded chapel. Kat, shocked, had turned away and made a surreptitious sign of the cross. Just in case. She had believed in God then. For a time there, she had prayed fervently, confessed her sins, felt true repentance, and attended the endless Stations of the Cross that on a spring afternoon could feel as long as eternity. She had believed in sanctity once, and in sanctuary.

Kat, listening to the choir in the small chapel in Forest Lawn, tried to remember when her religion ceased to matter to her. When did it fail to comfort? As a child she had prayed often, had loved benediction, communion. As an adolescent, the formal sung mass in the old chapel at the convent had always moved her. But at some time during her teens, during those years at St. Theresa's Convent School, she had lost her faith. For the first time, Kat was aware of the real meaning of this expression: *to lose one's faith*. Something gone, possibly forever, misplaced, not to be found again. *Lost.* Kat thought, *It's a shame that religion can no longer console us.* Scott had always claimed an agnostic view of the world, but he was not raised Catholic. To be able to find solace in the church, to find meaning now, surely that would help them both?

"Do you wish you believed in God, Scott?" she asked as they walked to the car.

He slowed his step, thinking.

"I guess it might help right now," he said. "Maybe. If I really believed there was life afterwards. But—" He shook his head. "I imagine that grief is painful for anyone. Whether they have a god or not."

They drove toward the exit of Forest Lawn, moving slowly down the wide access road. A number of funerals were in progress. *How did we get through that day?* Kat wondered. *How?* She had little memory of the graveside service. She remembered sitting in the limousine with her sister, waiting for Scott to thank the priest, and she retained snapshots in her mind of people standing around on the grass as she stared through the tinted glass of the car, thinking in a blank, disconnected way, *Oh, look who is here, how nice of them to come. How nice of them to come.*

The gathering of people at the house afterward was now just a blur. Maggie and Brooke had set out food, made fresh drinks, moved busily in and out of the kitchen. Kat, feeling uncomfortably like a monarch, was urged to sit in the armchair, with Scott standing beside her, as Chris's teachers, parents of his friends, her own work colleagues, and Scott's partners and associates came forward, murmuring, to offer condolences. After two hours of this, when Kat desperately wanted everyone to leave, Brooke and Maggie, by the simple act of collecting glasses and removing plates, persuaded people to the door and ushered them out. Brooke, who hugged people as easily as she breathed, warmly kissed the cheeks of total strangers as they departed. *We couldn't have managed without her on that day,* Kat thought as they drove out of Forest Lawn. *Nor without Maggie.*

Now, as they reached the exit of the memorial park, she glanced out the window. "Where are we going?" she asked when Scott did not turn onto the freeway.

"North Hollywood," he said.

"What?" asked Kat, astounded.

"The old building. We'll pick up a meatball sub on the way. Have a picnic."

Minutes later, they were at the fast-food drive-through window they used to visit with Chris years ago. Scott ordered the sandwiches and Cokes and handed them to Kat, then drove along Ventura. Soon, he turned off the boulevard and parked the car outside their old apartment building on Chandler Avenue. Kat understood then: Scott was making a formal pilgrimage to celebrate Chris's birthday. This had been their son's first home. They had driven the newborn straight from

UCLA Medical Center to this place. Scott had carried him into this building when Chris was just two days old.

"I don't believe it," said Kat. "It looks exactly the same."

Kat climbed out of the car and Scott joined her. They stood for a minute, looking at the two-story stucco building. Kat remembered a wicker bassinet and endless laundry and friends for supper and laughter. They had been short of money. Scott, waiting for bar results and working as a clerk in a small law firm, had not earned much then. But they had been happy.

"It's changed a bit," said Scott. "New coat of paint. You want to go around the back? Look at the pool?"

"It will be locked."

"Not necessarily. Somebody always used to leave it open, remember?"

Sure enough, when Scott tapped the metal door, it opened easily.

"See?" Scott said, stepping inside the pool area.

"This is crazy, Scott. It is absolutely nuts."

"Who cares if it is?"

She followed him to a small table on the shady side of the pool. Scott handed her the meatball sandwich, opened the Cokes, gave her one, then leaned to clink his can against hers.

"To Chris," he said.

Kat, biting her lip, trying hard not to cry, raised her can in a toast, then sipped the drink.

"To Chris," she said.

They ate in silence, lost in separate memories. A woman resident in a pink-flowered housedress with her hair in tight rollers emerged from the building, stared, and then went back inside. Two young black men studied them for a moment or two before clattering noisily up the stairs to the second level. Kat thought that she and Scott, sitting quietly with their picnic, obviously did not seem threatening or out of place here. They must look like they belonged.

"We swam in this pool. Can you imagine?" said Scott at one point.

"It was cleaner then," Kat said, then looked at him, eyes widening. "Wasn't it?"

He shook his head.

"I'm not sure."

After a while, Scott gathered up the sandwich wrappings and Coke cans and put them in an overflowing trashcan at the side of the pool. Then, he held out his hand to his wife.

"Let's get you home," he said.

He drove east toward the freeway, passing the park where, every Saturday morning, Scott would take Chris, just a toddler then, to play on the swings and the slide or dig in the sandbox. Sometimes, Kat would join them, though more often she would prefer to stay at home, doing laundry and other housework instead. She hated parks with high slides, monkey bars, dangers. Scott had slowed the car, was looking out at the sandbox where a few toddlers played.

"Remember when we used to come here? On Saturdays? Chris loved that big slide. And the monkey bars."

"I know. He was totally fearless. God, I hated to come here."

Scott looked at her, surprised.

"You did?"

"Yes, I was always so scared he would fall. I remember, years later, when he and Ben were going off somewhere and I was nagging about something, Chris said to me, quite seriously, that I was overprotective. Like it was a character defect. A serious parental flaw. Like crack addiction."

"From his point of view . . ." Scott said.

Kat looked out the window.

"It's not fair," she said quietly.

"No. It's not."

Once back at the house, Scott gulped down a mug of coffee. Five minutes later, he was at the door, briefcase in hand.

"Faster than a speeding bullet," Kat said. "Did you even taste that coffee?"

"Sorry. The work. Jesus. It just piles up."

"Sarah Harrison keeping you busy?"

"She's brought in a lot of new accounts, so I'm not complaining. But Sarah wants what she wants. She's not the easiest of clients," he said.

"I never thought she would be."

He paused on the step.

"Okay, I'll be home soon as I can. Maybe we can open a bottle of wine. Watch *The NeverEnding Story.*"

Kat regarded him sadly. Chris's favorite movie when he was a young child.

"If we can bear it," Kat said.

In the early evening, when Scott was still not home by the time she was ready to prepare dinner, Kat moved to call him just as the phone rang.

"Damn car," Scott snapped immediately. "It's acting up. I'll have it checked on the way home. You go ahead and eat, sweetheart. I'll pick up a hamburger."

Kat ate a small piece of cold lasagna from the fridge, picked at a salad. Afterward, she pulled the DVD of *The NeverEnding Story* from the cabinet, studied it for a moment. It would be too late to watch it when Scott got home. She took a breath and then slid it into the console. Kat heard only the first notes of the movie score before she switched it off fast. No. It was not a movie to watch alone. It was a movie to watch with a child. An hour later, she was in bed. She heard Scott's key in the lock. He closed the door quietly. She heard the soft thud of the fridge door, the clink of a glass. Then, silence.

ELEVEN

The moment Scott left for work the next morning, Kat pulled out her laptop. Telling herself that it was just a quick look, only curiosity, she checked medical websites, just as she had done years ago, for reasons why a woman did not conceive again after the successful and easy birth of a first child. Maybe there would be new research? Maybe things had changed? But the information was still overwhelming and inconclusive. They would need tests, both of them, just as the doctor had suggested years ago. And Scott would not agree to tests—she was certain of that. He would say it was too late. He would say those days were over.

One fact occurred and reoccurred on every medical website—it was more difficult for a woman to conceive after the age of forty. Kat had reached her fortieth birthday just five days after Chris's death. A birthday that, numb with grief, Kat and Scott had not celebrated, had barely acknowledged. She sighed, closing her eyes. She really was losing her grip. It was ridiculous to think like this. It was insane to even consider having another child. Could she cope with pregnancy right now? The hormone changes, the mood swings? Her moods were erratic enough. And to focus on getting pregnant? They would need passion for that.

Maybe Scott could muster enough. But could she? Maybe pregnancy simply wasn't possible. And yet, and yet . . .

They had always wanted more children. They had imagined, when they were first married, having three or even four. Two at least. They had talked, when Chris was accepted at Berkeley, of being empty nesters, and Kat had joked that they could always foster needy kids from time to time. Scott had not balked at that. He had smiled. But no, that wasn't the same. It wasn't what she longed for right now.

Kat closed the laptop, stood, and moved to the window to stare out blankly at the garden. She closed her eyes, recalled clearly—all senses stirred—the memory of the warm weight of Chris as a new infant in her arms. She remembered sniffing his head and thinking that he smelled freshly baked, like a blueberry muffin. His soft skin, the velvet pads of his tiny hands holding her finger, the fluttering of his eyelashes as he dreamed. What did he dream of, she and Scott would wonder, when he knew so little of the world? Maybe the warm, watery womb he had left behind?

Catching her breath, stunned by another wave of loss, Kat turned and held on to the sink for a moment to steady herself. Enough. Enough. She needed fresh air, activity. She needed to clear her head. She picked up her bag and car keys. Grocery shopping was a chore she dreaded—she feared bumping into anyone she knew, hated the awkward conversations, the stumbling sympathy—but she needed to pick up something for dinner and also some wine and Scott's whisky.

At the top of the hill, she realized she had chosen the wrong time of day. It was lunch break at the high school; seniors were all over the place, dragging along in groups or singly, heading to Wendy's or the market. The one privilege of the last year in school was the freedom to go out to lunch. How Chris had loved that.

Kat, hands tight on the steering wheel, tried not to look at the young people on the sidewalks and kept her eyes on the road until she swung into the market's parking lot. Most of the kids would be at Wendy's, across the street. She hurried toward the entrance of the market and there, so visible with that signature pink streak in her hair, was Chris's friend Vanessa—and Ben and Matt, too. Behind Vanessa, she could see another girl, a dark-haired girl. Kat slowed, ready to turn around quickly and head back to her car, but Vanessa had spotted her. The teenager frowned, lifted her hand in a wave. Kat moved toward them slowly, her smile frozen.

The boys melted away like spooks, disappearing around the corner. The girls waited.

Vanessa greeted her in a soft voice, her usual bright smile missing.

"Was that Ben?" Kat asked. "And Matt?"

"Yes—they had to go. How are you, Mrs. Hamilton?"

"Fine. Just fine. Thank you."

The two girls stood, in the small awkward silence, waiting for her to speak further. Kat felt paralyzed.

"It was Chris's birthday yesterday," Kat said finally, the words coming from nowhere, unrehearsed.

"I know," Vanessa said. "We had a little party for him. Just a few of us. His favorite beer. A cake."

Kat thought about this. What was his favorite beer? She had no idea.

"That's so nice," she said, swallowing. "Ben was there? And Matt? And Teddy?"

"Yes. All the boys who were with . . ." Vanessa faltered. "Who were there," she concluded.

"And how are they now?"

"Ben's okay. Teddy's still having nightmares."

"Oh," said Kat. "I'm sorry." Though she was not really sorry, she admitted to herself with shame. They were alive. A nightmare was a small price to pay.

"It was fun," the dark-haired girl said. "Chris would have loved it."

Kat looked closely at her: a slender brunette, pretty, with dark eyes.

"I'm Chloe," the girl said. "Chloe Martinez."

Love you, miss you. So this was the girl who had left flowers at Chris's grave. Kat felt a sharp pang of loss for all the things her son would never experience: the journeys not taken, the love affairs never begun. *I hope Chris had a massive crush on you,* she thought as she studied the young woman's attractive face. *I hope he kissed you behind the school bike sheds. I hope he felt joy. I hope he experienced that, at least.*

"Nice to meet you, Chloe. Well, I'm an idiot. I've come to the wrong market. They don't have Scott's whisky here. Different brands, different prices. I'll have to drive over the hill. Good to see you both. Give my best to the boys."

She was talking too fast. The girls must think she was a blathering fool.

"Bye," they said in unison.

Kat turned and walked quickly to the car.

Minutes later, she was back on her own street, pulling into the driveway of her house, still shaken. She was cursing herself for a wasted trip when she saw Brooke, smartly dressed in tailored work clothes, getting a package out of her mailbox.

"You want coffee? I've just made some," she called to Kat.

Kat crossed the street to Brooke's ultramodern home, a minimalist space of chrome and smoked glass she had inherited after her divorce. Newly promoted to art director at a small Century City advertising agency, Brooke made a good salary, but she freely admitted that her ex-husband had been generous to her. After two years of marriage, he had returned to his first wife and children.

"Back to his wife! Can you imagine?" Brooke said at the time. "The things he said about her. To hear him talk, you'd think she was an evil, frigid monster. I knew he was missing his kids, though. It was killing him. And, bright side, I get to keep the house. That will help mend my poor little broken heart."

"Your little broken heart will mend when you meet someone new."

"Me? Never. I intend to stay as free as a bird."

Now, as Brooke poured coffee, she looked over at Kat.

"So you went out alone, sweet pea? That's good," she said.

"Meant to go to the market and then didn't go inside. Met some of Chris's old friends and just bolted back here."

"That's okay. The market's not going anywhere. It will be there tomorrow and the day after. So who was the high-fashion gal visiting you in a Jag the other day?"

"Sarah. The old school friend I told you about. The one in Palm Springs."

"Oh, right. The rich widow. She looks pretty young for a widow. Well, if she ever gets tired of that Hermès bag, ask her for it. I've wanted one my entire life."

"Your entire life? You told me you were a tomboy most of your young life."

"Well, since I grew up. Since I stopped wanting a skateboard. So how are you, sweetie?"

Kat blurted out details of her Internet research, the newly awakened longing for a baby.

"You think I'm insane to think of it? Having another baby?"

Brooke, eyes narrow, thought about the question seriously.

"Not insane. No. But you're still grieving. It's maybe not a good idea right this minute. Not that I know shit about anything. What does Scott say?"

"Haven't really mentioned it to him yet."

"What's your therapist say?"

"Haven't told her."

"Well, that, babe, should be your first question to her at your next session. And maybe you should mention it to Scott *before* you get yourself pregnant."

"Saw some of Chris's old friends today," Kat said that evening as she and Scott had dinner. "During their lunch break. It was strange to see them. Without Chris."

He looked up, frowning.

"You were near the school?"

"At the market. I met the girl who left flowers at the grave. Chloe. Must have been Chris's girlfriend. Pretty girl. Nice, too. Seemed nice."

"Don't think I ever met her."

"She was with Vanessa. The boys were there, too, but they vanished before I could talk to them."

"I haven't seen the boys since the funeral," Scott said. "I thought Ben would drop by at some point. He used to pretty much live at our house."

"He probably doesn't know what to say to us."

"True," Scott said. "Maybe he worries we blame him."

Ben had been driving when a truck had blown a tire, veered out of control, and hit an SUV that then crossed three lanes of the freeway to hit the boys, traveling in a Mustang convertible in the opposite direction. According to all reports, Ben had been following the speed limit; he had not been drinking. He could have done nothing to avoid the accident.

"You did ask for the police report. Maybe he knows that you checked his alcohol level."

"Jesus, Kat. Any parent would do that."

She remembered Scott in those first weeks—checking maintenance records on the truck, on the road, talking to litigators at his office, researching tire statistics, desperate to find someone, anyone, to blame—the truck driver, the SUV driver, the tire company, even the county. If there had been a center divider, he told Kat, the accident would not have happened. His own colleagues had talked him out of litigating that. A freak accident. Nobody to blame.

"It wasn't Ben's fault," Kat said.

"He doesn't *know* that we understand that," Scott said. "Maybe he still feels, I don't know, guilty. Something."

Kat frowned. "God, I hope not."

After dinner, when Scott was working in his den, Kat took out the laptop and once more reviewed the Internet research on tests and pregnancy for an older woman. She wanted to talk to Scott about it. She knew he would think the idea totally insane, but she had to at least ask him. The words had to be said.

Finally, when Scott had been working for over an hour, Kat drank two fast glasses of wine, walked with rigid determination into his den, and stood in front of his desk like a schoolgirl facing the principal. Scott turned from his computer, frowning.

"What's up?"

"I want to ask you something," Kat said. She saw the concern on his face, and she took a long breath. "Would you even consider having another baby? Would you go for the tests the doctors suggested so that we could—"

She had no chance to end the sentence. He stood, moved around his desk to pull her hard against his chest.

"Kat, please. Please. It won't bring him back."

"I know it won't—" Her voice broke on the words. "But another baby. It would be so wonderful. Just to hold an infant. To care for another baby. Can you imagine?"

"Stop it, sweetheart. You're torturing yourself. You're not strong enough to get pregnant again, Kat. Not emotionally strong enough.

And we're so much older. No. No, it's just not an option. You need to find a different way through this."

She leaned against him, unable to speak further until, after a while, he released her gently.

"Make some hot tea," he said. "Maybe find an old movie to watch? I need to finish off this one report, then I'll join you."

TWELVE

In the late afternoon of the following day, Scott's voice on the phone sounded both exhausted and irritable.

"That damn car," he said. "It was supposed to be fixed. I'm leaving it in the shop. Have to get James to drop me. You better go ahead and eat."

"Again?" Kat said. "Well, of course. I love eating alone. In fact, I can't even remember when we last—"

"It's not my goddamn fault if the car—"

"No. Nothing is your fault, Scott—" She paused, biting at her lip. It *wasn't* his fault. Jesus. She was turning into a harridan. A cartoon wife.

"Do you want me to pick you up?" she asked in a small voice, praying he would say no. The idea of driving downtown frightened her: the kaleidoscopic clamor of the freeways; the huge, speeding trucks, too close. She waited while he considered this.

"No. Don't worry," he said, at last. "I'll get a ride."

She replaced the phone, walked into the kitchen. The house felt cold, echoing, and so quiet she could hear the clicking of the fridge. *I need to focus on something else,* she told herself. The job on the weekly paper would begin in a few weeks. She shivered. She didn't want the job.

She didn't think she could do it. The only job she really wanted right now, she admitted, was to take care of a child. A baby. A growing child. That tiny curl of desire was becoming impossible to ignore.

Two hours later, when Kat was beginning to worry that Scott was unable to get a ride home and she would have to pick him up after all, Sarah's green Jaguar pulled up to the curb. Scott stepped out and, seeing her at the window, waved. Kat hesitated and then moved to open the front door.

"James was tied up, so Sarah kindly offered to drop me," Scott called. He turned to Sarah. "Sure you don't want coffee?"

"No time," Sarah said, leaning out the window of the Jaguar and waving to Kat.

"It's a long drive to Ojai," Scott said. "Coffee might be a good idea."

Sarah looked over to Kat. The green eyes appeared bright in the fading light.

"Would it be a bother, Kat? I hate to interrupt your evening."

"Of course not. Come in."

As Kat made coffee, she listened to Sarah's and Scott's voices from the living room. They talked of contracts to be signed, documents to be filed with the court. She heard the name of Jeremy Woodruff, Scott's colleague, and then laughter. They seemed to have found common ground in their dislike of the pompous lawyer.

She carried in the coffee as Scott continued to explain about language that was essential, could not be excluded if they were to avoid problems later. It was Sarah who interrupted him, turning to Kat with a warm smile.

"Scott, enough of this shoptalk. I should get moving and leave you two to your evening."

"You're spending a few days in Ojai?" Kat asked.

"Just a quick visit. I have to meet the builder very early in the morning."

"You're extending the house?"

"I'm building an orangery. Remember the one at Lansdowne?"

"Oh yes. Of course. Victorian. It was beautiful."

"I want one exactly like it. The architect is having trouble with my phone descriptions. And I don't have a picture." She laughed. "They're not common in California. I'll have to walk the perimeter and try to make a sketch."

Sarah rested her head on the back of the armchair, musing. "Remember when you first saw Lansdowne? When I first took you there? You were so excited, you ran from room to room, even down to the basement, even up to the attic. You loved that house. Almost as much as I did."

"I was a council-house kid, remember," Kat said. "I'd never seen so much space. The bedroom you and I had, at the back of the house overlooking the garden? That was bigger than my entire home."

Sarah laughed.

"The house was falling apart and just so horribly tatty, and still you loved it," she said.

"Didn't look tatty to me."

Sarah stood then, gulped down her coffee, and was gone in a few minutes. She waved from the window of the Jaguar, gunning the engine as she headed up the street.

Scott followed Kat into the kitchen.

"She likes to replicate those old rooms, doesn't she?" he said, sounding puzzled. "That old bathroom in Ojai. This new project. And one of the rooms in Malibu is an exact copy of some room in a seaside cottage in Sussex."

"I remember the cottage in Sussex," Kat said. "Little gatehouse. Lovely place."

"Think she's trying to recapture her lost youth?"

"I doubt it," Kat said. "She had a miserable childhood. I can't imagine she'd want to recapture that. She was sent away to boarding school and moved from school to school. Always getting expelled. And her parents—well, I heard so many rumors. Her mother had a number of breakdowns. Her father lived in France. She won't talk about them."

"She must have been fond of this Helen. The one with the big house."

"She was. In a strange way. They were offhand with each other, never hugged much. But they had some kind of bond. I remember when Helen had a fall, Sarah was terrified she would die."

Sarah had been at Kat's house when the call came from Sister Agnes. A car was on the way to St. Theresa's to pick up Sarah to take her to the hospital in Sussex where her aunt was being treated; Sarah must return to the school immediately. Sarah had turned so pale, her eyes wide and bright with a fear Kat had never seen before. Kat's mother took one look at Sarah's face and then turned to her husband.

"My dad drove her back to school," Kat told Scott. "That was amazing in itself. He never drove anywhere except to work. That little car was kept ready for the next shift. Maggie and I *always* had to take the bus. Anyway, he said he'd drive Sarah back to meet up with the limo and I went with them, and Sarah curled up into a tight ball in the backseat, asking over and over where she would go, what would happen to her. She was terrified that Helen would die.

"I remember when we got to school, this big black car was waiting, and Sister Agnes was there and Mrs. Evans, the nasty housekeeper who hated me—"

"Hated you?" Scott interrupted. "Why did she hate you?"

"Wrong class. Lacked breeding. No right to be mixing with the likes of Sarah. She always treated me as if I were about to steal the silver. Anyway, Sarah just ran to the black car, didn't speak to Sister Agnes or pick up anything from her dorm. The car took off with her and Mrs. Evans in the backseat. I remember my dad watching her and saying—*Poor wee lassie.*"

"Nothing poor about the wee lassie these days," Scott said.

After dinner, Kat spent another hour researching on her laptop, then she stood at the bedroom window, chewing at her thumbnail. She liked the view from their hillside home: the twin boulevards of Tampa and Reseda pulsing yellow and red as traffic merged into shimmering neon trails. But on this evening, she was blind to the changing lights and shadows. There was a churning excitement building slowly in her gut. Maybe giving birth to another child was not a possibility. Maybe Scott would never agree to it. He would not go for tests; she was certain of that. And, yes, it would be difficult for her to conceive at her age. But there was another option. It was not ridiculous. It was not insane. But she needed more information on it. And she knew who could help her find it.

She checked her watch. Sarah would have arrived in Ojai by now; she would no longer be driving. Kat found the card with the gold lettering that Sarah had given to her and dialed the number on it fast, before she had a chance to change her mind. And then she said the words that, before this night, she would never have believed she would one day say to Sarah Cherrington:

"Sarah," she said, "I need your help."

THIRTEEN

Kat waited at the window a full thirty minutes before Sarah's car was due to arrive.

"Meet me for lunch in Beverly Hills tomorrow," Sarah had said when Kat called her in Ojai. Kat had murmured about hating to drive over the hill, about maybe meeting in a restaurant closer to home, but Sarah had interrupted, dismissing all this.

"No problem. I'll send a car for you," she said. "He'll pick you up at twelve thirty."

Kat had applied makeup carefully, had spent a long time arranging her hair, and at noon, wearing a simple blue linen dress, the most expensive thing in her closet, she paced from window to mirror to check her appearance. The mirror reflected a woman with tidy hair and a pale and anxious face.

Kat had no idea where she was going; Sarah had not mentioned the name of the restaurant. She assumed it was in Beverly Hills.

When a silver Mercedes pulled up to the curb, Kat hurried outside and saw a young man in a gray suit already standing beside it. He moved fast to open the back door of the car for her.

"Afternoon, ma'am," he said in a friendly way.

As the luxury car pulled out and made its way to the freeway, Kat, settling back into the soft leather of the seat, tugged at her dress so that it would not crease so much around the waist and hips, wishing now she had chosen something cotton, cool and crisp. She looked out the window as the Mercedes made its way over the hill, and she saw that, yes, Beverly Hills seemed to be the destination. The young man drove fast and smoothly, eventually pulled up outside a long, low building with a smoked-glass door, and Kat recognized the name of a restaurant she had only ever seen mentioned in the society pages.

She thanked the young driver and then, shaky, took a deep breath, lifted her chin, and walked inside the place fast, before she lost her nerve. Kat had an impression of frosted glass, of huge flower arrangements, soft lighting, white tablecloths, crystal, and silver. The maître d' approached her, greeted her with a silky "Good afternoon," and inclined his head, waiting for her to speak. Kat gave Sarah's name and he bowed slightly, turned at once, and led her through the busy restaurant to a table in the corner where Sarah waited, her phone in one hand, a netbook open on the table.

As they approached, Kat studied her. Sarah looked quite at home in these surroundings. She wore a gray silk suit, diamond studs in her ears, her hair swept to one side, as she had often worn it years ago. In profile, the two sides of her face could look quite different: one side so bare, the delicate bone structure clear and unobstructed, the other side hidden by a cascade of rich brown hair. *A Janus face,* Maggie had said once. *How appropriate.*

She clicked off the phone and stood as Kat reached the table.

"Aha!" she said, hugging her briefly. "You see, Caitlin darling, there is a world over the hill and beyond the Valley. Now, would you like a cocktail?"

"White wine would be lovely."

"White wine it is."

Sarah summoned a waiter, ordered a bottle of Chardonnay, and then turned her attention back to Kat. The green eyes sparkled. It was clear to Kat that Sarah enjoyed being in control, here in her own environment. She appeared to be well known to the other expensively dressed patrons who passed the table and nodded their recognition. Sarah acknowledged them coolly, her attention on Kat. Only once did she look up, her smile bright and immediate, to lift her hand in a brief hello. Kat turned to see a successful young actor, once hugely popular in a television series, now making movies, smiling at Sarah as he crossed the room.

"Oh—is that—?"

"It is," Sarah murmured, looking back at Kat. "And isn't he just delicious?"

"Yes," Kat said, surprised that the real-life actor was actually as attractive as the on-screen image. "He's just as handsome as I imagined. A bit shorter, though."

"They're all shorter," Sarah said. "He's nice, too. That's very disconcerting."

"You're disconcerted by nice?" Kat asked.

Sarah laughed.

"So tell me, Caitlin. What is it you need?"

Kat took a breath.

"Just some information, really. Just curious."

"About?"

"Your adoption charity. How does it work?"

Sarah looked at her levelly, her expression unreadable.

"It's matchmaking, basically," she said. "Matching unwanted babies with prospective parents."

"Ah. I thought so. Yes."

"Why do you ask?"

Kat, feeling foolish, hesitated. She shouldn't be here. This was a mistake. Sarah would talk to Scott, and Scott would be angry that she was pursuing something so clearly irrational.

"It's probably not possible—" she began.

"Everything's possible, Kat."

"I just wondered if Scott and I would qualify. If—"

"You're thinking of adopting a child?" Sarah asked. Her voice was gentle. She did not seem to think the idea insane.

"We haven't really talked about it yet. I'm just—oh, exploring it. As a possibility."

Sarah nodded slowly.

"It's a serious matter, Kat. You need to be very sure—"

"I know. I know."

"And, honestly, it wouldn't be easy. I believe grieving parents are generally treated with extreme caution. I would have to check." Sarah paused, thinking. "Did you choose to have just one child?" she asked. "Out of principle or something?"

"Principle? Oh no. No," Kat said. "Not at all. We wanted more. It just never happened. I never got pregnant again. We tried to find out why at one point. I had a preliminary examination; nothing was found. We were both going to have more tests, and Scott was meant to be tested, but—oh, I don't know. He just didn't. He was a senior associate then, trying to make partner, and he was so busy and we had Chris. We always encouraged Chris's friends to stay over, so the house was always full of children, and then—it just went onto the back burner."

"And you haven't discussed this with Scott yet?"

"Not properly. I thought I'd get some information first."

"He'll have to agree, I'm afraid. You must both want it."

"I know."

"And what does Maggie say about this?"

"I haven't told her yet. I've only just—"

"You haven't discussed it with anyone?"

"Only Brooke. My neighbor. Friend. Across the street."

Sarah frowned.

"The home-baking blonde?"

"Blonde, yes," Kat said, prickling. "And smart. And kind."

"Well, that's good," Sarah said. "And is she supportive?"

"She's not sure it's a good idea."

"Ah, I see," Sarah said, pausing as the waiter appeared with the wine. Sarah tasted it, smiled at the waiter. She had a way of looking directly into people's eyes, Kat noted, for a little too long. She did this with the young wine waiter, not flirting exactly, but—with a way of showing her absolute attention. She took control over ordering the meal. She consulted the menu, ordered for both of them, requested some special bread she liked, and olives, ascertained that the tiny lemon tarts she loved were on the dessert menu, then sat back and regarded Kat.

"Well, I can see why you want to do it. I should think you're a wonderful mother. But. It's a big decision," she said.

"Yes," Kat said. "I know."

"Also," Sarah continued, "a number of checks are made. Financial, employment, things like that. A home visit. And honestly, because of your situation, I don't think it would be easy.

"But," she added quickly, as if reading something in Kat's face, "it wouldn't be impossible. Listen, I don't usually get involved in the actual adoptions, but in this case, I'll do what I can."

"Thank you!"

Sarah smiled. "This is exciting for you," she said.

Kat felt a small surge of hope.

"Yes. It is. But I'm just exploring it right now. I really just want to get information."

"Well, I can certainly give you all that. I'll have the details delivered to your house this afternoon. The material is very comprehensive."

"Do the adopting parents have to be Catholics?" Kat asked.

"There's some flexibility. But, Kat, you *are* Catholic."

"Not anymore. I haven't been to Mass in years."

"Well, I think it's like becoming a godmother. You have to agree to raise the child as Catholic."

"Not sure how Scott would feel about that. It's all—oh, speculation at this point."

"Is it?" Sarah asked, eyes narrowing.

When the food arrived, salad with an assortment of berries and nuts, Sarah concentrated on tasting and enjoying it, just as she had at school. She urged Kat to try this or that, wanting her to like everything. The meal was delicious, Kat found, though the portions were small. Scott would complain if he were here. She looked up to find Sarah smiling at her.

"So odd to see you here," Sarah said. "I never imagined—" She shook her head. "Tell me. Your parents? Are they well?"

Kat, surprised at the question, put down her fork.

"Mum died four years ago. Of cancer. And my dad—he died nine months later. A heart attack."

"No. Dear God, how sad. And so soon after your—"

"He'd been drinking too much for months," Kat said. "And not eating at all. He simply stopped taking care of himself when Mum died. He was alone in the house when the chest pains struck. He didn't call for an ambulance."

"If he hadn't died this way, he would have starved to death," Maggie had said. "There's nothing to eat in the house. He must have just stopped buying food. Bottles everywhere. And nothing in the fridge."

"I think he pretty much gave up," Kat said now to Sarah. "He couldn't function without Mum. Didn't want to."

"I'm sorry," Sarah said, reaching across the table to squeeze Kat's hand. "So sorry. They were very kind to me."

She paused, biting her lip, thinking back.

"I remember your mother helping me on with my coat. She lifted all my hair from under my collar and then tucked my scarf around my neck and tied it. It was so—" Sarah hesitated, struggled for the right word. "So *gentle*, the way she did that."

Kat nodded, surprised that Sarah could recall, with such clarity, the kindness of a friend's mother, the gentle tucking in of a scarf, over twenty years later.

"It was a couple of weeks after that clinic visit," Sarah said, her eyes on Kat. "She didn't know, did she? Your mother? You never told her?"

"No. I never told anyone."

"She must have intuited it, then. Something. It felt like she knew. Her kindness."

"It's possible," Kat said. "I think she sensed when someone was feeling fragile. And she was a compulsive scarf arranger and tie straightener. And collars. She never met a collar she didn't want to smooth out. She was a very cuddly mum."

Kat reached for her drink, aware of a sharp pang of grief for the woman whose fussing had so irritated her and Maggie throughout their teenage years—and whom they both deeply missed.

"You were lucky," Sarah said.

"Yes. I know that now."

"Lucky to have a family like that. And lucky that you got to leave that soul-destroying school at the end of the day," Sarah said.

"I never thought being a day girl was lucky," Kat said. "I always felt I was missing something. Something exciting and fun in the evening."

Sarah laughed.

"Exciting and fun? The studious girls studied. The shallow ones painted their toenails. You didn't miss a thing, darling."

"It wasn't a bad school," Kat said. "At least we got an education."

"A *what*?" Sarah said, leaning back on her chair, frowning. "We got no such thing. English, yes. Latin, yes. Some history. Distorted.

But hardly any advanced math, limited physics. Shameful. And all that religion. Dear God. Remember Sister Agnes? The Gargoyle?"

Kat thought for a moment. Sarah had her own pet names for all the nuns: the Gargoyle, the Vulture, Jabba.

"Vaguely," Kat said.

"Of course you remember her. She had breath like a badger's bum. Listen—"

Sarah, leaning forward now, spoke in a hoarse whisper: *And therefore, gells, one achieves a state of grace—*

Sarah, always an excellent mimic, had conjured the nun's voice exactly. Kat shivered.

"Oh, stop it," Kat said. "Please. You sound just like her."

"And all those insane school rules?" Sarah said, not to be deterred, eyes bright. "Remember all the rules about that ugly uniform?"

Kat remembered Sarah wearing her school beret slanted over her eyes like she was a French model, the mandatory pleated skirt tugged up inches above her knees.

"You pretty much disregarded all that."

"Of course I did. It was ridiculous."

"I remember being baffled by the basic house rules," Kat admitted. "I never could see the sense in those. All the things that were considered *vulgar*. Vulgar to open a window wide? Why?"

"Oh, my aunts would agree with that," Sarah said. "Class thing."

"And no coughing. No eating while walking in public."

"No smoking in public, either," said Sarah.

"But no eating? Why?"

"I believe an ice cream at the beach was acceptable."

"Remember when they tried to enforce the thing that if you fainted during Mass you would be left on the floor until after the Consecration? When there was a kind of fainting epidemic?"

"Well, they had to do something. Girls were falling like trees. Power of suggestion. It stopped it. Remember? It actually worked."

"You fainted once, though, remember? Almost fainted."

"God, don't remind me. That girl with the nosebleed. Blood gushing all over the place," Sarah said, shuddering.

Sarah's hemophobia was well known to the pupils and nuns at St. Theresa's. A bloody knee during a hockey game, even on a player for the opposing team, would have Sarah retching into the bushes that lined the pitch.

On that school day, Kat had tried to catch Sarah when she became dizzy, and so both of them had gone down, landing on their knees. "I fell down with you, remember?" Kat said.

"Yes! Both of us on our knees like repentant sinners."

They laughed at the memory.

"What a weird place," Kat said. "Really. But I suppose we survived. With only minimal damage."

"You think?"

Kat found that the wine had begun to hit her hard; her head felt full of clouds. The waiter seemed to be refilling her glass constantly. She resolved to slow down.

"That's enough wine for me," she said to Sarah. "It's making me woozy."

Sarah laughed.

"Oh, drink up, silly. Why should you worry? You can take a little nap this afternoon. I have a board meeting. Entirely the most boring posse of board members I have ever met in my life. And then a meeting of lawyers."

"Scott? Will you be meeting Scott?"

"I will indeed."

"Did you tell him you were meeting me for lunch?" Kat asked.

Sarah regarded her with amusement.

"Aha—you haven't told him, then? Why not?"

Kat shrugged, the wine making her reckless.

"I told him I was meeting you," she said, remembering Scott's predictable surprise, his teasing threat to rat on her to Maggie. "But I didn't say why. As I said, we haven't really discussed adoption yet."

"Fret not," Sarah said. "Your secret is perfectly safe with me."

She looked over at Kat, her smile fading.

"You're serious about this, Kat, aren't you? About this adoption?"

"Yes. I think I am."

"Then, we must be sure to make it happen," Sarah said.

Sarah followed through as she had promised: a messenger delivered the adoption charity details later in the afternoon, just an hour after Kat had been driven home in the Mercedes by Sarah's driver. A card was attached to the package, referencing someone named Elizabeth Brady. Sarah had scrawled a note: Liz Brady was the person for Kat to contact; she should call Mrs. Brady if she had questions, but she must let Sarah know as soon as she and Scott decided to go ahead.

Kat studied the glossy brochure carefully. It was professionally produced with full-color photographs. It seemed that the charity coordinated the adoption process and also, if the mother-to-be had no insurance, helped with medical costs. There were nurses available, doctors on call. It was stressed throughout the brochure that all fees were paid by the charity, all medical costs funded by it, too; there was no cost to the adoptive parents. It was clear, Kat concluded, that this was no buy-a-baby scheme. She wondered if the goal was a donation to the charity. Certainly, she and Scott could afford to contribute something. It seemed wrong to accept so much without making any payment. The coordinator—in this case, Elizabeth Brady—would be on call 24–7 to answer questions and allay fears. A medical nurse would also answer questions by phone. It was an impressive setup.

Kat still had the package open on the coffee table when she heard Scott's car out front. Heart racing, she gathered the papers together, jogged upstairs, and placed them at the very bottom of her sweater drawer before hurrying to the window to check on Scott.

Yes, there was his car, parked in the driveway. She wondered why he was home so early when the closing was imminent, and she watched him as he climbed out of the car and began to pull boxed files out of the backseat. Something caught his eye then. He paused, leaving the files on the edge of the car trunk, and walked to the hedge. Kat studied him, puzzled, as he lifted an old basketball that had been hidden inside a dried-out shrub. He stood for a moment, twirling the ball absently in one hand. Then, he looked up at the basketball hoop above the garage door, ignored now, unused.

Kat, seeing the shadow that crossed his face, imagined the memories going through his mind, saw them herself, heard the same sounds: the *thump-thump* on summer evenings as father and son played ball in the driveway while she cooked dinner—their voices, loud, exuberant, floating on the summer air.

She remembered how, finally, tired of calling out that the meal was ready, that it would be cold or spoiled—and annoyed at being ignored, or fobbed off with *Two more minutes, two more minutes*—she would march out to the yard, try to intercept the ball herself, to call a halt to the game. She had done it once or twice, too. Neither her son, nor her husband, wanting to actually knock her over.

"Dinner!" she would yell, holding the ball high and victorious. "Now!"

"Two more minutes! I've nearly thrashed him."

"Yeah, right. Show me, old man. Give it your best shot."

She had a splintered, visual memory of leaping bodies, a spinning ball, the *whoosh* of the ball through the net, and the sound of laughter on the warm breeze. Why hadn't she just let them play for as long as it took, for as long as they wanted to stay out in the fading light? They wouldn't have cared if the chicken was dry, the steak cold. They could have enjoyed that time together. More of that time.

She wouldn't make the same mistake again.

Kat watched as Scott gave the old ball another twirl, then, shoulders drooping, head down, he took it to the trash bin and dropped it inside. He stood for a moment, as if regaining control of himself. Longing to hug him, but not wanting him to know that she was watching, Kat hesitated for too many seconds—and then it was too late. He was back at the car, lifting the files from the trunk, and a moment later, inside the house.

"Hi there." His work voice. Tired.

She hurried downstairs to greet him. He held the boxed files in both arms. His reading glasses were sticking out of his pocket, and his hair stood up on his head, as if he had been pushing his hands through it all day.

"You're early," she said. "What's up?"

"I'm going to work from here for a bit. Away from the damn phones. It's an absolute zoo downtown. I might go back later."

"I'll make you an early dinner. You could use some energy foods. Some protein."

"I could certainly use the energy. But hey, don't worry too much about me. A quick sandwich will do and some coffee," he said, then turned to her. "So how was lunch with Sarah Harrison?"

"Posh. Nice, actually. I think she's changed a bit. She's not so tough. It was a short lunch."

"Yep, she can do short. She shut Woodruff up in midspiel at the meeting this afternoon. That was something to behold."

Scott headed into his den, placed the boxed files on his desk. He seemed already distracted.

"A sandwich, then?" Kat said. "You won't want a drink if you're heading back to the office."

"No. Coffee for now. Lots of it. Anything at all to eat," he said vaguely. "Anything will be fine."

As Kat made coffee in the kitchen, she heard Scott talking on the phone, his voice irritable. She guessed he was talking to James, because there was an element of *I'm the boss* in the way he gave instructions. He slammed down the phone with a groan.

"Goddamn it," he said. "Fuck."

Kat picked up the coffee and his roast beef sandwich and stood in the doorway, holding them.

"It's going badly?" she asked.

"It's a closing. It's supposed to be hell," he said. "But no. It's not this damn thing. It's—" He shook his head. "You know Lindsay moved to Gibson, Harvey?"

Kat had a vague memory of Scott mentioning that a partner was leaving the firm but was unclear on the details. She nodded nevertheless.

"He's taken TDK Industries with him," Scott said.

"But isn't that—"

"Was," Scott said. "*Was* my client. My oldest fucking client, too. Damn. My fault. I didn't have time for them. I asked Lindsay to pick up the slack. Fuck."

"I'm sorry," Kat said, placing the sandwich and coffee on a corner of his desk, careful not to touch any papers. "Can you persuade them back?"

"No," he said, reaching for the sandwich, barely looking up from his paperwork. "And this thing? Christ. Being surrounded by fools who don't have their minds on the job isn't helping."

"Which fools? Who do you mean?"

"Ah, never mind. The work will get done. It always gets done."

Kat stood for a few seconds, unsure. She had wanted to show him the glossy brochure upstairs, tell him all that she had learned about adoption from Sarah. At some point they absolutely must talk about it. But—this was a bad time. He was already overwhelmed. She backed out of the door slowly.

Later in the evening, when Scott had returned to his downtown office, Kat paced the living room sipping her wine, wishing she had at least said something, put the idea in his head. Let him think about it, get used to the possibility of it, before they discussed it properly. Or perhaps it was better to wait until the closing was over. When he was calmer, not so distracted. He would be ready to listen. They would talk then. And she would convince him.

FOURTEEN

The next morning, the day of the closing, Scott jumped from bed before dawn. Kat stood in the doorway of the bathroom, watching him as he shaved. He looked exhausted: dark shadows had formed under his eyes and his skin had an odd gray sheen.

"You look done in," she said.

Scott studied his own face in the mirror.

"The color of dead fish skins," he said. "I look like Methuselah."

Kat touched his shoulder and turned away.

"You're just tired. You really need to rest."

"I've aged fifty years," he said.

When he called in the late afternoon to say that the closing was going smoothly, that all the papers had been approved, his voice sounded brighter.

"The end's in sight. Thank God," he said.

"Do you want me to prepare dinner? Or wait for you?" Kat asked.

A pause while he thought about this.

"Wait on mine, just in case."

"You don't think Sarah expects to take you all out for a celebratory meal, do you?"

"No. Well, whatever she expects, it's not going to happen. I'm too busy for celebrations. But anyway, you go ahead and eat, sweetheart. We can grill a steak for me when I get home."

Later in the evening, Kat opened the fridge door, pulled out cheese and ham and some salad items, set them on the counter, then shrugged, turning away. She was not hungry. She was restless and edgy. The feeling was not like the icy stupor of grief. It felt like something else; it felt very similar to fear. She wanted to call Scott to talk to him, but didn't dare. She couldn't talk to Brooke—she had gone out in the Miata earlier. She wondered about calling Sarah, just to be able to discuss the adoption idea. Discuss it with somebody. At least Sarah was sympathetic. She would listen. But Sarah would be involved in this closing, along with Scott. Maggie? No. Maggie wouldn't understand. Maggie would talk about healing, and stages of grief, and God knows what.

Kat made the sandwich anyway, but took only one bite. Instead of eating, she poured a large glass of wine and took it with her to the French windows overlooking the garden. The wind was strong again, Santa Ana strength, so that the palm swayed. She could hear a dog barking, somewhere over in the far canyon: a lonely sound.

She stood for a long time, sipping the wine, watching the trees bend. When the phone rang, she jumped.

"Kat," said Sarah. "Is our hero back yet? I have one quick question on this thing."

"No. Not yet," said Kat. "Is it over? Did it go well?"

"Oh, very well indeed," said Sarah. "Everything signed, sealed, and delivered, one assumes. Now, I wonder if he can give me a ring here. I'm downtown at the Ritz-Carlton. Where *is* that number?"

Kat could hear Sarah rustling about. She could hear, too, the sound of a shower. Sarah was obviously preparing to duck into it.

"Here it is," Sarah said, and read off the number of the hotel.

"It's the Ritz-Carlton?" asked Kat.

"Yes, the one near the office. I didn't really need to stay here after all. I thought the thing would take half the night but we finished early. I could have driven back to Malibu. Actually, I wonder if I could still do that?"

Kat held the phone, waiting, while Sarah thought about it. The noise from the shower shut off abruptly. Kat frowned, puzzled. It sounded as if Sarah had someone with her.

"No. I may as well stay here for one night," said Sarah at last. "Ask Scott to give me a ring. Tonight, if he can. If not, tomorrow morning will do. And how are you, Kat?"

"I'm fine," said Kat. "Thank you. I'll have him call you."

"And—" Sarah said, a hint of something odd in her voice, "I have some news for you."

"For me? What news?"

"I talked to Liz Brady this afternoon. I gave her details about a couple I know who are interested in adopting a baby. I told her your situation. Told her the truth. I believe, if you allow me to handle this for you, I'll be able to do it, though I may need to omit some of the less important facts. You'll need Scott's signature. That's all. Liz Brady will need to do a home visit. But she'll call you on that once the initial papers are signed and in."

Kat sat down abruptly; her body felt liquid, unreliable.

"Oh, it's really possible? That's such good news. Thank you, Sarah."

"My pleasure," Sarah said. "You'll need to have Scott sign the application. Then, let me know how it goes. Oh, I have to move."

The phone clicked. Kat replaced the handset and roamed the house, feeling an odd, burning excitement. A feeling so long dormant she had almost forgotten how edgy, how sharp these sensations could be. A baby. Would he be tall? Would he walk early, chuckle a lot, and not want to sleep at night? She held on to the dining table for a second, thinking about this. He might be tall and slender, and graceful. And good at languages. And musical. And beautiful. Or he might not. He might be short and stubborn and difficult, but, oh, it didn't matter. It didn't matter.

She found that she was crying as she sat down on the sofa.

Well. Well.

She wanted Scott home. She wanted to tell him.

Kat reached for the wine bottle and poured herself another large glass. She was drinking too much, she told herself, even as she sipped it. She should cut down and she would. Soon. But this—this was special. A toast to a new family. But wait, wait. Scott must agree. Must agree. It was not yet a final decision. Kat tried to steady her racing thoughts. Dear Christ—where *was* Scott? Sarah had said the closing was over. Why wasn't he home?

She thought of the shower shutting off in the hotel bedroom as Sarah talked to her on the phone. The abrupt way Sarah had ended the call. Surely, Scott was not there, in the shower? The pain of that possibility caused a clutching sensation in her gut, but Kat pushed the thought away at once. Of course not. He knew what Sarah was like; Maggie had warned him. They had both warned him. He wouldn't be taken in by her teasing games. Sarah was beautiful, though. And sexually willing. Kat dismissed these thoughts fast. No. He was late because he was working. He was always working.

It occurred to her that she spent much of her life waiting for him these days. Waiting for him to call, waiting for him to come home. She wondered whether he thought of her, alone here, as he busied himself with closings and trial preparations and all the things that kept his mind occupied and away from the reality of what was left for them now.

When Scott walked in, two hours later, Kat had finished the bottle of wine and started on another.

"Where were you?" she asked. "Sarah called hours ago. She said it was over."

"I had to go back to the office. I've lost one client. We neglected another client while we worked on this damn closing. I had to catch up."

"You've been ages. Ages and ages. Are you going to slowly work yourself to death? Is that the plan?"

"One of them," he said tiredly. He moved toward the bedroom. "I need a shower."

"Wait," Kat said. "I want to talk to you. Let me get you a glass of wine."

"No wine, Kat. And we'll talk tomorrow. I'm bushed."

"Now. Please."

He stopped, waited wearily.

"You were right about not having another baby," Kat said. "It would be difficult maybe for me. My age. Hormones."

"I know that."

"So why not adopt? So many children need homes, and a baby—"

"For Christ's sake, Kat. Leave it alone."

Kat looked at him, bewildered.

"What?"

"I can't talk about it right now."

"So when will you talk about it?"

"Please. It's been one hell of a day. I'm tired. Leave it. Please."

"No wonder you're tired. Work has become an obsession with you, Scott."

The word *obsession* slurred and Scott looked at her sharply.

"An obsession," Kat repeated carefully.

She reached for the wine bottle, to refill her glass.

"You've had enough of that, Kat, don't you think?" Scott said, and began to walk toward the door. Kat took a sip, called to his retreating back.

"You weren't screwing Sarah at the Ritz-Carlton, then?" she asked.

Scott stopped dead, turned around slowly, his face stiff.

"What the fuck kind of question is that?"

"Someone was with her. I heard the shower."

"And you thought it was me? Oh, for Christ's sake."

Kat stared at him.

"Listen," she said. "I'm sitting here all night, waiting. I want to talk to you. The thing finished hours ago. You could have come home. But you didn't. You could have called me to explain. But you didn't. You go to your office. Or somewhere else. Who the hell knows where you go? Is it me you don't want to come home to? Or the house? Or what?

"I wanted to talk to you about something important," she continued loudly, aware that she was mouthing the words in a theatrical fashion. "Important to us. Important to our marriage. And you don't care."

This was too much for Scott.

"Oh, get over yourself, Kat," he said, and turned again to walk out of the room.

Kat's annoyance, fueled by the wine, grew fast. She tried to stand up, intending to follow him, but found herself momentarily unbalanced and sank back onto the chair.

"And that's all you have to say?" she yelled after him.

He paused in the doorway and said, through gritted teeth, "Can you *try* to understand? I have a lot to do. A lot to catch up on."

"*Catch up on?* Oh, it's Chris's fault, then. For dying and making you get behind with your work."

The words had flown unbidden, unconsidered, from her mouth. Stunned and cold with shame, Kat gasped. She wanted to take the words back, unsay them, but they hung in the air. Scott stiffened; his eyes were gray slate as they regarded her.

Kat shook her head.

"God. I'm sorry, sorry. I'm so sorry. I didn't mean—"

But he turned away fast. The door slammed behind him.

She waited, rigid, for his return, listening to the sounds coming from the bedroom. A few minutes later, she heard the shower, and later still, the creak of the bed and the light clicking off. He had gone to bed.

When she entered the bedroom, his face was to the wall. Kat pulled off her clothes, did not brush her teeth or shower; she just fell into bed. Scott did not move when she lay down next to him, and though she tried to puzzle it all out, tried to understand what all this anger might mean, the alcohol did its devious work and she was swept immediately into a deep and troubled sleep.

She woke, some hours later, with an aching head and a mouth impossibly dry and gritty. She sat up, reached for the glass of water by the side of the bed, and gulped at it.

"Headache?" Scott asked.

She turned. The bedroom, in the early-hours light, was shadowy and gray. Scott lay on his back, staring at the ceiling.

"A monster," Kat said. "I deserve it, I suppose."

"Yes. You do."

She lay back down, turned onto her side, and studied his profile. Then, she reached across and took his hand.

"I'm sorry. I'm so sorry. I said stupid things. That thing about blaming Chris. That was unforgivable."

"Yes."

"I didn't mean it. I really didn't mean it. I'm so sorry."

He gripped her hand.

"Okay. I'm sorry, too. For being so late. I just got tied up."

"And I'm sorry I said that about Sarah Harrison," Kat said, watching his face. He didn't look at her; he continued to stare at the ceiling. "I didn't really believe it."

"So why say it?"

"I don't know. I just wanted to shock you, I think. Except somebody was with her at the Ritz-Carlton."

"Could have been anybody. A personal friend. James. Brian Saunders."

"Brian?" Kat said, astonished. "The new associate? He's just a boy."

"I think he amuses her. He's so keen to work on her new acquisitions. But last night? I have no idea."

"Or James?" Kat said, awake now. "You said James."

"Well, it's possible. Anyway, that's his business, not ours, Kat. Okay?"

"But what about Glenda? I thought James and Glenda were maybe . . . ?"

"We don't know that."

"I might have misread the body language. But no, I don't think so. That night at Sarah's house? Oh, poor Glenda."

Scott sighed, clearly not wanting to talk about the personal entanglements of his colleagues and clients.

"And so—you were talking about adoption? What was all that about?"

"We can adopt a child if we want to. It's possible. We can do it. Even though we've lost a child. I checked."

He frowned.

"Kat, you have to work through your grief first. You know that."

"It doesn't have to be right this minute. In a few months maybe."

"Nothing will change in a few months."

"You can at least consider it."

"Right. I'll consider it."

He didn't sound certain. He was fobbing her off. Kat looked hard at him. He looked so tired and sad. Obviously, he had not slept much.

"You don't mean it. Please don't lie to me."

"We have a lot of grieving to do, Kat. And other things in our lives to consider right now. And what about your new job? On that paper?" he asked.

"I don't want it. Not really. I'd never fit in there. I'd feel like everyone's old aunt. I'm going to call that young editor tomorrow and withdraw. I'd rather get something part-time. Until we decide."

She settled back in the bed for a few seconds, then shot up, sitting up on her pillows, snapping on the bedside light to check the date on her watch.

"Oh God, oh God," she said.

"What?"

"Martha Kim! Damn, I completely forgot. I had an appointment yesterday."

"You forgot?"

Kat fell back onto the pillows.

"Yep. Just vanished from my memory. Damn. I'll call her tomorrow. Apologize."

"How can she help you if you miss appointments?"

"How can she help me anyway?"

Scott was silent for a few moments. When he spoke, his voice was weighted with tiredness.

"You have to get back on track, Kat."

Kat thought about this for a while.

"And what track is that?" she asked finally. "Where exactly is this track going?"

He didn't answer. She turned to look at him. His eyes were closed, his breathing steady. He was already asleep.

FIFTEEN

Sarah's voice on the phone, two days later, surprised Kat.

"I have the full adoption application for you," Sarah said. "I think there's a good chance. You just need Scott to agree and sign the form."

"Oh. That might not be so easy. But thank you, Sarah."

"What do you mean—*might not be so easy*? Scott said no?"

"He doesn't want to talk about it right now."

"And you can't persuade him?"

"I don't think so."

"He loves you. Surely, he'll want to make you happy? You need to think out a strategy. That's how I approach problems. How about meeting me for lunch in Beverly Hills again? We can have some more of those delicious lemon tarts."

"I'm not sure that right now—" Kat began.

"Okay. That's fine. We can have lunch another time. But, look, I'll be in the Valley tomorrow, a meeting at the Warner Center. I can drop in for coffee and I'll bring the application package so you have it at hand. I'll bring lemon tarts with me, too. Is ten too early?"

"Ten is fine," Kat said.

After Kat replaced the phone, she turned, gazing out into the garden. The window in the living room was open, so the sound of the sprinklers hitting the ground filled the room. The breeze moved the curtains, swirling pale ghosts against a washed-blue sky. Kat listened to the sound of the spraying water for a while. *A strategy?* She had never needed a strategy with Scott before. They had always talked so easily. Somehow, like so many other things in their lives, that had changed.

At exactly ten in the morning the following day, Kat opened the door to someone who, at first glance, looked like a stranger. Sarah, dressed in a sharply tailored navy suit and a cream silk blouse, wore her hair pulled back severely from her face and lipstick of a deep bloodred. She smiled at Kat's surprised expression.

"You look very—executive," Kat said.

"I know. I'm on my way to do battle in the boardroom. This is my corporate-warrior outfit."

"Corporate warrior in killer heels. It's very smart."

Sarah carried a brown envelope and a white box tied with ribbon.

"Application," she said. "Just needs signatures. When you've both signed, give the package back to me. I can have a messenger pick it up. And look here—lemon tarts, baby ones. Like the ones we had before."

Kat took the envelope from her, placed it on the hall table.

"I'll get the coffee."

When the coffee was poured, the pastries set out on a plate, Sarah leaned across the coffee table in the living room to reach for one of the tarts. Kat did the same.

"Two bites and gone," Sarah said, demonstrating.

"Oh, these are so good," Kat said.

"Nectar from the gods."

"I love the sharp lemon. Almost sour. And then the sweet."

"That's the joy of them."

"I daren't think of the calorie count."

"If God had meant us to count calories," Sarah said, "she would not have created lemon tarts. And so—Scott. He's still reluctant?"

"More than reluctant. Dismissive of the whole idea."

"He'll come 'round. Knowing how you feel, he must—" Sarah began, and then frowned as Kat shook her head.

"He's stubborn," Kat said. "He's always been stubborn."

"All men are stubborn. They can be persuaded."

Kat smiled then.

"The voice of experience? So tell me more about the adoptions—do they try to match prospective parents with the babies?"

"All screened carefully," Sarah said. "They do their best to find a good fit."

"As long as he's healthy. That's all that matters."

"He?" Sarah asked with a smile. "He or she will be healthy. I can promise you that."

She leaned back on the sofa and delicately brushed a stray crumb from the lapel of her suit jacket.

"Must not dent this armor," she said.

"It's that kind of meeting?" Kat asked.

"Indeed it is."

"You're going alone?" Kat asked, wondering why Sarah didn't take a couple of her executives along. Or a couple of her lawyers.

"I love going alone. One of the things I learned from Sam, over our long marriage, was the simple art of intimidation," Sarah said.

"You were married a long time?"

"Eighteen years."

Kat blinked, surprised, the coffee cup halfway to her mouth. Sarah must have married only a year or so after leaving the UK. She had imagined Sarah freewheeling all over Europe, living a wild, party-girl life, before she settled down. Obviously, that hadn't happened.

"I didn't realize you married so soon. I thought you were in Antibes. Or studying in Montpellier."

"I was. I did. Briefly. But I couldn't keep it up—my pitiful allowance wouldn't even buy a *drink* in Antibes, and I hated living with Aunt Octavia. Loathsome woman, always so scared that I would steal her squat little toadstool of a husband. I couldn't afford another semester in Montpellier, so when I met Sam I saw an opportunity."

"An opportunity?"

"To change my life. He had everything I needed to do that."

Sarah smiled at Kat's quizzical look.

"He was older. Successful. Knew his way around. He taught me a lot. I wanted financial security and he married me for my breeding, as he called it. I was the original well-bred trophy wife." Sarah gave a short laugh, reached for another lemon tart. "Ironic, really, since it turned out that I could not, in fact, breed."

She looked over at Kat, something like anger flickering in her eyes. Kat frowned, waited.

"A consequence of that little clinic session years ago," Sarah said. "Or the surgery that came after it."

"Oh God. I'm sorry."

"No matter. I was not surprised. But it was a shock to Sam."

"He accepted it, though?" Kat asked.

"He had no choice."

"What was he like, your husband?" Kat asked, curious now.

"Not attractive physically. Not like Scott, say. Or James. No. Not that kind of man. Short, stocky as a fire hydrant. Because he was plain-spoken people assumed he was honest. He was not. He was devious, slippery in business, very focused. When he wanted something, he got it."

Kat had the clear impression that Sarah admired these qualities.

"He suited me. I had no interest in those European playboys with their easy, inherited wealth," Sarah said. "And I didn't want someone clingy and besotted. We were very busy most of the time. Always traveling, always on the move.

"We never bought a house, you know. Sam liked his funds fluid, had no faith in property. We rented here, there, and everywhere. After he died, the very first thing I did, after they'd taken away all the medical equipment, the ugly hospital bed, all the nasty stuff that was littering the house, was make an offer on Ojai."

"Oh, of course. You nursed him at home. That must have been hard."

"It was a nightmare. He hated hospitals. Thank God for agency nurses and a sweet doctor who was not too stingy with the morphine."

"Didn't he have a morphine pump? Aren't they calibrated? My mother, when she—"

"Yes, he did," Sarah interrupted, a hard edge to her voice. "And liquid morphine, too. For bad nights. Why? Why do you ask?"

The green eyes, narrowing, had turned cold. Kat had a flash of memory of that angry face in the schoolroom all those years ago.

"Just that my mother's morphine was calibrated," Kat began, then added quickly, "Anyway, so you bought Ojai? It's a beautiful house."

Sarah nodded; her smile returned in an instant.

"It is beautiful, isn't it? But Sam refused to buy it. When I finally, finally had control of the funds, I made them an offer—too much probably—and bought it. My first real home. Well, after Lansdowne."

Such a strange, rootless marriage, Kat thought as she listened to this. She could not imagine it.

"You were happy together, though? You and Sam?"

"Happy?" Sarah leaned forward, reaching again for her coffee. Kat could smell the sweet floral scent of her perfume. "We were fine. We both had little affairs, discreet ones. He preferred professional call girls—he had some rather odd sexual preferences that I didn't share—and he never minded my dalliances so long as they didn't involve business rivals or other powerful men. Lesser mortals were fine.

"We had a lot of parties. He liked me to dress up, flirt a little. I complained once about all those leering men, staring at my breasts, drooling, brushing against me.

"You know what Sam said? *Never mind. It'll get easier when you get older. When you lose your looks.*"

Her laugh sounded warm and genuine. "He would have traded me in for a younger model when that happened. But I learned a lot. About business, about finance. I love that."

"No surprise. You were a math whiz kid at school."

"You could have got into advanced math, too, if you'd applied yourself."

"No chance. And you're still good at the financial stuff," Kat said. "So Scott tells me."

"I am. Good at the planning and scheming, the wheeling and dealing." Sarah gave her suit jacket another light sweep with her hand. "As the gentlemen at today's meeting will soon discover. They're going to have to take me seriously."

"They don't already? Why? Because you're a woman?"

"Oh, you have no idea. At the last meeting, I asked to see spreadsheets. The board chairman told me he would send them to my accountant. I said no, I would like to see them now, see them for myself, please. He smiled, ever so kindly, and said, *My dear, these things are very complicated.*"

Kat laughed. "He didn't actually pat your curls and say, *Don't you worry your pretty little head about them*?"

"Not in so many words. But yes. That was the gist of it. Well, today I have my own spreadsheets. With some of the dead wood chopped off. A nephew who does nothing but harass secretaries, a son-in-law with the IQ of an avocado. Slugs in polished shoes, both of them.

"Those two," she said, making a decisive movement with her hand, "are for the chop."

She paused then, surprised by a sharp rap on the door.

"You're expecting someone?" she asked.

"No. Not at all," Kat said, standing. "Sounds like my neighbor. It's her knock."

She hesitated as she headed to the door and turned, about to apologize for this interruption, but saw a shadow, a cold look of annoyance that crossed Sarah's face. So Kat said nothing and moved forward to open the door.

Brooke stood on the step, holding a silver box half covered in cellophane. She carried it through to the hall table, talking, as always, in a breathless rush, her soft voice rising and falling in a musical cadence.

"I'm racing, sweet pea, but look what I found. Home spa! It's got oil and a candle and just about everything. Oh, and the best hair conditioner. Leave it on for five minutes while you soak."

She leaned forward, lifted a strand of Kat's hair, and rubbed it between her thumb and forefinger.

"Okay. It's still a *little* bit dry. Leave it on for ten."

"Brooke. Thank you, but—"

"It's nothing. It was all on sale. And jeez, I'm sorry about the hideous color of that little headband. It said magenta on the package, but I had a peek and it's the color of those awful lawn ornaments in Florida. Flamingo? Flamingo pink? You'll look like a teenager."

She laughed, touching Kat's arm gently.

"And listen. My new gardener. Have you seen him? He has *muscles*. And he's handy, too. Does Scott still need someone to fix that awning out back? This guy could do it. I'll send him over. Well, he's fixed the pool pump. And the heater. It'll stay warm for a couple of days if Scott wants a swim. Does he still have the key? You know how he—"

She stopped speaking then, finally aware of Sarah, who was watching, with an amused expression, from the sofa.

"Oh my God. You've got company. I'm so sorry," Brooke said. She looked over at Sarah and waved. "Hi there. Sorry to come barging in like this."

"This is Sarah. An old school friend," Kat said. Sarah lifted her hand in acknowledgment but did not stand.

"Hello, Sarah," Brooke said, her smile blazing.

"Sarah, this is Brooke," said Kat. "My friend and neighbor and an incorrigible bringer of gifts."

"How very sweet," Sarah said. "Pleased to meet you, Brooke."

"Oh, I just love your accent!" Brooke said. "Look, sorry to interrupt. We're not filming until later and I thought I could just race this stuff over to Kat."

"Filming? Ah, you're an actress?" Sarah asked.

"Oh no. God, no. Advertising. We're filming a commercial."

"Interesting."

"It's fun. Most days."

Sarah lifted her coffee cup, regarded Brooke over the brim of it. Kat imagined the two women conducting the fast assessment that those interested in fashion and status do when they first meet: Brooke guessing the designer of Sarah's business suit, noting the diamond studs in her ears; Sarah taking in Brooke's silk blouse, the neckline a little too low, the shimmering bronze of her lipstick.

Sarah soon looked away and put down her cup in a slow, deliberate manner. It was a subtle dismissal, but Brooke picked up on it immediately and turned back to Kat with a grin.

"Okay. I'm gone. I'll be around late afternoon if you need anything. So—later, alligator. Bye, Sarah."

A hug for Kat, and then she was at the door, waving good-bye.

Kat closed the front door and returned to the living room.

"Do people really still say that?" Sarah asked. "*Later, alligator*?"

"Brooke does. As a joke."

"Ah. I see. So Scott actually has a key to her house?"

Kat frowned, puzzled.

"Her house? Oh no. He has a key to the back gate. The pool gate. He used to swim there early mornings. We all used the pool—" she said, faltering. "At one time."

"How nice for you. She's quite the live wire," Sarah said.

"She's lovely. I would have been lost without her."

"Really? Well, I should move, too," Sarah said, standing. "Get a few of those heads rolling."

Kat reached for the coffee cups, noted the last lemon tart left on the plate, and longed to just pick it up and pop it into her mouth.

"Do you want that last tart?" she asked.

"Why not?" said Sarah, reaching for it at once and biting into it.

She glanced at Kat's face and laughed.

"If you wanted it," she said, "you should have taken it!"

As she walked Sarah to the door, Kat, still wondering about James, asked in a voice that she tried to keep casual, "You had a date, then, after the closing the other night? Someone to join you at the Ritz-Carlton?"

Sarah stopped and turned, amusement in her eyes.

"And you want to know who it was? Caitlin! A lady never tells. As of course you know," she said.

"Okay. None of my business. Sorry."

"But you're guessing it's the young stud James?"

Kat shook her head, cheeks pink.

"No. Well, maybe I just—" Kat stopped. "You're having an affair with James?"

"An affair? Good heavens, no. An occasional dalliance, one might say."

Sarah's mouth curled and her eyes were full of mischief as she looked at Kat.

"I have rather high standards, of course. But I have to say that boy really does know what he's doing. Woodruff, on the other hand, is like a first-time schoolboy *every* time. He simply does not have a clue. Or any control whatsoever."

"Woodruff?" Kat said, astonished. "I thought you disliked Woodruff."

"Well, of course I dislike him. What's there to like? But he's been useful, in his weird little way. But sexually, oh my goodness. His poor wife."

"Sarah!" Kat said, pretending shock. "Stop it. These are Scott's colleagues. I'll never look at Woodruff in the same way again."

"But I haven't told you about Miyamoto yet!" Sarah said, eyes sparkling. She laughed. "Just teasing, Caitlin. All right, enough of this naughty talk. I need to get going."

Kat opened the front door.

"Thanks for coming, Sarah. I know how busy you are."

"Busy indeed," Sarah said. "After this I have to get back to Malibu. I have your husband and team out there. Scott with Glenda, of course. Maybe James, too. We should get a lot done."

She paused before she walked to the car.

"Take care, Kat. Call me. Let me know when you've convinced Scott about the adoption. When the papers are signed. I'll stay on top of it for you."

"Thank you. Thank you so much."

Kat watched Sarah march to her car. The corporate outfit had transformed her—she even walked differently. She had always loved to dress up. Years ago, they would raid her Aunt Helen's attic for cast-off clothes, giggling as they tried on furs and hats with feathers and rows of yellowing pearls. Always just the two of them. Sarah never wanted to show the other girls those gorgeous heirlooms, a fact that baffled Kat. Only one time did they wear the old clothes out in public. Kat could recall the occasion clearly. A birthday party for a girl Sarah despised.

Tracey Sullivan, deputy head girl, was another day girl but one with a very different background from Kat. Her father, a self-made man with a dozen car dealerships, was well known throughout the Midlands. It was rumored that he contributed large sums to the convent school. He appeared in his own commercials occasionally, red faced, yelling. Sarah called him the Shouty Man and called Tracey the Shouty Man's Daughter.

"We should go to this party," Sarah had said when Tracey's birthday-party invitation appeared in her school locker. "Looks interesting."

"You're kidding," Kat said. "You hate Tracey."

"With good reason. I hear that she's whispering stuff about my mother. Vicious bitch."

"So why do you want to go?"

"It will be fun. We can dress up."

"Not me. I wasn't invited," Kat said, blushing, feeling oddly ashamed.

"What? Why?"

"I'm a day girl, remember. Council-house kid."

"That's ridiculous. She's a day girl herself."

"From the other side of the tracks. You know what she's like. She's such a snob."

"Come on. We'll go. Your invite is probably late."

An invitation turned up in Kat's locker the next day.

"What did you say to her?" Kat asked Sarah.

"Moi?" Sarah asked, eyes wide. "Nothing at all. Listen, let's visit Aunt Helen, borrow a couple of her outfits. Tracey will look like the Sugar Plum Fairy—you just know she will."

At Lansdowne, Aunt Helen waved them toward a huge closet.

"Help yourselves," she said, yawning. "But do bring back whatever you borrow because I may have to sell it all eventually. And please don't take the ermine stole. People tend to steal it and it's no longer insured."

Helen had an accent with the sharp edge of cut glass and dressed with the kind of shabby elegance Kat had only ever seen in movies: silver hair in a casual knot on her neck, a tweed skirt, a single strand of pearls. She had been engaged once, briefly, to an army officer from a family with a double-barreled surname and a history of military service. He had died, not in battle but in a boating accident in the South of France, a fact that Sarah found amusing and shared with Kat. Helen wore her ring still, a huge square-cut emerald surrounded by diamonds. At first, she terrified Kat. Later, Kat realized that Helen's air of superiority was not intended to intimidate but was simply the easy, unassailable confidence of her class.

On that day, Kat and Sarah spent most of the afternoon trying on different dresses. Helen sat like royalty on a high-backed tapestry chair and passed judgment on each of the outfits.

"Too Hollywood," she said when Sarah tried on a silky black gown with a low neckline. "One needs very large breasts for a dress like that, and shapely though you are, dear, you're not quite shapely enough. And not black, Sarah, please. Black is too brittle for you. Isn't this for an afternoon tea party? You need dresses to midcalf, what we used to call ballerina length. Think of something suitable for a summer wedding.

"No, no, no. You look vulgar, my dear," Helen snapped when Kat twirled out wearing a scarlet dress with a full skirt and a top layer of spangled net. "With your classic features, you must remain simple and understated."

Kat emerged finally wearing a beautifully cut silk dress by a French designer unknown to her but familiar to Sarah and Helen. It was a strange, silvery blue and felt soft against her skin.

"Perfect," Sarah said.

"Yes, that will do. That will do nicely," Helen said, squinting at her. "You look rather fetching, dear. That color suits your eyes very well. You do need heels, of course. Look at the back of the closet for some strappy ones. They should fit you. And you need pearls. Borrow the long strand."

"I can't wear your pearls," Kat said. "What if—"

"Child, they're fake. The real ones are in the bank vault with my other little baubles. Wear them. They're a good copy."

Sarah borrowed a short taffeta skirt, in a glorious purple, that was puffed out and shaped like a bell. She wore it with a strappy top of her own. It had a sequined Mickey Mouse appliquéd on it, the purple of his ears the same shade as the skirt.

"Amazing outfit," Kat said. "Unique. They'll all be gobsmacked."

"That's the plan."

The following Friday afternoon they were taken by minibus from school to Tracey's house, a fake Jacobean behemoth with cast-iron lions guarding the automatic gates. Sarah, delighted, laughed out loud.

"Look at the lions! Oh, this is even better than I imagined."

"It all matches," Kat said to Sarah when they were inside the house and she gazed around at the coordinating colors of the plush interior.

"Of course. *De rigueur*, Caitlin. Even the artwork. Now, what we shan't do," Sarah whispered, waving to the girls who called out to admire her outfit, "is fawn over Tracey. She was mean not to invite you right away."

"I'm here now! And we have to say *Happy birthday*."

"Really? Why? Oh, God help us, Shouty is here, too. I really do not want to listen to that man. Grab some food. There must be a quiet room somewhere. They won't have a library, guaranteed. Perhaps there's a garden room."

They found a bench at the end of the garden, and eventually other girls drifted outside, drawn by Sarah, as always, and she talked and laughed, the focus of attention, as if it were her own party. Kat noticed Tracey gazing wistfully out the window at them, as if she longed to take Sarah's place, there in the center of the group. Sarah turned and saw her, too.

"Like the family pet waiting for the rain to stop," Sarah said, and the girls around her laughed. Kat, noting Tracey's hurt face, felt a moment's sympathy for the birthday girl. Something in her expression must have registered, because Sarah leaned forward and said in a harsh whisper, "Don't you dare feel sorry for her, Caitlin. Don't you dare. She's a gossip and a liar. She deserves everything she gets."

When it came time to leave, the convent girls were taken back to the school in a minibus arranged by Tracey's father.

"Come back to school," Sarah urged Kat. "I can sneak you into the dorm."

"I can't. My mum's expecting me home."

Kat, the only other day girl there, walked to the bus stop alone and took the bus home and had the odd experience of walking down her council-estate street wearing a designer dress and pearls.

The neighborhood had been quiet that night, the breeze carrying the scent of stale beer from the pub on the corner and disintegrating waste from the drains. A dog barked somewhere; she could hear a child's faint cry. The road sliced across the estate, and Kat paused, looking around at the red brick, gray in the lamplight, the worn gardens, the crumpled and torn remains of tossed-away fast-food papers caught on the struggling shrubs. In each direction, the same rows of neglected houses were visible, bookended by the dark bulk of the apartments. Here she was, walking past rows of shabby houses, wearing a designer dress by someone French and famous she'd never heard of and would never remember again. For those few minutes, Kat felt that her future was full of possibility, of mystery.

"It was weird," she told Maggie later. "Totally surreal."

Shaking her head at these memories, Kat watched as Sarah's Jaguar turned the corner at the end of the street, and then she closed the front door and headed back toward the kitchen. The house felt so empty again. How silent everything seemed.

She placed Brooke's spa gift in the bathroom and then took the application package into the bedroom, hid it in her sweater drawer along with the glossy brochure. When she returned to the kitchen, she turned on the radio. A voice with a soft Scottish accent talked of lochs. Yes. That was better than silence. That would do.

SIXTEEN

Maggie's response to Kat's adoption idea was stunned silence, confusion, and then outspoken opposition. She was not happy about her sister's plans at all.

"That's not a good idea right now, darling," she said when Kat tentatively broached the subject. "You really do need more time."

When Kat explained that, yes, she did mean adopting an infant, a newborn, that she did not mean taking on a temporary foster child, Maggie's voice rose, her concern making her sharp. "No, Kat. You don't want to get involved in adoption. No. Really. Not now. You're not ready for something like that. You have to heal first."

"This will help me heal."

"That's not true. Not at all. Ask any grief expert. Ask your grief counselor."

But Kat had still not mentioned the subject to Martha Kim. Martha, she was certain, would not understand.

When the phone rang, only days after Sarah's visit with the application, Kat stared at it, not wanting to pick it up. It was the time Maggie usually called. She had not spoken to her sister since that first awkward discussion about adoption, over a week ago now. She could not keep avoiding her. She dithered a few moments longer, unsure, and then lifted the receiver reluctantly.

"Hi, darling, just wondering about you," Maggie said.

"I'm fine," Kat said. "Just fine. How are you? How's Adam?"

"He's happy. He loves, loves Paris. And who can blame him? So what's happening with you?"

"Not much."

"What about work? You're still looking?"

"In a way. I'm fine, Maggie. Honestly."

"I thought you would have found something by now. I hope you've put that adoption idea right out of your head, darling. You'd be better off getting a decent job. Occupy your mind. You're so smart, Kat. And hardworking. You're wasted sitting at home."

"I'll get a job eventually."

"Good. So how's Scott?"

"He's fine. Working hard."

"How's he coping with the evil Cherrington?"

Kat took a breath. She had told Maggie nothing about Sarah's involvement in the adoption process, nor that she had met Sarah a number of times since Palm Springs. Her sister would not approve. Maggie would, in fact, be very annoyed indeed.

"Oh, Scott can handle her, I think," Kat said lightly.

"Handle her? She hasn't tried to screw him yet, then?" Maggie asked.

"For heaven's sake. This is Scott!"

"He's a man, isn't he? Well, I suppose if Paul resisted her legendary charms—though Christ knows what they are—then maybe Scott can, too. Maybe she's set her sights on somebody higher up the food chain there. That Japanese guy?"

"Don't be daft. She's not screwing Miyamoto. Though I did hear gossip that she was having a fling with James," Kat said, and then wished she hadn't spoken. Her sister's loud yell of amusement echoed through the phone.

"You are kidding me! That gorgeous young guy? I would have thought he had more sense. She's what—ten years older than him? More?"

"Just a rumor. Probably not true."

"Oh, I bet it is. Blimey. The black widow never changes. No danger of her marrying him, though. He's not rich enough. Paul was telling me about her husband's empire. It's absolutely vast!"

"I know. Scott's handling some of the legal stuff. She inherited it all."

"She probably bumped him off to get her hands on it."

"Maggie! He had cancer. You know that."

"I bet she nudged him on his way."

"That's a terrible thing to say," Kat said, recalling, even as she spoke, the flicker of anger on Sarah's face when the morphine was mentioned. "It must have been hard for her."

"With that kind of money? Nothing's hard. Well, let me know what happens next with James. Somebody should warn him. Okay, darling, I better go. You're taking care of yourself?"

"I am. Honestly."

"Right, well, what are you doing for Christmas? We wondered if you and Scott wanted to come here."

"Christmas?" Kat said. She had not given it a thought, had not been aware of any Christmas activities at all, though she had not been to a mall or shopping area for some time, or any place where Christmas lights might be in evidence.

"It's less than three weeks away, Kat," Maggie said.

"God. I, well, we hadn't thought."

She sighed. What was the point of Christmas without a child?

"I think we'll just rest. Burrow," she said.

"Yes, I thought you might do that. Probably the best thing for you this year. Maybe next year?"

"Maybe," said Kat, wondering why Maggie thought that next year would possibly be any different. Chris would not be with them for next Christmas, either.

Maggie chattered a little while longer, then hung up with admonishments that Kat take care of herself, eat properly, get enough sleep. Kat replaced the receiver, stood with her hand still on it.

Christmas. God.

Brooke's signature rat-a-tat on the front door came late in the afternoon. Her smile was wide, her face alight.

"I only have a minute," she said. "I have to get on a call. But I wanted to tell you."

"Come in. Tell me what?"

"My news," she said. "I got a job offer. Overseas!"

"Good grief. Where?"

"France!"

"How? When? Come inside—I'll make coffee."

"No time now. I really have to take this call. But I'll check in later."

"When do you go?"

"It will be soon. Very soon. I don't have all the details yet. Just the salary. And wow—well, it's much bigger. It makes me nervous. Just wanted to tell you."

She bit her lip, then moved to hug Kat.

"God, I'll miss you," Kat said.

"You can visit. France! Imagine it."

"Brooke's been offered a job in France," Kat told Scott later.

"In France? Wow. What kind of job?"

"Not entirely sure. She didn't seem too clear. It's a big raise."

"Good for her. You'll miss her, though."

"I will. She's just so—easy."

Scott grinned.

"Oh, yeah. I've heard that," he said.

"You know what I mean."

"I do. She's a nice gal. But damn. What about my date loaf? You think maybe if she gave you the recipe . . . ?"

Kat smiled, shaking her head, as Scott turned and headed toward his den.

"And Maggie invited us to England for Christmas," Kat said. He stopped, whipped around fast at this; she saw the alarm on his face.

"And you said?"

"I said no, thank you. We're just going to be quiet."

"Right," he said, clearly relieved. "I hadn't thought about it. Not at all. Have you?"

"No. I know I don't want to cook," Kat said. "I couldn't bear the smell of turkey through the house. It would be too hard."

"You want to go out for dinner?"

"No. All the restaurants will be decorated."

Scott nodded, understanding immediately.

"How about if I cook?" he asked. "Something different. Something we've never had before?"

Kat looked at him and slowly shook her head.

"No. That will make it seem special in some way. It will be false. Harder."

She thought for a moment.

"It's on a Sunday. Let's just do a normal Sunday. You catch up with paperwork in the den. I'll read the papers or a book or something. Let's just forget about Christmas this year. Toss it aside."

"You don't want a gift?"

"Nope."

"Well. Okay. No gifts. Just a normal day, baby?"

"Yep. Just a normal day. I'll get a bunch of books from the library."

When Kat visited the library, a week later, she stayed longer than she had planned, and it was already dark as she drove up the hill. Homes that had looked quite ordinary on her drive down were now miniature Disneylands of lights. A Santa Claus, impossibly red and silver, climbed a roof; reindeers pulsated in yards. Lights twinkled everywhere, and Christmas scenes were elaborately portrayed in back gardens. Last year, she would have continued driving for a while, enjoying the displays, noting which houses she should bring Chris back to see, which ones she must mention to Scott. This year the lights looked garish and hurt her eyes.

"Ignore them, ignore them," she murmured to herself. "Toss Christmas aside."

At the top of the hill, she turned onto her own street and saw, with a jarring shock, the "For Sale" sign on Brooke's house. The sign must have gone up while she was at the library. So soon. It was all happening so fast. Brooke's car was in the driveway, so Kat tapped on the back door and Brooke appeared, hair tied on top of her head, plastic wrap in her hands.

"A sign up already?" Kat said. "When are you going?"

"Like this minute," Brooke said. "Here, come in and help a bit. I can hold down the boxes while you tape."

"You're actually selling?" Kat said, following her friend into the house. "Couldn't you just keep the house? Rent it out? Have somewhere to come back to?"

"I wish, but no. I need the money. It's expensive over there and I'll need to rent, and really, this house is too big for one person. It's a family house. Don't worry, sweetie. When I come back, I'll buy a nice little condo right up the street."

"*If* you come back," Kat said.

"If I don't, you'll just have to come visit me," Brooke said, handing Kat a large roll of packing tape. Kat noticed, then, the deep male voice audible in the background.

"What's that?"

"Language tape," said Brooke. "Shush. Listen."

"I don't understand," the recorded male voice intoned solemnly.

"Je ne comprends pas," said Brooke.

"Please speak slowly."

"*Parlez lentement,* dumbass," Brooke said, switching off the machine and lifting both hands, palms upward, in the universal gesture of despair. "I'll never sound right. And I hate that man's goddamn voice. He sounds as if he's *sneering*."

"Why isn't he speaking French?"

"Different tape. It's in little steps. He speaks French, I answer in English. He speaks in English, and I answer in French, then we both talk in French. After a hundred years, I'll be able to say *I do not understand.* And still sound like a freaking idiot."

"You sound pretty good to me," Kat said.

"Do I? Honestly? I never paid attention in French. Truth be told, I skipped a lot of classes final year. Cheerleading practice and too much time behind the bleachers with Steve Partridge. Oh, I was crazy about that guy. Dumb as a post, but his shoulders—I can see them now. Anyway, the French suffered. I bet you're fluent, though, sweet pea. I bet you've got a lovely little accent."

"Are you kidding? We were taught to speak French while remaining at all times recognizably English. I'm certain it was deliberate. I never open my mouth in France. Scott is better."

"I just don't have enough time to learn," Brooke said, sighing. "And that patronizing public radio person on the tapes is not helping."

"Your colleagues will speak English, I'm sure," Kat said.

"God, I hope so!"

As Brooke held down boxes, Kat taped them and learned that Brooke's job would begin in the new year, that she would spend Christmas with her folks in Florida and then fly straight to Nice. She was putting everything in storage for now.

"It's been so fast," Kat said. "It's amazing."

"It's been like a goddamn whirlwind. My boss at Global is mad because this new group, well, they want me right away, and so I couldn't give much notice and everybody hates me for leaving when we're so busy. The job sounds awesome, though. It's in Cannes! I'll be able to go to the film festival! You'll have to come visit. Imagine!"

Her eyes sparkled with excitement. Kat tried to smile.

"What kind of company is it? And how did they find you?"

"Beaugrand, multimedia company. One of their reps was at a filming I did for that start-up company in Studio City. Remember that? I think I told you about it. They're into everything in the media world. I'll be doing pretty much what I'm doing now, except I'll get a much bigger salary. But who knows? Who knows what it could grow into?"

Her words tumbled out fast. Kat smiled at her friend's excitement.

"It sounds fabulous. Your perfect job," she said.

"Yep. But look, sweetie, what about you? Are you still looking for work? Or have you just abandoned it now?"

"I'm looking."

Brooke regarded her calmly, not fooled.

"You turned down that newspaper job?"

"Yep. I was only offered it because Sarah put in a word for me."

"Okay. But what about your old firm? You liked it there."

"No. PR is out. It requires bounciness and smiling. I'm thinking of something quieter."

"Like what? Library? Art gallery?"

"Maybe something like that."

Brooke snapped a box into shape, began packing books into it.

"Scott must love having you home. Fifties housewife. Dinner on the table every night. All very pipe and slippers."

"Not quite."

Kat thought about it as she taped another box. She imagined a fifties marriage. Orderly. Correct. With precision timing. At dinnertime, the husband would arrive home to a table set, the meal freshly cooked. The wife sweetly groomed, brushed, and polished would greet him at the door with a kiss and a smile, her gleaming lipstick a fire-engine red. Her marriage wasn't like that at all. She'd often eaten before Scott arrived home. Was sometimes already in her nightgown, ready for bed.

"Scott's working such long hours," she said now to Brooke. "I miss when we'd arrive home about the same time, cook together. I miss us shoulder to shoulder, chopping and talking. And Chris setting the table, wearing those damn earbuds so we'd have to yell at him or go over and yank them out of his ears to get his attention."

"Didn't know Scott could cook," Brooke said.

"More of an assistant chef. Chopping and peeling. That kind of stuff."

"Get him back in the kitchen. Use it or lose it," Brooke said.

Kat smiled.

"Oh, I'll really miss you," she said.

"I'll miss you, too, sweetie. But you can visit. Cannes! Think of that."

Six days later, Kat and Scott watched from the window as a moving truck arrived to take Brooke's furniture to storage. Brooke stood on the sidewalk, talking to a man in black denim and shades. The red Miata was at the curb. After a few minutes, Brooke handed the young man the keys and he climbed into the car.

"She's sold the Miata, then," Scott said.

"Looks like it. Oh, it's—it's like she's liquidating everything. She's just disappearing altogether."

The car engine revved into life. The guy said something to Brooke and waved before driving off down the street. The sun, glinting on the red vehicle, blinded Kat temporarily, and then the car was gone, the sound of the engine fading. Brooke remained on the sidewalk, watching until the car disappeared, and then she straightened her shoulders and walked back into her empty house.

An hour later, she was standing in their hallway, hugging them both, as an airport-shuttle waited at the curb.

"Take care," Brooke said. "Take care of yourselves. Take care of each other."

"Please write," Kat said. "Phone. Skype. Send e-mails. Anything. Please keep in touch."

"I will. I promise."

Kat had her gift ready. She had struggled to think of something for Brooke, something light and easy to carry, and had discovered, online, a silk-and-cashmere beret and scarf on sale in an exclusive Beverly Hills boutique. The parcel had been specially delivered, and the matching pair had arrived wrapped in delicate tissue and sealed with a tiny satin bow. Kat had lifted a corner of the tissue carefully to inspect the gift and immediately loved the vibrant, glowing colors, the soft feel of the luxury fabric. Brooke would wear both beret and scarf with the necessary panache, and the colors would bring out the pretty blue of her eyes.

When Brooke stepped back, Kat picked up the package from the hall table.

"For you," she said. "Open it."

Brooke groaned.

"Kat, you didn't have to—"

"It's a tiny thing. Have a look."

Brooke placed the package on the table, untied the bow, opened the fragile paper slowly, and gasped when the glowing colors emerged.

"Oh, look. How beautiful! How absolutely beautiful. You shouldn't—"

"Try the beret on."

Brooke lifted the beret, placed it on her head immediately, and turned to study herself in the hall mirror. She adjusted the angle of the beret until she had it just right, picked up the matching scarf, arranged it around her neck, and then turned to show them, her smile huge.

"I love this gift!"

"Made in France! You look fabulous," Kat said. "And it will be cold there, remember. For the next couple of months at least."

"Looks good," Scott said. "Very Parisian."

Brooke removed the beret and scarf, placed them back in the tissue, and wrapped the package again carefully. Tears were now visible on her face.

"I don't know what to say," she said, her voice breaking. She hugged Kat again and then Scott. "Thank you. I'll wear them all the time. And I'll think of you."

They walked with her to the shuttle. A few neighbors had gathered: Barbara Round, the old lady from across the street who rarely left her house, had managed to reach her gate and stood there, watching and waving. A young woman, with a toddler in a stroller, stood next to her. The Johnson family, including twin boys, called out to Brooke and shouted good wishes.

"This neighborhood will never be the same again," Scott said as the shuttle pulled away.

"I'll really miss her," Kat said. "I wish she'd stayed through Christmas. I just like the idea of her being there, across the street."

"We'll get through Christmas," Scott said. "We'll ignore it."

SEVENTEEN

In the middle of the afternoon on the day after Christmas, Kat walked into Scott's den shivering violently, tears on her face. Scott, making notes on a yellow pad, looked up, registered her tears, and stood immediately. He sighed, came to her, and held her tight against his chest.

"I'm sorry," Kat said. "I was okay yesterday, but today I can't seem to stop crying. No matter what I do."

His arms tightened around her.

"Why don't we just snuggle under a blanket and watch TV," he said.

"It will still be Christmas programming. All merry and stuff."

"Okay. A movie, then. And some brandy."

Kat dragged the comforter from the bedroom and draped it onto the sofa while Scott found brandy and two glasses. Then, he flicked through the DVDs.

"What would you like?" Scott asked.

"Oh, I don't know. A classic, maybe. Something strange. Set in a foreign land. Different. You know."

"*Casablanca*?"

"Hmm. Possible."

"*Lawrence of Arabia*? *Out of Africa*?"

"No. Well, maybe. No." Kat looked at him. "*A River Runs Through It.*"

"Foreign? Classic? Different?"

"I know. I know. It's just that I love the part where the father and son recite Wordsworth together."

"It will make you cry."

"I *am* crying."

He nodded.

"Okay. *River* it is."

When the movie started, Kat sipped the brandy. It burned her throat; she could feel its warmth all the way down to her stomach. She settled back against Scott's shoulder. She wondered what Chris's friends were doing, whether Ben and Matt were thinking of their old buddy. In previous years, they spent this day, the day after Christmas, all together, sharing new video games, holed up in Chris's bedroom, playing music, laughing. The day must feel different for them, too. And for Vanessa. And the pretty girl, Chloe? She would be sad today.

Brooke would be in Florida with her parents, ready for her journey to France, bubbling with excitement and anticipation, most likely, longing to begin her new life.

When the movie finished, Kat dabbed at her tears with the corner of the comforter before she took Scott's hand.

"We could watch our old home movies, too," Scott said, kissing the top of her head.

Kat thought about it for a moment.

"Could you bear it?"

"I think so."

"Okay. Let's do it."

"So dim the house lights," said Scott. "We will now begin our movie marathon."

Kat watched the flickering images, pain squeezing her chest. Chris, in one of the home movies, was a sturdy seven-year-old, running after

Ben, both of them mugging for the camera. Kat stood in the background, her hair long, tied back in a ponytail. She was laughing at their antics and looked young and carefree.

"I can't believe we were ever that young," she said to Scott. "Or that happy."

"It's pretty hard to remember how it felt."

"You want to watch *The NeverEnding Story*? We didn't watch it together on his birthday."

"Of course."

He was about to press the button on the remote when the doorbell rang. He raised an eyebrow. Kat looked at her watch. It was eight thirty at night, too late for parcel deliveries or FedEx.

"Better check it," Scott said, sighing.

Kat knew, the moment she heard the cultured English voice, the soft gurgling laugh, who was at the door. Sarah stood in the doorway, her hand on the doorknob, looking as if she were ready to leave immediately.

"So, name the poet," she began, looking at Kat. "Something about coming in from the night with flowers in her hands."

"Pound," said Kat. Name the Poet was an old game they used to play.

"Correct," Sarah said. "I'm just dropping these off, and then I will fly away and leave you alone."

She wore a long velvet cloak with a wide hood. To Kat, she looked like Little Red Riding Hood, dressed all in black. It was evening wear of some kind, suitable for the opera or the theater. Her eyes were made up with a green shadow that sparkled in the soft hall light. She held a basket in her hands, full of a mixed bouquet of flowers—gardenias, white roses, baby's breath—and also a bottle of wine and some chocolates. She posed, Kat thought, like someone out of a child's book of fairy tales.

Kat, conscious of her own sweatshirt, tearstained face, and neglected hair, of the crumpled comforter on the sofa, the littered glasses, and brandy bottle, noted that Scott, too, looked uncomfortably aware of his old jeans and sweater. He ran a hand through his uncombed hair, pushing it back from his forehead.

"You're working today?" he asked Sarah. "It's a holiday."

"I don't do holidays," Sarah said. "And I believe you need these for tomorrow."

Sarah removed a folder from the basket and handed it to Scott.

"The contracts. James said you wanted to look them over."

"Yes. You've checked them?"

"James showed me a first draft. I assume you or Miyamoto will fine-tune?"

"I will. Of course."

Sarah turned to Kat.

"And the rest of this basket is for you, Caitlin. You will see, on the bottom layer, a dozen melt-in-the-mouth lemon tarts."

"Thank you," Kat said, taking the basket. "Will you stay for one? Or a glass of wine?"

Sarah thought for a moment.

"Just one. And the tiniest glass of wine. Then, I must rush. I have to be somewhere for drinks, then I'm driving on to Ojai."

"So how's it going? The renovation?" Scott asked.

Sarah perched on the edge of the armchair, polished off one lemon tart in two fast bites, then took the wine Scott handed to her and sipped it as she described the problems with her new orangery.

"Not as quickly as I'd hoped. I knew the exact color I wanted on the walls. I showed it to them on the color chart, the exact shade. Did they do it? No. They did not. The color was close, but it was wrong. So they must do it again." She sighed. "It's impossible. I should be there, of course, when they begin every morning. To check."

"How does it look, though? Generally?" Kat asked.

"At the moment, it's a mess. But it will be beautiful. You must come see it. You can stride from one end to the other reading from 'The Waste Land.' Just as you used to do at Lansdowne."

"She did what?" Scott asked, grinning.

"Oh, please," Kat said, blushing. "I did that once. We had poetry readings there sometimes. The old orangery had this wonderful echoing sound. Perfect acoustics. So we would read poetry in it. Just for fun."

"This was to entertain your classmates?" Scott asked.

"Our classmates?" said Sarah. "All those gray girls? No. This was just for us. We took turns. Aunt Helen came in occasionally, to listen. Sometimes, we would dress up, to perform for her. Wear her hats and her fur stole."

"Wish I'd seen that," Scott said.

"Be grateful you didn't," said Kat.

Sarah looked at her watch.

"I should think about moving along," she said.

Sarah stood, watched Scott as he placed the contracts on the dining table, and began to leaf through them.

"You've signed everywhere?" he asked.

"I think so. I hope so."

As he studied the documents, Sarah handed her empty wineglass to Kat.

"I'll call you in the new year, Kat," she said in a soft, conspiratorial whisper. "I have some news." Then she added, with a small smile, "Good news."

Sarah turned, moved toward Scott to check the documents with him. Kat, puzzled, took the rest of the pastries and Sarah's empty glass into the kitchen. *Good news?* She must mean about the adoption. Sarah had clearly not given up on it. When Kat came back from the kitchen, Scott and Sarah were still at the dining table, talking quietly.

"It's contained in the final clause," Scott said.

"Is that enough?" Sarah asked.

"Oh yes. It's absolutely watertight."

Kat, as she watched them, was swamped by a feeling, not unfamiliar, of being *outside*—here in her own untidy living room, among the empty DVD cases, the used glasses, the rumpled comforter that a few minutes before she and her husband had been sharing. Scott, despite the casual clothes and unruly hair, was now very much the lawyer as he talked business with a woman who spoke the same language.

"Looks good. We're right on track," Scott said finally, closing the folder. "But I need to check something with James before I sign off. Can you hang on just a few minutes longer?"

"Of course," Sarah said.

Scott disappeared into his den to make the phone call. Kat, awkward, moved back into the room.

"Another glass of wine, Sarah? Coffee?"

"I'm fine. Sit down. Talk to me."

Kat pushed the comforter to the side and sat on the sofa. Sarah, sitting down beside her, looked levelly at her.

"It's hard, isn't it? This time of year. I hate Christmas."

Kat nodded.

"This one is hard. I loved Christmas before."

"I've always hated it."

"Even as a child?"

"Even more so as a child. My mother was always so unstable at any kind of festive season. More unstable than usual."

Kat, curious, leaned forward.

"She had problems, didn't she? I remember Helen . . ."

"Oh, you have no idea. I never knew what she would do. Whether she would be locked in her room, sobbing, or whether she would be racing around, dressed in weird clothes, talking, laughing, drinking. That's why I never took anyone home. Except you. I couldn't risk everyone laughing at me."

"They wouldn't have laughed."

"Of course they would."

Sarah regarded Kat steadily for a moment or two.

"You asked me about my parents once. Remember? And I got cross?"

"Yes. All I know is that they were both gorgeous," Kat said. "I remember the photograph on the piano at Lansdowne."

The picture showed a lovely young woman in a white dress of some filmy organza material; she had flowers in her hair. The woman was a true beauty, very much like Sarah. In the photograph, her young husband stood beside her, his dark hair falling into his eyes. He was laughing.

"Your mother was beautiful. You look like her."

"Apparently," said Sarah. "And they left me. Well, my father left first. One day, he just picked up his briefcase and was gone. I was riding. I came back to the stables and he was getting into his car, his new Jaguar. He had his briefcase and he waved to me. Didn't come to me, hug me, do any of the things one might imagine a father would do if he were leaving for good. He waved. That's all. I never saw him again. I was eleven years old. He moved to France. His new woman was French. When he died, I saw it in the newspaper."

"I'm sorry," Kat said.

"And my mother," continued Sarah with contempt. "My mother officially died when I was thirteen, but she was gone that same day, the day he left. She was never really alive anymore, not for me. Not that she was ever really there. Not in any sane way. Of course, in the end she did it properly. She overdosed on Seconal and slashed her wrists. Leaving her thirteen-year-old daughter to find her."

Kat blinked.

"You? My God, Sarah."

"Yes. It wasn't pretty."

Sarah shuddered at the memory. Kat, recalling Sarah's blood phobia, wondered if her mother's suicide had triggered it. So traumatic an experience must have left a scar.

"What a terrible thing for a child to witness."

"I got over it."

Sarah looked up then as Scott came back into the room, carrying the file.

"All in place," he said. "Thank you for bringing these."

"My pleasure," Sarah said, standing. She placed a hand on his arm, looked up at him, and smiled. The traumatized child had vanished, the sparkling charmer returned. "It's always my pleasure."

Kat felt a tiny warning twinge and got to her feet. Scott had stepped away; she could not see his expression. She guessed he was uncomfortable at this attempt to flirt with him, if that's what it was.

"And thank you for the goodies," Kat said.

"Oh, you're welcome. I know how hard it is," Sarah said.

Then, like a black moth, Sarah floated forward, kissed Kat's cheek, and, after a moment's hesitation, kissed Scott, too, before she disappeared into the night with a wave. It was so theatrical that Scott, after closing the door, turned to Kat, smiling and shaking his head.

"She's really pretty dramatic," he said.

"Maybe just a wee bit over the top?"

"God, yes. Just a little bit. So what's this all about?" he asked, his voice teasing. "You reading Eliot aloud?"

"Oh, don't. Please. Sarah performed and I listened. I was the audience. The orangery audience."

"That Sussex house must have been impressive."

"Lansdowne? It was a beautiful house once upon a time. When I visited, it was just big, crumbling, and freezing. Lovely in the summer but icy cold in the winter. And pretty much falling down. That's one of the reasons why she never invited any of the other girls to stay."

"Just you?"

"Just me. Council-house kid. Lower standards and easily impressed. She knew I wouldn't judge. Though she never invited anyone to her parents' house, either. Mostly because of her mother. Her mother got very depressed and would lock herself in her room and refuse to come out."

"You should feel privileged, then. Sarah ever stay with you?"

"In our tiny house? No way. There was no room. Maggie was at home. We only had two bedrooms, remember. My mum and dad had one. Maggie and I shared the other. Sarah came for tea a few times. But—I didn't invite her often. I was embarrassed about the estate."

The council estate, four short streets of terraced houses in a compact grid, housed mostly retirees and small families. It had fewer problems than the larger Midlands estates that were plagued by gang wars, drug dealing, random violence, and all the other inevitable consequences of poverty and neglect. Even so, Kat hurried Sarah past the graffiti fences, talked fast as they walked to the bus stop, hoping her curious friend wouldn't notice the neighbor's old car up on blocks, the small unsupervised child, barely dressed, swinging on a gate, the toothless woman sitting on a doorstep, drinking cider from a plastic bottle. Sarah looked around, eyes bright, as if she were visiting a new planet, and paused at intervals to stare openly.

"She was fascinated by the people on the estate. The bad kids and hoodlums. And, of course, they all stared at her."

"She creates a stir," Scott said. "They talk about her all the time in the office. I've never known so much office gossip about a client. All the female associates and paralegals chatter about her clothes."

"I bet they do," Kat said.

"Yep, Mrs. Sarah Harrison has got everyone curious. Still, let's have another glass of her wine."

Kat settled back down on the sofa, pulling the comforter around her. Scott returned and handed her a fresh glass of red wine.

"For you," he said.

Kat took the glass, raised it for a moment, and then sipped it. Scott clicked the remote so that the theme song of *The NeverEnding Story* filled the room.

EIGHTEEN

On a bright, crisp day in the middle of January, a day with a thin winter sun, Kat, sipping coffee in the kitchen, thought about Sarah's visit on the day after Christmas. She had said she had news, good news, but there had been no phone call from her.

Kat hesitated by the phone, holding the stiff card with the gold lettering tight in her hand, then took a breath and dialed the number on it. Sarah answered at once.

"Kat? Hello!"

Kat could hear voices in the background: another phone was on speaker.

"Hold on, Kat," Sarah said. "Just one moment."

Some rustling was audible and Sarah's voice from a distance.

"Call you back, gentlemen," Sarah said. The background sound deadened. A moment later, Sarah was back on the phone. "Kat?"

"I'm not interrupting you, am I? Was that a conference call?"

"Nothing important. How are you? Such a lovely surprise to see your name pop up on my phone."

"It's just that you said you had news and—"

"I do, I do," Sarah said. She dropped her voice. "I've been looking at prospective young mothers and I've found two—well, one is just perfect. One looks a little bit like your son's girlfriend. Chloe, is it? Pretty Hispanic girl. But the other is ideal. She's—"

"Chloe?" Kat interrupted, startled. "How do you know about Chloe?"

Silence while Sarah thought about it.

"Didn't you tell me? Perhaps Scott did. But, listen, Scott is here right now, out on the patio, and I need to get back to business because—"

"Oh. Sorry. I had no idea."

"How about if I call you back? Tomorrow? Tomorrow morning? Will that be a good time?"

"Anytime," Kat said, feeling foolish and intrusive. Scott would be furious to find his client distracted by adoption talk during a business meeting. "I'm so sorry to interrupt your—"

"No. Don't be silly. I'm longing to tell you details. Really. Tomorrow? Okay?"

Kat hung up the phone, biting at her lip. An idiot. She was an idiot. Why hadn't she just waited like a normal person for Sarah to call? And why was Scott talking about Chloe, about family matters, to Sarah? He never had time to talk at home. Irritable, Kat reached to straighten the curtains and saw that a "Sold" sign had just gone up on Brooke's house. A fast sale, then, cash most likely. Brooke had deliberately priced it low so that it would move quickly. Someone had left the front gate open, and it swung and rattled in the wind. The blank windows, the missing lawn furniture, made the place look even more abandoned. It felt, to Kat, as if Brooke, with her wide smile, her warm hugs, and easy laughter, had simply vanished. As if she'd never lived there, right across the street.

Scott returned from work in the late afternoon, angry, slamming into the kitchen, throwing his briefcase onto the chair, and then tugging hard at his tie.

"That asshole Woodruff should be hung from a fucking pole," he stated.

"Well, hi to you, darling. Had a nice day?"

"Sorry."

"What's going on?"

"War zone. Woodruff's doing a whole number on Sarah Harrison. He wants to get his hands on one of her Italian subsidiaries. Apparently, there's a big merger rumored. He aims to get in on the ground floor. It's creating a cold war between us."

"But she's your client, isn't she?"

"Well, yes, I handle most of her matters. He's been doing a lot of social stuff with her. Says he moves in the same circles. Load of bullshit. He must pay somebody so that he gets invited. Asshole."

Kat studied her husband as, tense and bristling with annoyance, he shrugged off his jacket. Sarah and Woodruff as a social item clearly bothered him.

"Why are you so worried? You think he's trying to ease you out?"

"No. Well, maybe. He's certainly trying. She gave him some weird little acquisition deal in the UK. Your old 'hood, as a matter of fact. Bunch of dealerships."

Kat turned, frowning.

"Car dealerships?"

"Yeah, think they were. Asset-stripping deal. She wants them closed down."

"Why?"

"Not exactly sure. She was talking about ugly. Blot on the landscape. Stuff like that," he said. "Anyway, Woodruff got the deal. Not that I wanted it. Sounds a bit goofy."

"The Shouty Man's business," Kat said.

Scott frowned.

"The what?"

"I remember the dealerships. The guy who owned them was on TV. We called him the Shouty Man. Tracey, his daughter, was at my school."

"Really?" Scott said. "Well, Mr. Shouty Man's daughter must have done something to piss Sarah off. She gave Woodruff another weird UK deal, too."

"Weird? Why was it weird?"

"Some little guy she was buying out. Falconbridge or something."

"Falconbridge?" asked Kat, fast. "A solicitor?"

"Yeah. Probate. Sarah is buying out the leases to his office building, wants to close the place down. God knows why. The old guy is due to retire any minute."

Kat leaned back against the kitchen counter, remembering Sarah's hatred of the solicitor who had controlled her trust fund, recalling, with shame, her own part in the distressing drama around Sarah's pregnancy. She had gone along with Sarah to visit the lawyer's office, had waited outside while Sarah pleaded for money for a termination, although the mystery boy involved had already given her cash and she had no intention of having a termination in any case. She wanted to keep the child, she told Kat. Why not? It was hers. Mr. Falconbridge had asked for the boy's name; Sarah had refused to divulge it. She begged him for money, she said. She told him it was her trust fund, and she was entitled to it. Then, she tried to threaten him. He would not be persuaded.

On the bus back to school, Sarah told Kat further details of the confrontation. When the solicitor refused to give her the funds, she told him that fine, she would keep the baby. She requested that he help her sell it.

"He was always telling me I had to be careful with money. So I told him it was a good way to make some," Sarah told Kat. "People love society babies. We could get a really good price."

Kat, scared, not sure whether to believe her friend and worried about her erratic behavior, had secretly called Aunt Helen, and the shocked woman had taken over. She arranged for an abortion, although it was later in the pregnancy than Sarah had indicated, and Helen had struggled to find a doctor willing to do it. Sarah believed that Falconbridge had telephoned her aunt and had been furious at his betrayal. Kat had never told her the truth.

"She hated that solicitor," Kat said now to Scott, feeling a surge of guilt for the deception years ago. "I'm surprised it took her this long to go after him."

"She didn't have the means to go after anybody until after Sam Harrison's death," Scott said, heading to the cupboard, pulling out a bottle of scotch. "But she's sure making up for lost time. She's got a couple of vendettas going on right now. Sometimes she makes great decisions, and sometimes she makes no sense at all. They make sense to her, I guess. Ah, it will resolve. It always does. I need a drink. You want something?"

Kat nodded.

"White wine?"

"Coming up."

Kat began slicing up the French loaf, placing it in a basket. So Sarah was catching up with her old enemies, one by one, like some dark knight crusader. They couldn't have known, that old-fashioned solicitor and those judgmental middle-class girls, that the aristocratic beauty with no available money would one day have such power. Though they might have guessed, even then, that it was not a good idea to cross her.

Kat set the table as Scott, calmer now, switched on the TV to watch the news.

"So you were out at Malibu?" she asked.

Scott did not look at her; he kept his eyes on the television screen. "What? No. Sarah came into the office."

Kat, frowning, set the knife she was holding down slowly, thought for a moment, and then turned to look at him.

"But I talked to Sarah this morning. She said you were out at her beach house."

Scott took a long swallow of his drink, then spoke rapidly.

"Oh, right. We were out at Malibu in the morning," he said. "Checking some blueprints and—"

Kat, cold with shock, moved closer so that she could see his face. She had never known Scott to lie to her.

"So why did you lie about it?" she asked.

He glanced at her quickly, looked back at the screen.

"I didn't lie," he said. "Not really. Got a bit confused, that's all. And Christ, does it matter? You're always saying things like *You've been out at the beach*. Makes it sound like I'm just lazing out there in the sun, and in fact I'm busting my fucking ass—"

"What do you mean I'm *always* saying things?" Kat said, anger sharpening her voice. "I made a comment about you being out at the beach once. Just once. And, why were you talking to Sarah about Chloe? You barely say a word to me about anything."

"What?" Scott asked. "I don't even know Chloe. And I don't talk to Sarah about anything except business." His eyes were still fixed on the TV.

"Well, I didn't say anything to her."

Kat paused then, doubting herself. Had she described Chloe to Sarah? She had talked to Brooke. Or had she? She could be confused. She was so forgetful these days, so unfocused, somehow things just slipped away from her, out of her grasp. Scott had never seen Chloe. How could he describe her?

Unsettled now, crossing the room to stand in front of Scott, she felt a seismic shift, as if the floor were not quite steady beneath her feet.

"But you were out at Malibu, weren't you? Please don't lie to me, Scott, for God's sake. Ever."

He looked at her directly at last.

"Sorry," he said. "Sorry. It's just been one hell of a day. I wasn't thinking."

"In the future—please think."

NINETEEN

Sarah's promised phone call came the next morning. Scott had left for work early, and Kat, resolving to tidy up the neglected house, had just dragged out the vacuum cleaner.

"Now, are you ready for some news?" Sarah asked, a pulse of excitement audible in her voice. "Some really good news?"

"Yes. I was hoping you would call and explain. I've been wondering."

"Well, I wanted to be sure. But there's a young woman, five months pregnant, who might agree to you both. I haven't talked to her myself yet, but Liz Brady has."

"What?" Kat said. "She's pregnant now?"

"Yes. Perfect match for you. Teenager. Accepted at Stanford. Doesn't want to give up her scholarship. Doesn't want a baby. She's Catholic. I don't have details about the father—she refuses to give them—but I assume he's a student also."

"But she might change her mind?"

"Well, that's a risk you'll have to take. But no, I don't think so. She seems very determined. And smart. Educated. A really good fit," Sarah said, clearly delighted at having found so good a match.

"What about her parents? Maybe they'll want to take the baby."

"No chance of that. Her mother's dead. Her father's some high-ranking oncologist. She's planning to follow in his footsteps."

Kat, barely able to breathe, struggled to speak.

"And she'll agree to us?"

"I'm absolutely certain I can persuade her."

"Five months?"

"Yes. That gives you time to convince Scott. He's still unsure?"

"Yes. But—maybe, maybe if I tell him about this girl—"

"He can't possibly say no, Kat. This young woman is perfect! I'll send you details. You must get that paper signed now, though. At least get the application in so that she doesn't sign up with someone else. Tell Scott there'll be opportunity later to change his mind. But just to sign the darned paper. Now."

Sarah waited as Kat struggled to take this in.

"Oh God, I hope, I—"

"She's so right for you, Kat," Sarah said. "A musician, too. Can you believe that? Clarinetist in the school orchestra. Doesn't mean the baby will be musical, of course, but chances are . . ."

Kat let out her breath.

"Oh God. She sounds wonderful. Have you seen a picture?"

"Yes. I'm looking at it right now, in fact. Right here on my screen."

"Don't suppose you could—?"

"You haven't signed anything yet, Kat. That would be absolutely against the rules."

Kat sighed.

"Of course. I understand."

"But when have I ever followed rules?" Sarah asked, laughing. "Check your e-mail. But—please. Make sure Scott signs. Tonight."

"Oh God, I hope he agrees!"

"He will. Of course he will. Have some faith in him, Kat. Trust that he loves you."

Kat raced to get her laptop, waited, tapping her foot, while it loaded up, and then she clicked on to e-mails. Yes, there was one from Sarah. With an attachment. A photograph.

She stared for a long time at the picture: a young girl with freckles, blue eyes, curly fair hair tied back from her face. A serious young woman.

Kat sank back onto the sofa, her knees weak. "Oh, Scott. Please, please," she whispered. "Please say yes."

Kat cleaned the house in a fog of alternating fear and soaring hope. Scott must agree to this plan. He must, he must. And if he did . . . Right now, at this very second, a child was growing. A tiny bean at this point, but a growing child. A baby.

The house sparkled by midafternoon. Kat pulled out steaks from the freezer; she baked potatoes, prepared an elaborate salad, and then opened a bottle of red wine and poured two glasses.

Scott, swinging in from work, placed his briefcase on the armchair, surveyed the carefully set table, and took a swallow of his wine.

"Hey, this looks good. And I'm starving."

He had taken only one bite of his steak when Kat, unable to hold back the words any longer, told him of the pregnant teenager who wanted to have her baby adopted.

"We have to sign the application, that's all. We have months to get used to the idea."

Scott placed his fork down and very slowly pushed his plate away, his eyes never leaving her face.

"No," he said. "I'm sorry, Kat, but no."

His voice was quiet, sad. There was no irritation in it. Kat sat back in her chair, trying to remain calm.

"Why not?"

"There are a million reasons why not," Scott said. "But I really don't want to go 'round in circles with you again."

"You don't want to discuss it?"

"What is there to discuss? We talked about it before."

"We talked about getting tested. About trying for our own child. We talked vaguely about adoption. We didn't talk seriously about adopting a particular baby. A baby who would be a really good fit for us. Perfect, in fact. You're just going to dismiss it out of hand, without talking about it properly? Without even thinking about it?"

"Kat, I *have* thought about it. Because it's been pretty clear that this was where you were headed."

Kat stared. Clear to whom?

"That's not true. How can you know that?"

Scott pushed his chair back, as if he was leaving the table.

"It doesn't actually matter what I want, though. Does it?" Kat added.

He shook his head. His mouth tightened; she could see annoyance building in him.

"Seems to me you're unconcerned with my feelings. Listen, Kat. No adoption agency would agree to parents who are still grieving for a child they've so recently lost. It's not fair to the adopted child or to the parents. It's not possible. You have to accept that."

"It is possible. I've checked—"

"Bullshit. Maybe in a year or so."

"In a year or so? Why not ten? Or twenty? Why not wait until you retire? We can be the two old codgers, waiting at the school gates. Won't interfere with your work then."

"This has nothing to do with work! Taking on a stranger's child, beginning again with broken nights and all that worry and work for a stranger's child? No. Sorry, but I won't do it. And I don't want you to continue thinking about it."

He began eating again, not looking at her.

Kat sat rigidly still at the table, watching him.

"We'll have a few months to think about it some more. Then, well, surely you'll feel differently?"

"No. I won't. Ask me again in a year or two."

"And that's it?"

"Yes. This discussion is premature, Kat. Really. Wait a couple of years. Then, maybe we can foster a child. Just see how it—"

"No! No. That's not what I want. We can look after an infant. Bring him up from the very beginning and care for him and give him a good life. We can!"

"*Him?* You've already decided the child must be a male?"

He stood then, pushing his plate away, the meal abandoned. Kat continued talking stubbornly, willing him to stay in the room and listen to her.

"No. No. Of course not. He or she. It doesn't matter. But look, Scott. We have space now. Money. We were in a one-bedroom apartment when Chris was a baby, and of course it was tough. But we have a bigger house now. You won't be disturbed at night, I promise. I'll do the night feeds. I'll move the baby over to the other side of the house so you won't be disturbed. You can work as late as you do now. Work as late as you like. A baby won't interrupt your life at all, I promise."

Scott gave a long sigh.

"Listen to yourself. How healthy is that? For you or the child? Kat, please. This is totally irrational."

Kat stood, ran upstairs to the bedroom, slamming the door. Scott was behind her only seconds later, pulling her close.

"Stop. Stop it. You have to deal with realities. Okay? Not fantasies. Not conjecture."

"Spoken like a true lawyer."

He took a deep breath.

"You have to get yourself together first. You have to start to heal."

She pushed him away.

"Heal? Shit. You've been talking to Maggie. You'll be talking about *closure* next."

"I just don't think you need more stress in your life."

"Is that how you see a child? Just a lot of stress?"

"You don't need this, Kat."

She shrugged.

"And you know what I need?"

He moved to the window and stared out into the garden. It was a clear night, the Santa Susana Mountains visible in the distance. Kat waited. At last, he turned from the window.

"I can't talk about this now, Kat," he said. He regarded her steadily. There was no warmth in his eyes. "We'll talk again at another point."

He turned, walked out of the bedroom. Minutes later, she heard the clink of the wine bottle and glass. He was pouring himself another drink.

Kat called Sarah as soon as the door to Scott's den closed.

"Oh no. Surely not," Sarah said. "How can you bear it? And there's no persuading him?"

"No. Not right now," Kat said, a tremor in her voice, tears close to the surface. "He might talk about it again sometime. But not now."

"Oh, Caitlin. Well, I'm so, so sorry, but this girl won't wait. How devastating for you. This must hurt terribly."

"I don't know what else I can do."

"It's hard. He *is* a lawyer. He has that nitpicky legal mind. I never dreamt he would be so intransigent. But look, all things are possible. I could ask Liz Brady to keep your file open. In case he changes his mind."

"He won't change his mind."

"Don't give up. Please."

"But how can they do that? Keep the file open?"

"If I tell them to do it, then they'll do it."

Sarah paused, thinking.

"You must try to persuade him," she said eventually. "Try to tread softly, perhaps. Not force him into anything. But I'm certain when he understands how badly you want it, he'll reconsider. He loves you, Kat. He must want you to be happy."

"Don't know about that."

"Of course he does," Sarah said. "Try to build a bridge. Anyway, I know this is probably the last thing you feel like doing right now, but I wanted to ask you about visiting my Malibu house. A partner from Milan will be here. We may merge a couple of subsidiaries."

"It's a business thing? No. I don't—"

"He's only here for one evening and he's fun and interesting. It will be drinks by the pool, just a few minutes of business talk with Scott. And Glenda, of course. I wish you would come, Kat. I really do."

"I'd really rather not. Scott and I at the moment, well—"

"It would be a new client for Scott," Sarah said softly. "He will definitely appreciate it."

"Ah. I see."

"So? You'll come? Please come."

"Maybe," Kat said.

Kat ate a sandwich before Scott returned from work the following evening, set the table for one person, and served him a simple grilled chicken breast and fries. Scott looked at her over his eyeglasses.

"You're not eating?"

"I ate earlier. I wasn't sure if you would be late. Again."

Scott shook his head, said nothing more, and ate the meal while reading the newspaper. Afterward, he stood, placed his plate in the dishwasher, and turned to her.

"Sarah has invited us out to Malibu," he said.

"Oh, really," Kat said coldly. "Why?"

"To meet an Italian businessman. A possible client. It's just drinks, conversation. It will be short."

"Have fun."

"She'd like you to come."

Kat, ignoring Sarah's advice to tread softly, looked at him defiantly.

"And why should I?"

"You might enjoy it. I would like you to be there."

"Oh, really? Would you now? So I can help you snag the Italian client that Woodruff wants? Right? That's so very, very important."

"For Christ's sake, Kat. It's drinks in Malibu. I'm not asking you to walk over burning coals."

"I'll do anything to help you. You know that. Pity you don't feel the same way about me. You don't seem willing to do anything I might want."

Scott gave a heavy sigh.

"What you want, Kat, is not my presence for something simple like drinks with a stranger. You want a lifetime commitment to something we are not ready for, cannot handle, are not even sure we can do."

"Do? Of course we can do it. We did it once before."

"I don't mean having our own child. I mean being approved for the adoption."

"We might be able to have our own child if you would agree to get checked out," Kat snapped.

"Really? And are you planning an immaculate conception, because getting pregnant involves—" He stopped, froze. "Jesus. Sorry," he said, swallowing.

Kat stared at him. She wondered if she'd heard correctly. The words were cruel. Scott was never cruel.

"Immaculate conception?" she asked, her voice iced.

"I didn't mean that."

"What *did* you mean?"

"Fuck, I don't know. I don't know what the hell is happening to us. Look, are you coming to this thing, Kat? Or not?"

He was expecting her to say no. She knew that.

"Well, damn it, yes. I'll come," she said. "Why on earth not?"

TWENTY

The interior of the car felt hollow and echoing on the drive to Malibu. Scott said little; Kat stared out the window. On this winter's day, the ocean looked gray and choppy; clouds scudded across the sky as the wind picked up. The palm trees bowed like dancers. Kat wanted the evening to be over. She wanted to be in bed, with the comforter up to her chin.

Sarah's Malibu house was a white stone villa right on the coast, surrounded by assorted cacti and swaying palms. Scott parked on the wide, curving driveway and then turned to her.

"You going to stay mad and sulk all evening?" he asked.

"I'll be your little ray of sunshine, just watch me."

"Kat, we have to get beyond this."

She looked at him. He returned her gaze, unflinching, determined. *He is not going to change his mind,* she realized. *He is never going to change his mind.*

"I wish I knew how," she said.

"You think maybe you could just give it a try?"

"Well, yes. I think from now on, both of us should simply devote our entire lives to your career."

"For Christ's sake, Kat," Scott snapped.

Kat blinked, startled. Her husband's face was closed, tight as a fist. She had seen him angry before; she had seen him irritable. She had never felt so distant from him.

Then, Sarah was in the doorway, calling to them to come inside, to have a drink.

"Welcome, Caitlin," she said. "To my little beach house."

"Little?" Kat said.

The house had marble floors, and the view from all the windows was of the ocean and an infinity swimming pool that was designed to look like it was floating on top of the water. Kat paused at the entrance. To have Ojai and this house, too? Sarah, as a schoolgirl, must have dreamed of something like this.

Sarah, at her elbow, studying her reaction, asked, "You like it?"

"Of course I like it. Who could not? The pool is beautiful."

Sarah led them out to the glassed-in patio, a light space that had views of the water from three sides.

"Come, have a drink. It's a buffet meal and ready to serve. I've sent the car for Luca Bianchi. He should be here any moment. And, oh, here's Glenda to translate for us. I hope her Italian is as good as she says it is."

"Glenda doesn't exaggerate," Scott said.

Glenda had made an effort. She wore an elegant dress in a soft violet shade, had a new hairstyle, blunt cut and curling into her chin, that flattered her narrow face, and she wore earrings that sparkled with amethyst stones. She appeared anxious as she walked toward them.

"And looking very pretty today," Sarah said, as if to a little girl just off to a party. Kat saw Glenda's small smile at this, noted her glance at Scott.

"Thank you, Sarah," Glenda said. She smiled at Kat, gave a little wave. "The client not here?" she asked.

"He's not actually the client yet, remember," Scott reminded her.

"He will be, I'm sure," said Sarah. "Oh, look. Here's the car."

Kat turned to see an attractive middle-aged man step out of Sarah's Mercedes. He looked like a stereotypical wealthy European playboy: a light linen suit, unnecessary sunglasses, thick silver hair brushed back from his face. His age was evident in the deep vertical lines that ran down each side of his mouth. He wasn't very tall, but his view of himself as an alpha male was evident in the tilt of the head, the confident stance, the way he surveyed the house, the grounds, even the beach, as if he owned it all. As if he *could* own it all.

Sarah hurried toward him, and he greeted her warmly with kisses, hugs, exclamations in Italian. She laughed as she led him to them. Kat took a breath. She noted the flash of slightly prominent white teeth, the smooth, graceful walk. The song "Mack the Knife," with the shark and its pearly teeth, played in her head.

As he approached, he removed his sunglasses and looped them into the top pocket of his jacket. Sarah introduced him to Scott.

"Scott Hamilton, my attorney," Sarah said as Bianchi shook hands with Scott. "I hope he can advise us today. And this is his wife, Kat." Bianchi lifted Kat's hand to his mouth and kissed it, his eyes meeting hers. His eyes were the palest blue, like a winter sky. It was a cool, careful assessment. She tried to smile but was made shy by the measuring gaze.

"Kat with claws? Or Kat with a soft purr?" he asked.

"Both," she said. He laughed.

"And this is Glenda," Sarah said. "Scott's associate and our legal terminology translator."

"Ah, and your Italian is good enough for this big job?" Bianchi asked Glenda.

"I hope so," Glenda said.

He raised an eyebrow and unleashed a torrent of language, the rising notes at the end of each sentence indicating that they were questions. *He's testing her,* Kat thought. *He's a games player.*

Glenda gazed back at him, her smile in place, and she answered at once in Italian, fast and fluently. Kat and Scott smiled. Sarah actually laughed out loud.

"Aha. Our Glenda has obviously been to Italy often," Sarah said.

"Every summer when I was a child," Glenda said. "My grandmother lives in Positano."

"A beautiful place," Bianchi said, smiling warmly now. "I am glad you are here," he added. "My English is, I think, good. But with legal matters, I must be clear. Yes?"

"Of course. I'll help all I can."

Bianchi gave a low, formal bow. Kat noted that Scott grinned as Glenda looked to him for approval, obviously proud of her score for the home team.

Immediately, Sarah's cook began setting out food. Kat looked at the table laden with cold salmon, sliced rare beef, cheeses, salads, fresh fruits. It was an impressive spread for just five people.

"Wow, this looks good, Sarah," Scott said.

Kat turned, surprised, to look at her husband. The jovial voice, the easy smile. There was no trace of the cold anger he had exhibited in the car. He appeared comfortable and at ease, ready to enjoy the evening, as Sarah waved an arm for them all to sit.

"Please. Help yourselves," she said.

Bianchi was seated opposite Kat. She watched as, superficially charming and alert, he switched from only slightly accented English to fast Italian, which Glenda immediately translated. Occasionally, he would exchange private words with Glenda, and they would laugh together. Glenda had relaxed, blossoming under his attention. *She's really quite attractive,* Kat thought as Glenda giggled at something Bianchi said. Scott, always curious about European politics, asked Bianchi about the new players on the political scene in Italy, but Bianchi was not inclined to discuss politics. He talked of his trip to New York, of his recent visit to the UK.

Kat, uncomfortable and awkward, listened and thought—*a year ago I might have enjoyed this. I would have found it amusing at least. Most people would think themselves lucky to be here: a beautiful view, a lovely house, good food, and the company, if not quite as charming as it appeared on the face of it, was at least interesting. I have lost the ability to feel pleasure,* she thought. *Feel joy. Feel love. Is my life now to be this quiet, claustrophobic panic?* She wondered how long she would need to sit there, pretending to be a normal person, wondered how long it would be before the people around this table talked of work and she could escape to sit quietly inside Sarah's house or to walk around the pool, stare at the ocean.

Sarah picked up the conversation, guiding it back to the Milan merger. Kat, trying to follow Glenda's swift translations, Scott's interventions, found her mind drifting again and wondered if Bianchi would remember her as the woman at the dining table who had nothing to say. She caught Sarah looking at her. As the maid cleared the table, and documents were produced for Scott to check, Sarah tapped Kat's arm.

"Would you excuse us?" she said to the group. "You don't need us for a moment. Must show Kat my little den."

As they walked into the main house, Sarah said, "Kat, you're so quiet, so pale. You're not ill?"

"No. I'm fine. Thank you."

Sarah gave her a long, sympathetic look.

"You haven't been able to change Scott's mind yet, then?"

"He's never going to change his mind no matter what I do," Kat said. "I'm quite certain of that."

Sarah stopped in her tracks and turned to Kat.

"Even though he knows how you feel? What this adoption means to you?"

"Even so."

"I'm sorry, Caitlin. So very sorry. No wonder you feel so . . . well. Damn."

"Yes. Anyway, what do you want to show me?"

"Come look."

A few moments later, Sarah opened a door off the main entrance hall. The room she showed to Kat was enormous, with a private terrace looking out onto the ocean. The walls were a pale blue, the sofas a cream linen; the French doors opened to the patio and had a view of the coastline. The fresh-air smell of the ocean filled the room.

"The Sussex cottage," said Sarah. "Expanded!"

Kat looked around, astonished. This was the room Scott had mentioned, but he had no way of knowing how perfect it was in every detail. It was as if Sarah had exactly re-created the Sussex gatekeeper's cottage they had stayed in years ago: the colors, the furnishings, even the framed Mary Cassatt prints and bookcases along one wall. A cobalt-blue glass bowl holding sharp-green apples had been placed on a side table. Kat remembered one just like it.

"It's exactly right," Kat said. "Only bigger."

"I know. I was there recently. Had it painted but kept the same color scheme and just updated the kitchen. I so love the place."

"I remember it well. It was beautiful."

"A retreat," said Sarah. "I use it for a bolt-hole. Mrs. Evans brings me an evening meal down from the main house, and the rest of the time I fend for myself and walk and hike and do a lot of physical things. Get back into shape. Walk along the cliffs with the wind on my face. Breathe that lovely fresh air."

Kat could taste the Sussex wind, the salt in it.

"You're lucky to have such a place," Kat sighed. "A place to hide."

"But you can use it, too. I'll give you a key," said Sarah. "Come on, so I don't forget. Have a key. If you need to go, it's there. You remember where the cottage is?"

"Yes, but really, I can't," Kat began. But Sarah was already heading toward her office.

"Come on," she called. "The key's in my desk. An extra one. Go whenever you like. You don't even have to tell me. Call in at the main house and tell them you're staying, and Mrs. Evans will cook dinner for you."

"Sarah, I can't do that. Really, it would be impossible. It's not so easy just to drop everything and pop over to Sussex from LA."

"You don't *have* to go," said Sarah, turning to look at Kat. For a moment, Kat felt like a schoolgirl again. How difficult it was, always, to deny Sarah. She would insist and cajole, and in the end people just gave in. She made it seem churlish, mean-spirited, to refuse. Kat felt a bit like that now. She followed Sarah to a large office at the back of the house. A mahogany desk was littered with files. Kat saw one labeled with a company name: *J. De Beaugrand.* It sounded familiar, and for a moment she struggled to understand why. Was that the name of the company Brooke had joined? No. How could it be? Then, Kat spotted another folder labeled *Falconbridge* and felt a sharp bite of recognition. That name was definitely familiar. She turned to Sarah.

"Richard Falconbridge?" she said. "Wasn't he the solicitor who controlled your trust fund?"

Sarah nodded.

"Yes. And about to get his comeuppance. No more than he deserves. He betrayed a confidence. The oily snake."

"He never told Helen the whole story, though, did he?" Kat said.

Sarah looked hard at her.

"Ah, you remember that? The baby-sale threat?" She gave a short laugh. "I thought the blue blood might be worth rather a lot of money. No. He didn't tell Helen that part. But he should have given me the money. I needed it. And it was *my* trust fund. What was left of it. You know what was funny that day? I told him if he didn't give me the cash, I'd tell everyone he'd tried to touch me—and he laughed, just laughed in my face. He said that half of London would know I was lying, that he had no interest in the fair sex of any age or type, and Charles, his partner of twenty years, would happily testify to that. Then, he must have called Helen. Slimy little worm."

She turned back to the desk, fumbled in the drawer.

"Here," she said, handing Kat a silver key to a Yale lock. "The cottage key. This is it."

Kat held it in her hand. It felt heavier than it should.

"I'm not sure—" she began.

"My goodness, nobody's *making* you go, Kat," Sarah said. "But keep the key in your pocket. Just in case. That place is soothing. It soothes the soul."

She turned, touched Kat's arm.

"Come on, back to the fray. Let's see how Scott and Glenda are managing Luca Bianchi."

Kat hesitated, staring out through the windows at the group, talking loudly now on the patio. She saw Bianchi gesticulating and then laughing, his white teeth flashing. Scott appeared to be laughing, too. Her husband looked like a stranger.

"They all seem to be getting along rather well," Sarah said. "That's good."

"Yes."

"You don't find Luca amusing?" Sarah asked.

"Not much impressed by polished playboys."

"Oh, he's not exactly a playboy. Tough businessman underneath all that polish. Women usually adore him. Look at Glenda—she's positively glowing. Though much of that, I suspect, is because he's making her look good in front of Scott."

As they watched, Bianchi leaned forward as if to whisper something. This was followed by more laughter, and Kat felt herself shrinking inside, not wanting to return to that table and produce more false smiles. She touched her head. A headache was beginning behind her eyes. Sarah, noticing the gesture, frowned.

"This is hard for you, isn't it, Kat? Feeling as you do."

"Yes. Well, tonight I'm not really able to—"

Where were the words? What could she say? *I feel inarticulate. Unnecessary. Lost.*

"You came. You made an effort, even though you're obviously very hurt and upset. If you want to leave, Kat, then do. Please. Go home, rest. Have one of those long, scented baths you used to love. I won't be offended. Honestly. Not at all."

"I can't leave. Scott will be furious if I try to drag him away now."

"So don't drag him. I have my car and driver here. He's hanging around, waiting to drive Luca back to the hotel. My driver can easily take you home and come back for Luca. It would be simple."

"Oh no. I can't do that. It wouldn't be—"

"Of course you can do it. This evening will be all business from now on. Why should you be bored and unhappy? You're an adult, Kat. Make your own choices. Plead a headache."

With that, Sarah strode back out to the patio.

"Kat has a bad headache and so the car will take her home," she said to the group. "Luca, you won't need it for a while, will you?"

"Of course not." He stood up at once, looking concerned. "I am sorry."

Scott also got to his feet. He walked over to his wife, took her arm, began to lead her away from the group.

"I'll drive you. Just wait a little longer, Kat. Please. We're almost done."

"No. No. I'm just going to take a painkiller, go to bed. You stay. Finish whatever you have to do."

He looked at her, uncertain.

"Please," she said.

The driver appeared only moments later, and Scott and Sarah walked with Kat to the car.

"I won't be long," Scott said.

Sarah hugged her briefly.

"Feel better," she said. "It breaks my heart to see you like this."

In the back of the car, Kat turned to look out the window. Scott and Sarah stood together, watched the car until it reached the end of the drive, waved, and then began to walk back to the others at the patio table.

As the car waited to enter traffic on the busy Pacific Coast Highway, Kat turned once again to look back. She could see directly on to the softly lit patio: the Italian with the white shark smile and cold, assessing eyes was talking, laughing, his arms gesticulating. Glenda, next to him, leaned toward him, like a flower to the sun. Scott and Sarah, joining them, both smiling, pulled out chairs and sat together on the opposite side of the table. A happy foursome, enjoying time together on a winter night in California.

TWENTY-ONE

As the driver pulled into the driveway of her home, parking on the apron in front of the garage, Kat stared at the house for a moment, baffled. The drive from Sarah's villa had been a blur of lights, a timeless fog. She had no memory of it. She recalled only *What now?* playing in her head like a mantra and the image of Scott across the table, laughing. A stranger.

The house felt cold. Scott's coffee cup was in the sink; a square of crumbs indicated that he had buttered his toast on the countertop without using a plate. The peanut butter lid was at an angle. Kat noted these small domestic details in an oddly detached way, as if this house, this kitchen, this snacking husband, were all unknown to her.

A blinking light on the telephone indicated that someone, mostly likely her sister, had called. Kat lifted the receiver and then replaced it hard. She didn't want to talk to Maggie. Nor to anyone else. What could she say? She felt a sudden, violent claustrophobia, as if a trap were closing over her head. Fearing another panic attack, she sat down on the kitchen chair, pushing her feet to the floor, trying to find balance. The room seemed to spin and then settled.

And so, what now?

She took a long bath, got into bed, listening all the time for Scott's car. He would not be too late, surely? They had already begun to talk of contracts and agreements. How long could it take, this business chatter? When, an hour later, he had not returned, she felt the anger surge, a fast snapping in her head. Who knows what he was doing back there, in that luxury home by an infinity pool.

She recalled clearly the image of Scott rejoining the group on the pretty patio, the ocean view behind him, smiling as he pulled out a chair for Sarah. But who could blame him for preferring the company of a beautiful woman, a suave European, and a charming young associate to that of a wife who could no longer function in the world? With these thoughts, Kat felt the anger abate, the return of a hollow emptiness, and knew that it was not simply a case of bridging a gap—that the space between them was huge, a crater, unbridgeable.

Sarah was right. She needed to get away. Get away from the California sun. The light was too bright, too harsh. It dried everything. She wanted to walk, alone, in the shade, through cool, green, English lanes. Feel the rain on her face; listen to it tapping against the windows. She would like to spend time in solitude, so she could think clearly. And decide on the best way to live her leftover life. Decide, perhaps, if she wanted to live it at all. It was her decision. Hers alone. And one that must be made peacefully, away from everyone. She did not have to tell Scott exactly where she was going. She would say she was visiting Maggie. She did not have to tell Maggie the real reason for her visit, either. She had two bottles of pills saved now, hidden in her underwear drawer. And she had the key to the cottage in her purse.

She pretended sleep when, a long time later, Scott returned home, stumbling a little in the bedroom. He undressed quickly, edged into the far side of the bed. She could smell chlorine. He had been swimming, then, in that luxury pool. She allowed the surge of pain and then squeezed her eyes shut. She would be gone tomorrow. She could think about it all then.

When Scott returned from work in the late afternoon the following day, Kat had her flight booked, a suitcase half packed on the bed, the saved bottles of sleeping pills tucked into an inside pocket.

At the sound of the car pulling up, she turned from the closet, a sweater in her hands, and hurried to the window to watch Scott come into the house. He stood for a moment and then straightened his back before walking up the path. She moved slowly downstairs to greet him.

As he entered the kitchen and came toward her, his face was already creased with concern.

"How are you?" he asked. "Do you feel okay now?"

"Okay? Of course I'm not okay. I feel like—I don't know what I feel like."

Like Eliot's ragged claws, scuttling across the seabed. She shook the half-remembered quote from her mind.

"I'm sorry," Scott said. "I'm really sorry. That fight. I was—"

"Forget it. It's over now."

"And to be so late home last night. I'm sorry. I tried to leave. I kept trying, but—"

"So why didn't you? Why didn't you leave?"

"They couldn't agree on the final clause. Sarah being stubborn. Bianchi, too."

"So you decided to go skinny-dipping instead?" Kat asked, impassive.

"No. Of course not. Sarah thought that we were all getting foggy, that we needed a dip in the pool, and she produced swimsuits. The others were keen. It was idiotic, really. I swam for about two minutes and then got right out and got dressed. I thought, *Fuck this,* and picked up my jacket and car keys and said good night, but Sarah wanted me to check one paragraph in the documents and Bianchi came over to talk. Stood there, dripping, in his miniature Speedo. I said I had to leave—I was worried about you. He said he understood."

"Oh, I bet he understood," Kat said.

"No. I think he meant it. Anyway, he said we could finalize the agreement in the morning. He'd come to my office. So I got out of there and came home. You were asleep."

"Did he? Come to your office this morning and finalize it?"

"Yeah, he did. Amazing."

She turned away.

"Good. Anyway, do you want a glass of wine?" she asked. "Or a scotch?"

"Wine is fine."

He was watching her carefully. He knew her too well. He was waiting for her to say whatever was on her mind. She poured the wine, handed it to him, and then spoke in a rush.

"I want to go to England for a little while, Scott. For a break."

"That's a good idea. Maybe later in the year we can visit, and go on to France, too, and—"

"No. I mean now."

He shook his head.

"I could maybe do it in a month or so, but I can't go now," he said. "I've got a merger coming up and a whole load of—"

"You don't have to come with me. It's a break I need."

"You want to go alone?"

"Yes."

"That won't help, Kat. It just won't."

"But that's what I want to do."

His eyes met hers; the pain in them clutched at her heart for a second.

"Are you sure?" he said.

"Yes."

"You belong here with me, Kat," he said. "Not in England. Look, I'm sorry you're so upset."

"Upset? Is that what I am?"

"Well, disappointed, hurt, whatever." He stopped, looked at her, frowning. "You really think a trip will help?"

He looked so anxious that, for a few seconds, Kat came close to changing her mind, but the need for solitude reaffirmed itself and she nodded.

"Yes. I think so," she said. "It might help both of us. You can work late if you need to. Work all night if you want. You won't have to worry about me waiting here. We have different ways of dealing with things, Scott. Work helps you. That's fine. Really. But right now, you can't help me. And I don't think I can help you much. I've got to find some way of my own."

He scrutinized her face, considering this.

"You must do whatever you need to do, Kat," he said.

TWENTY-TWO

Maggie, wrapped in a thick woolen coat, her face solemn, waited at Heathrow Airport.

"Are you okay, darling?" she asked, hugging her sister. "Such a surprise, your call."

"Sorry," Kat said. "Should have given you more notice."

"Oh no. No. I'm really happy to see you."

Kat had said nothing to Maggie about visiting Sarah's cottage and was already dreading that conversation. Maggie would be confused by such a plan. And likely be angry, too.

"Scott called," Maggie said in the airport parking lot as she started up her car. "He said to call him. He didn't seem too sure how long you would be staying."

"Well, that's because I'm not too sure myself."

"You didn't tell him how long?" Maggie asked. "Did you talk about it?"

"We did talk," said Kat. "A bit."

"Is there a problem with Scott?" Maggie asked a minute or two later.

"Not with Scott," Kat said. "With me."

"He told me about your adoption plans," Maggie said. "I know it's a disappointment, darling, but it really is for the best that you don't—"

The best?

"Maggie, please," Kat said. "I don't want to talk about it."

"Okay, fine. Fine," Maggie said, giving her sister a sidelong glance. "You look tired, Kat. A long bath and a warm bed, how does that sound?"

Kat smiled at her sister.

"Perfect," she said.

Maggie and Paul's house, a Victorian brick structure, was set back from the road and surrounded by lawn and old oaks. Paul waited in the doorway and hugged Kat with the gruff affection he had always shown her. He was tall, thin, unchanged over the years; the absentminded academic look had stayed with him. Peering over his glasses, he inspected her and nodded.

"Not quite the pitiful creature your sister has been expecting," he said. "But in need of some fresh air, certainly."

"In need of a drink is what you mean," said Kat.

"Indeed," he said. "What will you have?"

Later, in the pitch-black of the bedroom, Kat lay sleepless. She felt calmer now, felt a kind of relief. She didn't have to pretend anything for Scott's sake. Once she was away from Maggie and Paul, alone in the cottage, she need not pretend anything for anyone, or even talk to anyone at all.

She turned restlessly in the bed and looked out the window. As dawn approached, the tree branches came into focus, charcoal etched against the sky. How to tell Maggie that she intended to go to Sussex for a visit? How to explain the cottage? Maggie would hit the ceiling, of course.

Maggie was fiddling with a brand-new cappuccino machine in her sleek modern kitchen when Kat, sipping her breakfast orange juice, finally found the courage to speak about her plans.

"I thought I'd go to Sussex for a few days," Kat began.

"That'll be a nice break. I'll come," Maggie said, tapping out the coffee. "We can stay at the Old Ship. Remember that time we all stayed there?"

"No. You don't have to come, Mags. I know you're busy."

"Oh, it's fine. I can take a couple of days off."

Kat took a breath.

"I might go down first, meet up with you later. I've a key to the old cottage near Wystandean."

Maggie turned around, the little metal jug in her hand. The machine hissed behind her.

"What old cottage?"

"The old gatehouse. Sarah's cottage. She gave me a key."

Maggie regarded her sister, a small frown furrowing her forehead.

"How could she just give you a key?"

"It was when we were at her Malibu place."

"You actually went to that woman's house?"

"She's Scott's client, Maggie," Kat said.

"So what? Come on, Kat!"

Kat heard something in her sister's voice that she had not heard for many years. Even when Maggie was a child, anger had brought her close to tears.

"Why would she want you to go to her cottage?" Maggie asked.

"She said it helped her, was healing. After her husband died. I used to go there before, years ago. It's a beautiful place."

"And this is not a beautiful place?" Maggie asked.

Maggie turned back to the machine. Her shoulders were rigid and she gave a hard sigh. Kat regretted mentioning the Sussex cottage so soon.

"Maggie, please."

Maggie turned to face her. She was hurt, obviously, that her sister was leaving, but there was something else in her expression, and Kat realized, with a shock, that it was fear.

"Whenever Sarah Cherrington gives something, she wants something back," Maggie said. "You know that, Kat. I can't imagine why she would lend you her cottage. Unless she's going to borrow something of yours."

"She's just trying to help."

"She does not ever try to help. She manipulates. She controls."

"She thought I would want to be alone. To think about things. She's right."

"Alone?" Maggie cried. "You don't need to be alone. That's the last bloody thing you need. You need people around you, people who care about you. She's bloody insane, is what she is. And so are you, Kat. So are you."

Maggie's voice broke, and she turned quickly and walked out of the kitchen. Kat followed.

"Mags, please. I'll just spend a day or two down there. Walk on the beach, on the Downs."

"You can walk here."

"Look, later on you can visit me there if you like. We can hike."

"I wouldn't set foot in that woman's house. Remember what she did to Sven? To my wedding? And remember what she called me, the night before I got married? *A lumpen great cow,* that's what. At three in the morning on my wedding day. Remember?"

Kat remembered arriving in Rugby after stumbling upon Sarah and Sven. Maggie had been in their bedroom, hanging up her wedding gown. She had turned, excited, and taken one look at Kat's tearstained face before fear crossed her own.

"Oh my God, what's happened? Tell me. Tell me."

"Sarah Cherrington and Sven—" was all Kat could say.

Maggie stared at her, disbelieving.

"No. Not Sven."

"I just saw them. I don't think he'll be here tomorrow, Maggie. He won't be best man. I don't think he'll come."

Maggie rushed to her sister, held her shoulders.

"I didn't think he even liked her," said Kat, crying hard.

"Oh shit. We should kill that bitch."

"It takes two, Maggie. Sven was . . . touching her."

"We should still kill her."

Sarah had arrived at their home at three in the morning, throwing stones at the bedroom window. Kat, in a restless sleep, had woken to find Maggie already up.

"That Sarah person is actually here," Maggie said, pulling on her robe. "Right outside our bloody house. I'll deal with her."

"Maggie, just ignore her."

"*Ignore her?* Are you barmy, Kat? She'll wake the whole house. You want Dad to go down there? Jesus. She should be put away. You stay here."

Maggie hurried downstairs. Kat heard their murmuring voices, and curious, frightened, she pressed hard against the window and listened. She could hear Sarah sobbing.

"I just want to say sorry to Kat, that's all. Sorry, sorry."

"You're drunk," said Maggie. "Who's in the car? Is Sven with you? Where is he?"

Kat peered out at this. Sven wasn't with Sarah, surely? But it was Dick Hawkinson, a friend from university; she recognized his old VW, the bearded face looking out.

"A friend. He drove me. I just want to tell Kat—" Sarah began.

Maggie interrupted her at once. Her voice, still quiet, sounded hoarse with anger.

"Get yourself out of here now, Sarah-bloody-Cherrington," she said. "Or I will kill you with my own bare hands. And if I see you again near my home or my sister, I will punch that pretty little face of yours. You are an evil witch. An evil, bad person, and you bring pain to people wherever you go."

Sarah had backed away up the path, staring, amazed, at Maggie. The shy, blushing Watt sister, the quiet one, had turned into a demon of fury.

"And don't you dare turn up tomorrow," snapped Maggie. "I don't want you at my wedding."

Sarah had recovered enough to turn at this, and her voice rang clear and loud.

"I've no intention of coming to your wedding," she said. "Why would I want to? To see a lumpen great cow like you in a white wedding dress? You're a fucking joke."

Sarah said nothing more. She climbed unsteadily into the VW, and they drove away.

"Maggie, it's the cottage I want to see," Kat said now. "And walk the Downs, and along the beach. Sarah won't be there. She doesn't even know I'm in England."

Maggie shook her head.

"You are going alone to a cottage in the middle of nowhere, and you think it makes sense? The way you feel right now?"

"Yes," said Kat.

"You'll give me the address?"

"I'm not sure of the actual address," Kat said. "I know where the cottage is, though. I remember. I'll call you when I know the address. And maybe in a couple of days, you could come?"

Maggie, her face troubled, studied her sister.

"Mags, I love you—you know that," Kat said. "If anybody has helped me, it's you. But I just want to hike and think. And remember."

"Remember?" Maggie said. She was still unsure, but this was emotional territory she did not understand, grief she had never experienced, and Kat saw confusion in her sister's face.

"Yes."

"For God's sake, Kat," said Maggie, sighing. "I wish you wouldn't. I think it's bloody stupid. But damn—be bloody stupid. I can't stop you."

Kat moved forward to hug her sister, but there was still so much unspoken and she felt as if a chasm had opened between them. Maggie, too soon, turned away from her and returned to the kitchen.

TWENTY-THREE

The cottage looked exactly as Kat remembered it, exactly like its reproduction in Malibu: a bleached-wood floor, a few Chinese rugs, a long sofa of soft cream linen with periwinkle cushions.

The place was uncluttered. A few prints, including a Mary Cassatt and a Renoir, decorated the white-plaster walls. And yes, there was the cobalt-blue bowl, now empty of apples. The windows were wide, with wooden shutters painted a soft blue. When Kat opened them, salty sea air whooshed into the room. The view of the sea filled the entire window; gulls swooped into the surf. On the horizon, Kat could see boats heading toward the Brighton Marina. She stood for a few minutes, simply staring at the view, before turning to explore the rest of the place.

Only the kitchen looked different, larger. It had obviously been remodeled. She found a microwave, a fridge, and a cupboard stacked with staples: long-life milk, tea, coffee, and a variety of cans.

A fire in the fireplace was set but not lit. Kat took one of the long, thick matches and lit it, and immediately, the flames brightened and burnished the room with gold. She remembered sitting by the fireplace with Sarah, waiting for the call from Helen that would summon them to dinner at Lansdowne. In the large bedroom—the bedroom that had been Sarah's—the bed was already made up, sheets turned down, towels laid out. It was as if this cottage was always ready for visitors, or for Sarah.

Kat took a can of baked beans from the cupboard and a variety of cheeses and crackers, and setting it all out on thick pottery plates, she settled down in front of her now-blazing fire. It was so quiet. There was no sound but the sea, no lights but the fishing boats out there. The edginess she had felt in Los Angeles, the pain and disappointment, had faded, leaving only a strange emptiness. But she did not feel lonely. *Chris,* she wondered, *did you come here with me?* She felt the tightening in her chest that she had previously recognized as the ache of loss or grief, but it had changed slightly. It felt warmer, some warmth spreading across her chest.

"See how nice it is here, Chris," she said aloud, just in case. *Who is to know if the dead hear us?* she considered. *Or whether God exists, or if there is life afterward. Who has the answers?*

After dinner, Kat wondered if she should call her sister, just to reassure her. She pulled out her cell phone, saw a flashing light indicating that the battery was low, and remembered that her charger still sat on the dresser in Los Angeles. *Damn.* She looked around for a landline. The phone was not visible in the den, or the sitting room, or in the kitchen, either. She looked in the smaller bedroom, and then, with mounting puzzlement, she returned to the larger bedroom to check again. Distracted for a moment, Kat looked at the framed print on the wall—Rothko's *Violet, Green and Red.* The same print Kat had hung in the Birmingham apartment. She remembered Scott's words about Sarah needing to replicate things. It was true. Even here.

Kat shook her head and continued her search for the phone. After five minutes, she began to figure out the answer to a question she had never thought to ask. There was no phone in this cottage. She bit her lip. Well, that solved that problem. She would go to bed instead.

When Kat woke, at dawn, she heard the sound of the sea and the frantic squawking of gulls. It was cold in the cottage, the fire long out, and a mist of vapor fogged the windows. Kat dressed quickly, warmly, for her walk to the village.

The air smelled of damp grass and undergrowth as Kat moved briskly along the path from the cottage, hesitating at the lane that led to the big house. The road had a sharp bend, so she had to stride up the hill for a few yards to see clearly, but she was curious about the home Sarah had described as "hideous"—the house that had replaced Lansdowne. She paused on the curve; the driveway now led straight and steeply to the house on the hill, a modern structure, with a wide building alongside it, a garage for the owner's collection of cars. One of the garage doors was open. Kat could see the glint of a Jaguar. A black compact was parked in the driveway. She studied the house: not hideous, certainly, but all angles and glass and lacking the charm and elegance of Lansdowne. After a few moments, she turned back to the empty lane. She could taste salt in the wind. There was no sidewalk, so she kept to the edge of the road, but only one flatbed truck trundled past, the driver tooting his horn to warn her.

The village was little changed: a small Saxon church, the haberdashery, and the neat lawn of the village square, with its carefully manicured borders. The timbered pub, though, looked closed, a new "For Sale" sign nailed to one of the beams.

Kat decided that she would walk toward Wystandean and then circle back through the next village. An hour into her hike, she found herself outside Elmwood Hall, the school from which the young Sarah had been expelled. Kat tried to imagine Sarah here at that age. The girls she could see playing hockey looked about fourteen years old. Sarah had been fourteen when they first met, with that thick braid down her back. But these girls seemed younger, sweeter, with their pink, raw cheeks, their bright, clear voices.

It was midafternoon by the time she returned from Wystandean, choosing the cliff path back to the cottage. It felt freezing near the cliffs; the wind had a biting edge to it, so Kat pulled the neck of her sweater up around her mouth and tied her scarf tighter. The Channel was choppy, the water a gunmetal gray, edged with white foam. To the east, she could see the chalk headland of Beachy Head, high on the list of the world's suicide spots.

She stood on the edge of the cliff staring at the water, studying the rock formations. Years ago, Sarah had shown her this place. Sarah's young friend Joanna had jumped to her death from here. It would be simple enough, Kat thought: the rocks below were jagged, hard, and a long way down. Instantly. *You will die instantly,* she told herself. *And be with Chris. And if not with Chris, there will be nothing. Our little life is rounded with a sleep.*

Kat moved to the edge, thinking hard. This must not be an impulsive thing. She must think about it carefully. If she were to do it, then it must be a considered decision. It must be the right decision. It occurred to Kat that this did not frighten her, or even disturb her, this option to end her life. It was simply that: an option. It was something she could do now, or later. Or not do at all.

She inspected the sloping bank to the lower rocks. A better place would be fifty yards farther north, where the rocks were sharper, spiking in a circle. It was an interesting rockscape, with a maelstrom in the center: swirling, turbulent circles of water, where a body could be lost, possibly sucked down into the cavernous dark. But that would leave Scott endlessly searching for her. Maggie and Paul, too, forever scanning the surface of the water. No. Better the simple dive into the Channel; her body would wash up, eventually, with the tide. She walked to the promontory, stood at the edge, and looked down. Yes. Yes, this would do. This would be a good place. She would not need the pills.

Kat stood still, biting at her thumbnail. What would one think before the water took over, spinning a body swiftly into that dark void? What was Virginia Woolf thinking when, not so far from here, she walked from her house to the riverbank, put down her walking stick, and filled her pockets with stones? *Something similar to the thoughts I have now,* Kat concluded. *That it is time for it to be over. It is simply time for the pain to be over.*

At the edge of Kat's consciousness was the certainty that she would come back to this. And when the time was right, she must write two letters: one to her sister and one to her husband. She must not leave them wondering and searching. They had talked of healing, Maggie and Scott, but Kat knew that this was not why she had come to Sussex. She did not believe that healing was possible. *I am broken,* Kat thought, *in some deep, unfixable place. And possibly Scott is, too. Perhaps he can find a way back. I thought I had found a way. A new baby. A new beginning. But there is no way back for me now.*

The sound of twigs crackling underfoot jarred Kat so severely that she jumped. She turned. A shadow moved near the trees on the far side of the path. Kat waited, holding her breath. The shadow stepped out into the light. Sarah. For a moment, Kat thought that she was imagining it, that the image she saw was only in her mind. Sarah smiled.

"Hello, Kat," she said softly.

Kat, too stunned to reply, simply stared, wondering how long Sarah had been there, watching her, hidden in the shadows.

"Sorry to startle you," Sarah said. "I thought you might be up here."

Kat stepped away from the cliff edge. "I didn't expect—"

"I did try to call. Scott said you were in England. I hoped you'd be at the cottage. Cell phone reception is abysmal there and you didn't bother to plug in a phone. Why didn't you collect the phone from Mrs. Evans?"

"I didn't think—" Kat said, bewildered. "You're here for a vacation?" she asked, unsure of how to word the questions spinning in her head. It was Sarah's cottage, after all.

"Only for a day or two," said Sarah. "I thought I'd rest here before taking on the big city. I have meetings in London."

She smiled at Kat's unsure expression.

"Don't worry, Kat. I'll be in the other room. I won't get in your way. You can stay in the big bedroom. I see you've made yourself nice and cozy in there. Ignore me if you like."

Kat swallowed. Ignore Sarah? She was not so easily ignored.

TWENTY-FOUR

Inside the cottage, evidence of Sarah's presence was everywhere. A sweater had been thrown onto a chair; a scarf snaked across the kitchen counter. A white phone had been plugged into an outlet to the right of the fireplace, and Sarah's laptop was open on a small table beside it. Sarah had lit the fire; the coals glowed in the dim light. Two bottles of red wine had been placed on the dining table.

Kat took off her coat and stood with it draped over her arm, like a hospital visitor.

"I'm going to have a bath," she said. "I'm frozen to the bone."

Sarah had thrown off her jacket and taken one of the seats by the fire. She stretched her hands toward the flames to warm them.

"I bet you are. That's a bitter wind. But hurry. I asked Mrs. Evans to cook her *coq au vin*. And we have two bottles of excellent Bordeaux."

Sarah's green eyes gleamed with reflected light from the fire and what appeared to be pleasure and anticipation for the evening ahead.

"Go have your bath and we'll have a drink."

"I'm glad we have a phone," Kat said. "I need to make a call."

"I wouldn't call Scott just yet. A small legal crisis in LA—he'll be tied up in meetings."

"I'll call later."

Kat stood, waiting, until Sarah reached out, unplugged the telephone, and handed it to her.

"There's a phone outlet to the left of the dresser. And please, Kat," she added, in a coaxing tone. "Don't look so put out. I don't mean to be a bore. I rather thought you might enjoy this. For old times' sake."

Kat smiled faintly and escaped into the bedroom. She saw that the book she had left open on the bed was now closed and had been placed on the bedside table. The closet door was ajar. Sarah had been looking around, of course, snooping through clothes and papers. She used to do the same thing years ago, when they shared an apartment. Nothing was out of bounds for her, not private diaries, not personal letters. Strangely, this snooping did not bother Kat now, though it used to infuriate her. There was nothing private here. Sarah's curiosity was simply an irritant.

Kat found the outlet for the phone, pushing a lamp and a photo frame out of the way to reach it. The old silver frame with the picture of Chris at his junior high school graduation had tipped onto its side. She straightened it, studied it. Chris wore a white shirt and a serious expression. It was a formal school picture. Why had she brought this one? Instead of one of him laughing? She had grabbed this photograph from the hall table instead of choosing a better one from upstairs on the dresser. *Shows what kind of glazed fog I was in when I packed,* she thought. *I must have been in some kind of fugue state.*

When the phone was plugged in, and she had checked the dial tone, Kat sat on the bed and took a deep breath. It was midmorning in Los Angeles. If Sarah was right, and Scott was in a meeting, she could leave a voice mail, ask him to call her back. She hesitated, holding tight to the phone. Their conversations had been so angry lately, or polite and false. What could she say to him that was true? *I love you. I've always loved you. But it's not enough.*

She rested against the wall, uncertain. In that time on the clifftop, she had made a decision: she would not be returning to California. But what words could she use to tell him that?

Sighing, she replaced the phone. Later. She would call him just before bed. From the kitchen, she could hear the sound of a wine bottle clinking against glass. Sarah, too impatient to wait, was pouring herself a drink. Kat ran a bath and climbed into it, adding more hot water and ducking down so that she was entirely submerged. The air in the bathroom felt cold. Sarah's voice was now audible in the other room, talking to someone Kat assumed was the formidable Mrs. Evans. Kat slid down under the water. She would wait until Helen's former housekeeper left. She could easily visualize the pinched face, the pursed mouth. No. She had no interest in seeing that woman again. A few minutes later, Sarah knocked on the bathroom door.

"Dinner is served, madam," she called. "And quite delicious it looks, too."

Sarah was enjoying herself, Kat realized, as she sat up in the bath and reached for a towel. Her voice sounded as young, as lively, as it had all those years ago.

"Be right there," Kat called.

Sarah had set the table. The *coq au vin* steamed in a large casserole in the center; there was crusty bread, country butter, and Sarah's wine. Sarah looked up, appeared to scan Kat's face as if searching for something.

"You didn't reach Scott?" she asked.

"Didn't try. I'll call him later," Kat said. "Well, this looks good."

"Doesn't it, though? You'll excuse me, Kat, if I should pitch forward into it. I'm so tired. Jet-lagged beyond belief. After this, I may just lumber off to bed."

"Lumber away. Fine with me."

"So," said Sarah, helping herself to the casserole, "where else did you go, besides the clifftop?"

"Oh, walking about. A little hike."

"Where? Tell me."

"Into the village. It hasn't changed much."

"Nothing changes here."

"The pub looks closed. It's for sale?"

"Yes. Somebody will buy it and convert it, most likely. Pubs are closing all over England."

"Mostly, I walked along the cliff path," Kat said.

"You saw the place where Joanna leapt into eternity?"

"Was it there? On the path to Wystandean?"

"Yes. The bit that juts out."

Kat longed to ask the question but faltered, unsure.

"Why did she do it?" Sarah said.

Caught out, Kat nodded.

"A boy, of course," said Sarah with a small, strange smile. "He got another girl pregnant."

Kat thought back to the Brighton clinic. Could the pregnant girl have been Sarah? The boy involved had never been named, not by Sarah or Helen, and described to Kat as just a village boy Sarah had met when she visited her aunt. There had been no mention, then, of a young girl's suicide.

Sarah regarded her steadily, a challenging look.

"That's very sad," Kat said.

"Yes."

Sarah, lifting the wine bottle to refill their glasses, said nothing more.

"This is delicious," Kat said, after a while. "Mrs. Evans hasn't lost her touch."

"She was happy to cook something interesting. She calls her employer 'that pie and pint man,'" Sarah said.

"She doesn't like him?"

"Despises him. Refuses to stay overnight at the big house, drives home every night to a tiny bedsit. Says it would not be at all appropriate to live in with a man like that." Sarah laughed. "Well, you know what a snob she is—"

"I certainly do," Kat said, remembering her fear, whenever she visited Lansdowne, of the housekeeper's thin-lipped hostility.

"She says he's in trade. Lowest of the low in her book. Actually, he's a trader in the city and makes an absolute mint. Sam knew him, was able to negotiate her contract as part of the deal to buy the land. I promised Helen I'd look after her."

"Why didn't you employ her yourself?"

"God no. Can you imagine? It would be like living under a cloud of constant disapproval. Besides, she wouldn't want to live outside the UK. Her roots are here in Sussex. Family members have been in service in this area for decades. To the best families, she says. Her grandmother was employed at Goodwood House."

"Ah. That explains her attitude to me. Working class riffraff. Doesn't know her place."

"We have our standards," Sarah said in a perfect imitation of Mrs. Evans's voice. She smiled, shaking her head. "Not just you, Caitlin. Oh no. She hated Sam, too, though in truth he felt the same. When I asked him if he would employ her, he said he would rather hire an ax murderer and take his chances."

Kat smiled.

"No persuading him, then."

"No persuading Sam into anything. Well, perhaps when we were first married . . . But later, no. When we learned that I couldn't have children, I rather lost any leverage with Sam."

Kat looked up at this, surprised, and caught a glimpse of Sarah's expression: stiff, eyes cold, as if a shadow had crossed her face. At once, Sarah blinked, brightened, and it was gone.

"Come on, eat up," she said. "There's a delicious lemon tart for dessert."

After dinner, Kat cleared away the dishes while Sarah had a bath, then settled in front of the fire with the Margaret Atwood novel she had taken from the shelves. Sarah emerged from the bathroom after a while, her hair wet, hanging down her back. The gardenia scent of her shampoo and body lotion filled the room. She wore an emerald-green dressing gown of a thick embossed silk and had a peach towel draped around her shoulders. With the rich colors and her dark hair, she looked exotic and young.

"Let the hair dry thoroughly before bed," she said. "Otherwise, it's double pneumonia, as every Englishwoman knows."

Kat smiled.

"What are you reading?" Sarah asked.

"Atwood again. *Cat's Eye.*"

"Oh yes. Great book. *Robber Bride* is here somewhere. Let me see if I can find it."

Sarah found the book easily and took the other chair. It was quiet, the wind had dropped, the room felt cozy and warm. Sarah pulled over a footstool and put her feet up.

"This is so nice, isn't it, Kat?" she said.

"Yes," said Kat, hoping that Sarah would not want to talk, that they could both read peacefully, the only sounds the crackling fire and the distant beat of the waves.

"Like old times," said Sarah in an odd voice. "The happiest days of my life."

Kat looked up, alert.

"With your husband?" she asked. "You were here, like this?"

"Sam? Oh no. Not at all. He hated Sussex. I've *told* you what my life with Sam was like."

"So when? When were the happiest days of your life?"

"You know when."

Kat stared, puzzled. Sarah's eyes glimmered, strangely bright in the firelight.

"I realized a while ago," said Sarah. "That I was truly happy once. Just once. For quite a short time. Those times in our flat, or here in the cottage, or up at Lansdowne with Helen."

"It was fun," Kat said slowly. "But I'm sure you've had happier—"

"No," Sarah said. "No. I haven't."

Kat felt the first stirrings of unease. She put down her book.

"Really?"

"Really. Lansdowne was the first place I felt safe. And later, when we had our little flat, I was happy. But I destroyed it all, didn't I? With Sven. Destroyed everything."

Kat shook her head, uncomfortable.

"Years ago, Sarah. Forgotten."

Sarah reached for her wine, drank deeply from it, then circled around to lift the fresh bottle from the dining table. She opened it quickly, refilled her glass.

"I thought you would forgive me, Kat. I really did."

Her voice was soft, more regretful than accusatory, but she spoke fast now, as if the words might damage her mouth, as if the buried regrets must be spat out at speed.

"But you couldn't, could you? You cut me off. Everyone hated me. I was so hurt. After all I'd *shared* with you. You knew me, Caitlin. Like you were my family. I'd never had that before. Isn't that what families do? Share history? Share experiences. Forgive. It was painful. And I had forgiven you, remember."

"Forgiven me?" Kat asked. "For what?"

"For telling Aunt Helen I was pregnant. I know it was you."

Silence in the warm cottage. Kat looked away, biting at her lip.

"Helen told you?"

"No. Mrs. Evans told me. I blamed that awful solicitor at first."

Kat recalled then, a snapshot bleached by light, the young girl she had known, shaking under the duvets after the clinic visit, her skin the color of alabaster. For those seconds, Kat's uneasiness was replaced by pity.

"I'm sorry," she said.

Sarah shrugged.

"You weren't to know the consequences of that botched surgery, were you? None of us knew."

"No. Even so."

"Never mind. I forgave you. Forgave both of you. I thought you and Helen were the only people who cared about me. Nobody had before. And later we had our flat and university and a life and I was happy. Imagine? I was actually happy."

She paused, studied Kat, eyes intent. Kat, made even more uncomfortable by this scrutiny, frowned, waiting.

"What is it?" she asked at last.

"I know what you plan to do, Kat," Sarah said. "I know."

"You know what?"

"I saw how you looked, up there on the clifftop. I know you have pills with you. I just want to say that I understand."

Chilled, Kat shook her head.

"Sarah, I really don't want to talk about—"

Sarah tossed her hair over one shoulder and began to rub at the ends of it with the peach towel, her eyes never moving from Kat's face.

"You needn't be alone, you know. I won't intervene. If you're at all nervous, I can—"

"Stop," Kat said, getting to her feet. "Please."

She moved so abruptly that she banged into the table and the wineglasses shook. She straightened them without looking at Sarah and walked to the window, aware of Sarah's eyes on her back. She looked out into the night. It was dark out there; the shadowy trees swayed in the wind, and she could see the ocean, a black swirling cauldron.

She swallowed hard; her throat hurt. The sea remained black, rough, fathomless, a possibility that still beckoned.

"It was quite clear to me that evening at Malibu," Sarah said softly. "You were so very unhappy. And who can blame you? So much to bear these last few months. The loss of a child, the disappointment over the adoption. Scott's terrible neglect and indifference. Too much."

Kat stepped back from the window, moved away from the black nightscape of seething water and swaying trees. She turned into the room, studied the beautiful face of the woman she had known since adolescence and who now regarded her with an expression of gentle sympathy.

"I don't have to leave, you know," Sarah said. "If you'd prefer that I stay."

A warning bell sounded in Kat's head. There was something smug and strange in Sarah's voice. A kind of triumph. As if she had won. As if she had achieved something.

"Stay here?"

"Yes. Stay with you. I can walk with you to the cliff path. Or, if you decide to take the pills, I can wait with you here until it's over."

Kat felt as if an icy breeze touched the surface of her skin.

"Sarah, honestly—"

"Or not," Sarah said quickly. "If you don't want that, I can make sure that Mrs. Evans finds you. She's very capable. She'll know what to do. Whom to notify. Nobody will know I was here."

Kat turned back to the window, unable to look at Sarah.

"I really don't want to discuss—" she began.

But Sarah wasn't listening.

"It's absurd, isn't it?" she said. "How my life is littered with suicides? Do you think I exude some kind of pheromone? A chemical that makes people reach for the razor, or the liquid morphine, hurl themselves off cliffs? Well, who knows. People hurt themselves, don't they? Sweet Joanna, smashed onto the rocks like a broken Barbie. Foolish, drunken Sven, tumbling down the stairs, talking the entire time."

It took a moment for the words to register fully with Kat.

"You were there, then, when Sven fell?"

"Hardly matters now, Kat, does it? My concern, right now, is you."

Shaken, Kat said nothing. Her breath seemed to be caught in her throat. The atmosphere in the cottage was so heavy and oppressive, as if the air had been cut off, as if the oxygen were slowly vanishing from the room. She wanted to get away. But she did not want a confrontation. She moved from the window, her head down, avoiding Sarah's eyes.

"I'm tired, Sarah," she said. "I think I'll just go to bed."

"So early? Okay. Fine. But listen, I'll be here, you know, if you need me tonight."

Once in the bedroom, Kat closed the door carefully. Her hands were trembling as, silently, she tugged the suitcase onto the bed. She opened it slowly, holding her breath. She could be packed in minutes, could leave in the early hours when Sarah was asleep. She lifted the items from the bedside table, placed them gingerly in the case. The closet door creaked as she opened it, and she stood rigidly still, listening, before reaching inside it, taking out one item at a time so that the hangers did not clash together.

She had placed some of the sweaters into the case when she heard a click behind her. Sarah stood in the doorway, her face stiff.

"What are you doing?"

"Looking for something."

"The pills? They're in the pocket. Inside."

Kat, trying to hide the tremor in her hands, pushed the suitcase away and reached for her nightgown, as if preparing for bed.

"It's okay. I'm just going to bed."

"Of course. It's only that—well, you looked so distressed."

She leaned against the doorjamb, studied Kat carefully, eyes narrow.

"You're not packing, are you, Caitlin?" she asked finally.

When Kat did not reply, she moved closer.

"You were meant to stay here," Sarah said, her voice rising. "Isolated. Alone. Like I was."

Meant to stay.

A moment of stunned disbelief, and then, like a window thrown open, a blast of icy air, Kat saw clearly and understood. Sarah had destroyed many lives since she gained access to her husband's funds and companies. She was not finished yet.

Kat gripped the sides of the suitcase to steady herself and turned to look at Sarah, a slow fear growing in her gut.

"How long have you been planning this?"

Sarah laughed. A startling sound in the claustrophobic bedroom. Her amusement seemed real, the laugh unforced.

"Oh, I can easily answer that. Since the morning I saw your picture."

"My—?"

"In the newspaper. It was quite a shock. I'd just met the lawyers, been given full access to Sam's funds. I was exhilarated that day. I walked around my Ojai house. I imagined the renovation. I imagined the scores I could settle. Then, I took a little break. Coffee and the newspaper. And there you were. A photograph of Scott receiving some lawyer's award. A charity function. You were wearing black, too. So odd, don't you think, both of us wearing black that day?"

"And I became one of your scores to settle?" Kat asked, trying to keep her voice level.

"Not at first. No. You looked so sad. That young gangster was there on the podium with Scott, and you were seated behind them, next to James. You looked so small. So alone and lost. Just as you looked when I first saw you at St. Theresa's. I researched you, of course. Learned all about Scott and the death of your son. I have people who can find out everything."

Kat recalled the expensive flowers at the grave. Sarah. Of course. *And that's how she knew about Chloe,* she thought. *She knew about her even before I did.*

"It was so easy to arrange a meeting," Sarah continued. "I was looking forward to it, actually. I thought I could forgive you."

She paused to study Kat's stricken face.

"Thought I could," she repeated slowly.

"But—?"

"There you were in that glitzy Palm Springs ballroom and not lost at all. Not alone. Your handsome husband at your side. Your rottweiler sister there, too. And everyone saying, *What a devoted couple. So loving. So very close.* I'd already been damned for ruining the love of your life. You can see how the irony of it was hard to resist."

She shook her head, musing, thinking back.

"But Scott—stubborn, difficult. He leapt away if I as much as touched his arm. It was really quite amusing. So then I thought, well, perhaps with the right circumstances he and Glenda might . . . But then you came to me for help. A solution! Simple one, too."

Kat took a slow breath.

"So the adoption—that was just a game you were playing?"

"What do you think?"

"We would never have been approved, would we?"

"Not by that agency. Not by any agency, probably."

"So you lied about it to me, said something different to Scott, simply to create a rift between us?"

Sarah shrugged.

"It worked rather well, didn't it?"

"And the Stanford student? All fabrication?"

"No. Not entirely. I have access to the applications. I read them occasionally, out of curiosity. She's real. And she was perfect. She even looked a bit like you. Did you notice that? But no, not possible for you."

Kat recalled her growing hope when Sarah told her that adoption was possible, the elation she felt when she saw the picture of the Stanford girl on her computer screen.

"Don't you understand how cruel that was?" Kat asked quietly. "To mislead me like that?"

"Cruel?" Sarah repeated. "For God's sake. No crueler then you were to me. You deserved it, Caitlin."

Kat, mouth dry, turned away. She needed to get out. Get out fast. To the station, to a hotel, anywhere. Quickly, she began to pack the suitcase as Sarah watched like a cat from the doorway. Aware of Sarah's eyes on her, Kat felt gauche and clumsy as she folded underwear, reached into the closet for pants and sweaters.

She had gathered together the toiletries on the dresser and then, remembering that a cab could take a long time this late in the evening, picked up the phone and asked the operator for the number of a cab company, when Sarah leaped forward and snatched the phone from her hand, unplugging it from the wall.

"No, Caitlin," Sarah said.

Kat took a small step backward. Sarah's whole body was poised, tense like a spring. Her eyes were focused on Kat's face with a frightening intensity.

"I don't think so," Sarah said. "No telephone calls. No taxicabs. You stay here. Alone. Unhappy. Isolated, just as I was. You have all you need. The pills in your case. The clifftop just a stroll away."

"You can't stop me leaving."

"Really?"

Sarah stepped forward, gripped Kat's wrist tightly in a wrenching motion. She stood so close that Kat could smell the gardenia shampoo in her hair.

"You have nowhere to go," Sarah said. "There's nothing left for you in Los Angeles. No good friend. Your little pal is happy in my company in France. You have no husband. Your marriage is over. Poor

Scott. Finished. Disgraced. How will he like that, do you think? The embarrassment. The awful shame of it. Such a successful career. Over."

"Scott?" Kat asked, fear for her husband swamping her. "What have you done to Scott?"

As she said his name in the electric tension of that room, Kat had a clear picture of her husband entering the kitchen after work each day: the way he loosened his tie, the way his hair would spike upward. His smile.

Kat pulled herself free. A bracelet of red remained on her skin where Sarah's fingers had circled her wrist. As she reached for the last item to pack, her makeup bag, Sarah took the small floral bag out of her hand and dropped it to the floor.

"You won't need that, Caitlin."

Heart pounding, Kat watched as Sarah moved to the suitcase.

"You will need these."

Sarah reached inside the suitcase for the two bottles of pills, placed them, with a sweeping flourish, on the dresser. That done, she tossed items out of the suitcase, scattering them around the room. As she lifted the picture frame, tangled in clothing, she looked hard at Kat. Then, she hurled it to the floor. The sound of glass breaking, splintering, echoed through the small cottage.

Kat gasped, bent to lift the shattered photograph. She pulled out the picture of her son, pushed it into her purse before she began to pick up the broken glass from the floor near her bare feet.

"Handsome lad, wasn't he?" Sarah said.

Kat looked up. Sarah regarded her with a small smile, the green eyes cold as stone.

Kat felt as if a twig snapped in her head; her ears felt full of rushing sounds. The anger she had battened down—at the driver of the truck, the woman in the SUV, at Scott for burying his own grief in work—now focused on one target: Sarah. She felt a soaring, spiraling loss of control and stood, a long shard of glass in her hand.

"What the fuck do you want, Sarah?" she whispered. "What?"

Sarah took a step backward.

"You should be careful with—"

"Tell me. You just want to hurt people. Is that it? Is that your plan?"

"Don't—"

Kat moved closer, holding tight to the curving glass.

"You didn't need to destroy Scott, Sarah. Or me. We were already destroyed. Can't you understand that?"

"I—"

"You want blood? Is that it? Is that what you want?"

She saw Sarah flinch. Kat, trembling visibly, stepped forward.

"You want another bloody suicide? Is that it? You want to watch?"

Kat gripped the shard of glass, turned her other arm to expose the soft inside flesh, then looked directly at Sarah.

"Watch!"

In one fast movement, she slashed downward.

"See!"

The flesh paled, then reddened. The severed skin opened and began to bleed. Blood ran down her arm, and Kat took a sharp inward breath at the throbbing pain. Sarah cried out, pressed back against the wall, her face chalk white.

Kat moved fast then. Grabbing only her purse, she pushed past Sarah and out of the bedroom. She heard Sarah's scream.

As she pulled at the front door, a cold wind blew into her face, whistled through the cottage. The trees were bowed in the wind, the sea a black, turbulent mass on the horizon. She could hear the sucking sound, loud and ugly, of the stones in the surf.

She ran down the path, her bare feet slipping and sliding on the stones. As she reached the country lane, she heard Sarah's angry voice behind her. It sounded close. Kat, struggling to ignore the insistent pain, pressing her arm against her body in an effort to stop the bleeding, tried to run faster. She did not dare cross to the cliff path with Sarah so close behind, and she felt the fear rising, choking her. Kat heard then, over the sound of the wind, over the sound of Sarah's voice, a car engine, and saw, at the edge of her vision, headlights. A car coming down from the big house.

If she could just dart across. Move fast. Sarah would be distracted by the car, would have to pause, wait for it to pass. Kat took a jagged breath, counted one, two— She ran. On the other side of the road, she whipped around to see if Sarah had stopped. At the same moment, she heard the screech of brakes, the snapping of breaking branches in the roadside shrubs. Kat caught one glimpse of Sarah's face before the vehicle hit. So focused on Kat, so intent on catching up with her, Sarah had not realized how close the black compact car was. Her face showed no fear, no caution. Only a cold, determined rage.

As the car screamed to a halt across the lane, its lights illuminated the figure now crumpled on the ground. Sarah lay perfectly still. Blood pooled behind her head, almost black in the slanted beam of the headlights. Her body had landed at an odd angle, one knee bent outward in an impossible position. The peach towel was still draped around her neck.

Shouts and footsteps were immediately audible from the main house. A heavyset man with a smooth shaved head ran down the hill, pulling a cell phone from his pocket. Kat heard him calling for police, for an ambulance.

Kat, shivering violently, moved forward, pausing as a woman climbed out of the black car. An older woman with a wide, pale face, gray hair pulled back into a knot on her neck, walked stiffly toward Sarah. Kat heard her low moan as she knelt on the road. She looked up and saw Kat. The two women stared at each other. Then, the sharp shock of recognition. Mrs. Evans, eyes narrowing, mouth a thin, hard line, waved her hand in a contemptuous gesture—*Get back, move away*—before she turned again, keening softly, to Sarah. Kat stood frozen, felt time stretch and stall, as they waited for endless minutes for the ambulance they all knew would be too late.

TWENTY-FIVE

On the morning of the anniversary of Chris's accident, as a warm breeze carries the scent of juniper and litters the sky with pink paper-thin clouds, Kat stands at the open bedroom window, aware of the air on her damp skin. She has just bathed and still has the towel wrapped around her.

"Going to be a hot one," Scott says, coming up behind her. She leans back against him, murmuring a good morning. He, too, is fresh from the shower and smells of shampoo and pine-scented soap. His kiss, soft on her neck, triggers a memory of last night's lovemaking. Since her return from England, shaken, close to collapse, wanting only to find Scott, Kat has rediscovered the soothing quality of physical closeness. She would like to stay like this, his arms around her, the breeze lifting the curtains. Scott kisses the top of her head, releases her, and reaches for his shirt.

"Better get going," he says. "Before the traffic builds up."

"You've got the whole day off?"

"Yep. Took a vacation day."

It is his first vacation day since he accepted a position with the large public-interest law office on the other side of the city.

"Civil liberties focus, so it's interesting work," Scott said when he described the job offer to Kat. "But it's a huge drop in income."

"If you'll like the work, then take it. We'll manage."

When Kat first learned the details of the loss of his partnership, she had wanted Scott to fight the board decision. It was too late, he told her, shock and disbelief still in his voice. Sarah had removed all her files on the day she left for England and cited his incompetence as the reason. She had taken Bianchi with her. The decision had been effective immediately. It was all in place.

"I had to resign," he said. "It was such an enormous loss to the firm."

The shock of Sarah's death has now faded in the Los Angeles legal community. Scott has discovered, through tentative inquiries to former colleagues, that all her old matters are now being handled in Europe. Kat wonders if anyone mourns her, besides Mrs. Evans, the housekeeper, so wretched at the accident site.

"Next time we go to England, we should take some flowers to that lane by the cottage. Gardenias maybe. Some remembrance," Kat said to Scott one evening.

"Remembrance? For that woman? After all she did?"

"For the girl she was, not the woman she became."

He shook his head, touched her cheek with the back of his hand.

"You're nuts," he said.

At odd moments, Kat experiences flashes of memory, fragmented images of those hours in Sussex. She recalls Sarah's visible fury just before the car hit and the blood pooling on the asphalt; she remembers the roiling sea and clifftop, the sucking sound of stones in the surf and the crash of shattering glass. At these times, she reminds herself that Sarah, in trying to destroy her life, had actually saved it. There is an appealing irony in that, one that Sarah would certainly have recognized.

In the kitchen, dressed and ready to leave for Forest Lawn, she makes coffee.

"One quick cup," she says, handing a mug of coffee to Scott.

He takes it, regards her steadily.

"You're okay now, Kat?"

"As okay as I can be. Considering the date."

Soon after they were reconciled, she had apologized to Scott for her obsession with the adoption plan and the conflict it caused between them.

"I was impossible," Kat said to him. "Crazy. I'm so sorry."

"Not impossible. No. Just grieving. And manipulated by Sarah."

"Oh, it was more than that. I believed what I wanted to believe. I thought I could just rewind and begin again. Start over with a new baby—and change the ending. Change the ending! As if I could. As if I could replace Chris. As if he could *be* replaceable." She stopped, sighing. The words she needed to explain her mixed emotions eluded her.

"I should have been more understanding," Scott said. "I was just so busy. I was overwhelmed."

Now, Kat turns away, makes a small adjustment to the bowl of roses she has picked from the garden. The rich red and gold colors glow in the thin morning light. She reaches for the card she will attach to them and writes a few lines from a Carver poem she loves. When she is almost at the end, she hands the pen to Scott.

"Write the last two lines," she says. "This is from both of us."

He hesitates. This is the kind of sentimentality that, just a year ago, Scott would have mocked, but on this, the anniversary of their son's death, he is not the same man. He takes the pen and reads the first four lines from "Late Fragment."

"I hope he felt that," he says.

Kat looks at her husband quizzically.

"Chris? Or Carver?"

"Chris. I hope he felt what Carver describes. I hope he felt beloved on the earth."

"Of course he did," Kat says, hugging her husband. "He was loved. He knew that."

The grave site, when they arrive just before noon, is already piled with flowers. Kat places her roses by the others and bends down to read the cards. Ben and Matt have left a balloon displaying a picture of a rock band. Chris's former English teacher has placed a bowl of white camellias by the side of the grave and written out, in her graceful script, the entire Frost poem, "Nothing Gold Can Stay." There is a bunch of mixed flowers from Brooke, now back in the neighborhood, her new job having ended as abruptly as it began, and another one from Maggie and Paul. Kat smiles when she sees, right in the center, a vase of purple-and-white tulips from Chloe. Attached to it, and clearly visible, is a picture of Chris with all his friends around him.

We love you, Chloe has written. *Don't you forget it.*

"Look at all this," Scott says. "It's amazing."

"We have to remember that he wasn't just ours," Kat says. "A lot of people loved him."

She turns back to her husband, holds his hand briefly before kneeling down on the grass and bowing her head.

"Find peace, sweet son," she whispers.

Kat feels Scott's arm around her shoulders as he crouches beside her at the graveside.

"We miss you, Chris," he says aloud. "We miss you, son."

A soft breeze carries a dampness from the ocean a few miles away. Kat thinks she can taste salt in it. Scott stands, reaches for her hand to help her to her feet.

ACKNOWLEDGMENTS

Many thanks to Julia Kenny, my agent, and to Carmen Johnson, my editor at Little A, for excellent support and guidance.

I'm grateful to the talented writers at Zoetrope Writers' Studio for their encouragement and friendship over the past fifteen years. Too many wonderful people to list here. You know who you are. Special thanks to a few pals, both inside and outside the studio: Steve Augarde, Jo Barris, Brian Burch, Jai Clare, John Cottle, Terry DeHart, Lucinda Nelson Dhavan, Pia Z. Ehrhardt, Marko Fong, Avital Gad-Cykman, Alicia Gifford, Debbie Ann Ice, Webb Johnson, Lucinda Kempe, Roy Kesey, Andy Morton, Jean Saunders, Tom Saunders, Kay Sexton, Maryanne Stahl, Wendy Vaizey, and Bonnie ZoBell.

My thanks to three superb writers, Pamela Erens, Charles Lambert, and Ellen Meister, for taking time out from their busy lives to read and endorse the manuscript.

To my son, Nick, brother Jim, and in-laws, Linda and Chris—thank you for cheerleading with such enthusiasm and style.

Finally, I owe so much to my sister, Helen Chappell, and to my good friend Bev Jackson. My love and heartfelt thanks to you both.

ABOUT THE AUTHOR

Mary McCluskey's prizewinning short stories and essays have been published on Salon.com and in the *Atlantic*, the *London Magazine*, *StoryQuarterly*, London's *Litro*, and other literary journals in the United States, the United Kingdom, Australia, and Hong Kong. She divides her time between Stratford-upon-Avon and Los Angeles.